Aeon Pneuma

Spirian Saga Book 4

Rowena Portch

Aeon Pneuma

Originally published in America by Rowena Portch, in 2011 as ***Aeon Pneuma***

FIRST AEON ENTERPRISES EDITION, JANUARY 2013

www.Aeon-Enterprises.us

Cover illustration and book design by
Aeon Enterprises

ISBN-978-0-9886275-3-6

V2.0_r2

Printed in U.S.A.

ACKNOWLEDGMENTS

Gregg, you are a wonderful mate. Thank you for sticking with me through all my adventures in life. I know it's hard to be married to a female with a gypsy soul. God bless you, my angel. You are and always will be my best friend.

Daughter, Erika. Your skill of storytelling inspires me to continue writing. I know your own novels will be a huge success. Thanks for your undying support and cheerful spirit. Most of all, thank you for my wonderful grandchildren who make me smile.

Nick, Andrew, and Zach, you are the most gifted sons a mother could ask for. Not only do you encourage me to continue pursuing my dreams, you call when I need to hear the words, "I love you, Mim." Thank you.

To the females in my life, Mum, Evelyn, and Georgian, bless you for the girl time, the laughs, your support, and most of all, your unconditional love. I couldn't make it without you.

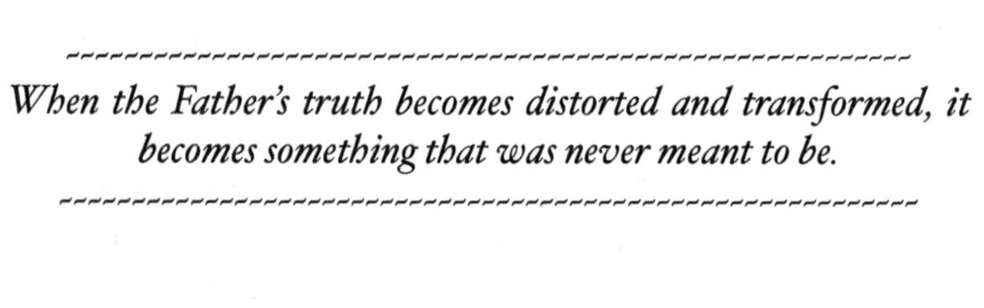

When the Father's truth becomes distorted and transformed, it becomes something that was never meant to be.

Chapter 1

-Elle-

SOME PEOPLE BELIEVE THAT HEAVEN and hell is what you experience after you die. I believe they exist right here on Earth. I have experienced them both.

Practicing karate was my slice of heaven, my sanctuary and solace next to my placid career as a novelist.

I thought about that as I entered the martial arts studio in Gig Harbor. It was more of a shed, really, with peeling paint and a sagging roof, but our sensei, Master Mac, was great, and my friends were even better. As usual, I was the first to arrive for class.

Master Macalister Kinelli Sobopriatiario held a seventh-degree black belt in Kempo; an art that cleverly integrated Judo, Jujitsu, Aikido, and Kung Fu. He was thirty-two years old, one year younger than myself. His steel-gray eyes followed me as I bowed and entered the dojo. They were a perfect match for his long silvering hair that he wore tightly bound at the base of his thick neck. I often wondered if he dyed those silver strands, seeing he was too young to have earned them himself.

"Good evening, Miss Alder." His silky voice was well rehearsed. It was no secret that he was a player and popular with the ladies. "You look very nice," he commented.

I looked down at my gray sweat pants and matching shirt. "Uh, thanks." I clutched the bag hanging over my shoulder and hurried to the ladies dressing room. One look in the mirror was enough to convince me that Master Mac needed to have his eyes checked. My hair was in disarray from driving my Miata with the top down, and my face was still blotchy from the cold. I wasn't what most would consider a striking blonde. I was actually fairly simple. I wore my thin, straight hair in a braid that fell just past my shoulders. My blue-green eyes had an almond shape to them and my lips were thin and lacked any sort of shape. My teeth, however, were perfectly white and straight—a trait from my mother's side.

I had spent the past four hours with the police, who were interrogating me about the recent robbery of my studio apartment. I wondered if they had forgotten that it was my apartment that was vandalized and I was not the one who did it.

My nerves were shot and I hoped Master Mac had a challenging workout planned today. I stripped out of my sweats and dressed into my gi. I wove what straggling strands of hair that I could back into my braid then tucked my bag under the bench.

Jamie strolled in, already dressed and looking like an expensive doll that shouldn't be played with. Her curly auburn hair haloed her head and framed a magnificent pair of kelly green eyes. She had full lips that begged men to kiss her. She certainly didn't lack in the man-friends department.

"Hey, Chicka, what's up?" she said, her tone inquisitive. "You parked like you had a few too many. Is everything all right?"

I rolled my eyes. "I'll tell you about it after class."

She smiled with anticipation. "This oughta be good."

As a historical fiction novelist, I should be living a quiet, simple life in the woods somewhere overlooking a placid lake. Sounds simple enough—just not for me. Trouble always sought me out and found me as if I had a built-in GPS with a target marked "DESTINATION." My parents claimed I invite trauma. Honestly, I couldn't see how. I don't date or excessively socialize, and I spend most of my free time typing on my computer—hardly the disposition of a drama-seeking female.

As Jamie and I walked into the dojo, Kael ran past us, his thick brown hair plastered down by his bicycle helmet. "Hi girls," he said in passing.

We giggled.

"Is that man ever on time?" Jamie asked.

"Rarely," I muttered.

Jamie and I took our place in the front of the class next to Neal, a brown belt. He gave us a smile that looked more like a smirk. Since he outranked us, he stood to our right.

Jamie rolled her eyes. She and I were green belts, soon to test for our brown. We both knelt and fastened our belts before standing again.

Pearl, a quiet but charming young woman who liked to keep to herself, and Jim, her boisterous husband stood behind us. They were both from South Africa, very dark, and wittingly funny. It was fun to have them in class.

Master Mac stood before us, clasped his hands together

and offered a slow bow. We all followed suit. "Neal," he said. "Please lead the class in a five-minute stretch."

Halfway through our stretches, Kael jogged in toward the rear of the class, dropped to his knees, and fumbled with his belt. Master Mac groaned, showing him again how to tie it properly.

"Kael," he chided. "You are a purple belt now. You should know how to tie this correctly." He tied the belt snugly, then pointed to the ground. "Fifty pushups for being late."

"Yes, Sir," said Kael.

By the time we completed our stretches and were well into our warm-up, Kael completed his pushups, red-faced and breathing hard.

Master Mac drilled us through our punches and kicks, and then told us to pair up for sparring. Neal was in the middle of asking me to be his partner when Kael grabbed my gi sleeve.

"Not this time," he said, rather protectively.

"Careful," I said to Kael. "People might think you have a thing for me."

"I do," he admitted with a smile.

I knew better than to take him seriously. We had been a little more than friends for nearly seven years and had never once kissed. I mock-punched him to the stomach, clipped his chin with my elbow, then took him down.

"Best keep your guard up," Master Mac instructed him.

"Yes, Sir."

Kael stood, rubbed his jaw, and then glared at me as he took a stance. He kicked out at me before moving in for a punch. I stepped aside, grabbed his outstretched fist and flipped him to the ground.

He groaned. I offered him a hand up.

Master Mac stepped in. "Never sacrifice your balance for speed or force," he said. With power and grace, he demonstrated his point precisely, landing me on my backside.

Kael helped me up.

"Got it," I groaned. "Thanks, Master Mac."

Master Mac nodded, smiling down at me as if he had enjoyed planting my keister on the hard carpet. According to him, he couldn't afford cushy mats. Personally, I thought the carpet-covered concrete was a cruel way of teaching us how to fall properly. Despite his roguish nature, the man had a certain draw to him and he definitely knew it. "Keep your feet on the ground, Miss Alder," he chided.

"Yes, Sir," I replied, my face as red as the sun in the mural on the wall.

We continued to spar, then moved into some grappling and defensive techniques. The class was blissfully exhausting, exactly what I wanted—a slice of heaven.

The hot shower afterward was even more rewarding. I braided my wet hair, squeezed it with the towel, and then tucked my clothes into my bag.

"Ya gonna come out for coffee with us, Master Mac?" Jamie asked, toweling her curly head dry. Her attraction to the stunning man was no secret. Unfortunately for her, he liked his women challenging and hard to get. Jamie, bless her heart, was much too willing.

"No, Jamie. Thanks for asking though."

She sighed and gathered her things.

"Elle?" Master Mac called out to me.

I looked at Jamie and Kael who stood waiting at the door. The glare in Kael's eyes did not escape my notice.

I cleared my throat. "I'll meet you two at the coffee

shop, okay?"

"I'll wait," said Kael, his thin frame and boyish face in sharp contrast to the domineering karate master.

I shook my head before turning my attention to the devastatingly handsome man standing far too close for my comfort. I cleared my throat and took a step back. "What is it, Sir?"

"There is a test coming up next week. I think you're ready for it."

I frowned. Typically, Jamie and I tested together. He had never asked me outside of her presence. "Um, did you want me to inform Jamie for you?"

He shook his head. "She is not ready. It will just be you and two others."

I knew better than to deny his offer. That would have been disrespectful. Kael and I had plans to see a movie that weekend. We would have to postpone it. "Thank you, Sir. What time should I be here?"

"Saturday, 10:00 a.m. sharp."

I looked down and away from his piercing gray eyes. "Okay, I'll see you later, then." I started to walk away. He grabbed my gi sleeve.

"Miss Alder, you'll need these." He handed me my purse and duffle.

Again, my face heated. He had a knack for turning me into Jello and he knew it. "Thanks," I said, taking the bags.

He smiled, as if quite pleased with his ability to affect me so easily. Then again, he affected most women that way.

Kael shook his head as I walked toward him. "Honestly, Elle, I don't know what you see in that man. He is a player and a crude one at that."

"I'm not interested in him, Kael, or any other man for that matter."

"I knew it," he said, slapping his helmet onto his head. "You're into women."

I laughed. "No, I'm not gay."

"What is it then?" he asked, releasing the lock on his bike. "I've known you for years and have never heard you talk about a single date."

I shrugged. "I'm just not interested, that's all."

He swung his bike around and stared at me with deep brown eyes. "Any chance of changing that?" His question came out as if it were only meant for my ears. He didn't wait for an answer before pushing off and swinging his leg over the seat. "I'll see you at the coffee shop," he said over his shoulder.

"Okay," I replied, under my breath and out of earshot. He was such an odd bird, Kael. A good friend, perhaps the best and closest friend I ever had. Still, I felt as if there was so much more I was missing. I just couldn't identify it.

I tossed my bags onto the passenger seat before settling into my car. It was my liberation toy; my last defiant act against my unsuspecting parents. Daddy had bought me a very practical Mazda GLC, silver in color, and very inconspicuous. With the phenomenal contract of my first book, Czar, I traded the reliable sedan in for a shiny new Mediterranean-blue Miata.

I drove it with the top down as often as the moody Washington weather permitted. The little rain that fell this time of year hardly ever damaged the tan leather seats. I kept them well conditioned just in case. Now that summer was just around the corner, I would have more time to enjoy my ride. Then again, this was Washington where rain was more of a commodity than a condition.

I took off down the street and headed toward Cutters Point Coffee on the other side of Highway 16. There was an accident that had just occurred, causing the traffic to jam up the overpass. I inched my way forward and finally, as I approached the wreck, I saw Kael's red bike, twisted and bent, his bags strewn over the road.

I jammed the gearshift into park, got out and rushed toward the chaos. My legs could not carry me fast enough. Kael lay still on the ground, his limbs bent at awkward angles. He wasn't moving.

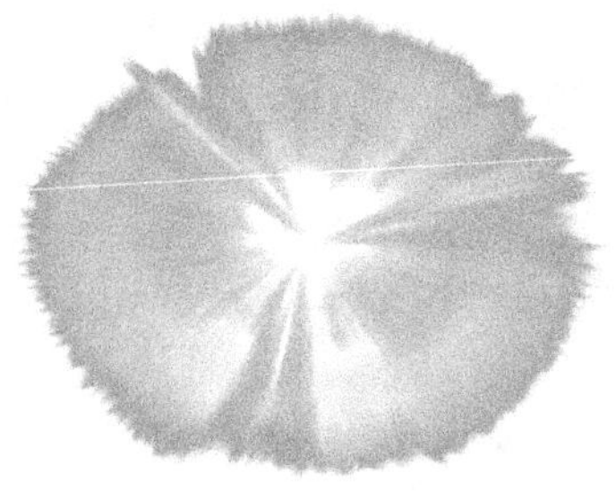

Chapter 2

-Avel-

When the High Council asked me to accept this mission, I thought they had all gone mad. Some bloke—a black wizard— had found my father's *Book of Light* and had distorted and transformed it into its exact opposite, *The Book of Shadows*, a common practice of alchemy. My job was to inhabit the body of a man on the verge of death, get close to the woman who had found the book, and destroy the black wizard who had altered my father's work—bloody petty mission for a Spartan warrior.

Archangel Raphael was assigned as my ward during this quest. Looking down at the mangled body about to be mine, I completely understood the Council's choice. Raphael was unmatched as a healer, especially when several miracles were in order.

"Remember," Raphael said, "you are to blend in and assume the life of this young man. Speak in English, and try to rein in your temper, will you?. Your gifts as a spirit will only linger for a few days before you become fully human."

I sighed. "So I've been briefed, my friend."

The old man stood before me, resembling the character Gandalf from Lord of the Rings. He completed the image by carrying a long white staff and wearing a long white robe. It wasn't at all what Raphael really looked like, but as an Archangel, he could manifest any image he wanted.

"Interesting choice," I commented, looking him up and down.

"I thought so," he replied. "You must hurry, the body grows cold." With that, he struck me with his staff.

The pain that followed was indescribable. It felt synonymous with being frozen alive, and then slowly thawed. Every bone and muscle screamed in agony as Raphael leaned over my damaged body and meticulously mended it back together. Bystanders stood back, mumbling with disbelief. They could not see the old Angel, of course, but they hardly missed the fact that my crumpled legs were now straight and moving. I sat up and raised my hand to my throbbing head. The bleeding had suddenly ceased and the gaping wound at the back of my scalp slowly closed.

A young woman pushed through the crowd and hovered above me. The body I now inhabited recognized her as a friend, Elle Alder. She grabbed my face between her hands. "God, Kael. Are you all right?" Her eyes scanned my body.

"Help me stand," I said.

"No," she replied. "Help is on the way. You need to see—"

"Help me bloody stand!" I repeated, adding a

demanding emphasis to my tone.

She frowned, hesitating before draping my limp arm over her shoulder. "You really should wait until the ambulance gets here."

"I don't need an ambulance. Grab my bag and help me to your car."

She slung my bag over her shoulder with a humph. Her hand gripped my wrist. "Kael, you were just in a horrible accident. You need to wait here—"

I pulled away from her and grabbed my bike. "Where's your car?"

She pointed to a Miata with the door swung open. "Over there."

I shifted my bike to one arm then hauled her back to the car. "Are you going to drive, or should I?"

A police car arrived at the scene. A young dark haired rookie had gotten out and was currently working his way through the crowd that was still gawking at me and my mangled bike.

"I think you should talk to him," said Elle, apprehension in her voice. "I'm sure you hit your head pretty hard."

I had studied the ways of this new world prior to my mission. Leaving now was sure to attract more attention than I needed. It was best to simply talk to the officer and assure him that I was in no need of medical attention.

Elle opened the car's trunk and placed my bag inside along with hers. I lowered my bike down and waited for the inevitable.

The cocky young officer had odd-shaped facial hair that looked as if it were painted on, rather than grown. He wore dark sunglasses, despite the fact that gray clouds had rolled in. The truck driver who hit me stopped him briefly to proclaim his innocence, waving his hands for emphasis.

Several bystanders pointed the officer toward us, mumbling indistinct words and expressions. The officer pushed his way through the crowd.

"Bloody perfect," I mumbled.

"What's with that word, 'bloody'?" Elle asked. "I've never heard you use it before."

I frowned, not really wanting to explain right now. Besides, our mutual friend, Jamie, was waiting at the coffee shop. All I needed was for her to worry and add to the growing confusion. "Call Jamie and let her know we're running late. I don't want her to worry."

"What should I tell her? 'Sorry, Jamie, Kael was hit by a truck. He was broken to pieces, but is much better now. We'll be joining you soon'?"

"Tell her we're stuck in traffic, nothing more." I left to meet the officer walking toward us.

"Are you the young man who was hit?" he asked.

I stifled a laugh at his comment about me being young. Compared to him, I was ancient. The thirty-five-year-old body I inherited, though, could have passed for twenty, maybe younger. I would have to remedy that, and soon.

"I am."

"Care to tell me what happened?"

"No. I'm late for an appointment."

The officer looked up from his clipboard. "It can wait."

I recounted the incident, in grueling detail. The officer's statement filled three and a half pages before he left to speak with the driver who slammed into me. Since I refused medical attention, and the right to press charges, I was free to go.

I gathered my crumpled bike and wedged what was left of it behind the seats of Elle's car. When the front wheel was removed, the bike fit snugly in the cramped space, though it towered precariously high.

I sat in the passenger's seat. "Drive," I told Elle.

She stared at me with doe-like eyes. "I think I liked you better before you got hit," she said, jerking the car into gear and merging into the traffic ahead, just past the scene. She reached into the glove box and pulled out a package of wet towelettes. "You might want to clean yourself up if you don't want Jamie to ask questions."

I pulled down the visor and inspected the damage. Good Father in Heaven, I looked much worse than I imagined. Kael's face looked like a child. The small, delicate hands I had inherited looked like those of a ten-year-old. How in God's great Kingdom was I supposed to face a black wizard when I looked like Harry Potter?

Elle yanked a towelette from the container and wiped the back of my head. She parted my hair and inspected my scalp. "Where are your wounds?"

"Archangel Raphael healed them," I explained.

She laughed. "Yeah, right."

"He was there, kneeling beside me. Did you not see him?"

"I'm driving you to the hospital," she said, veering her car to the right.

I grabbed the wheel and forced it to stay in the left lane. "And tell them what, Elle? 'My friend was in an accident and hit his head. There are no wounds, mind you, because he claims an Angel healed them.'"

She turned her blinker on and pulled left into the shopping center.

Slamming her hand against the steering wheel, she screamed, "I knew this was going to be a crappy day. I just knew it!"

"Your day is what you make it," I said.

"Were you visited by Plato as well?"

I shook my head. "No, I haven't seen him in years. He's very busy, you know."

"Right," she said, sarcasm lacing her tone. She pulled a brush out of her bag. "Here, clean yourself up. You look like something my brother would be proud of."

Images of an older man employing the looks of European grunge came to mind. "Is your tongue always so sharp?" I drug the brush through my hair trying to obtain some semblance of style.

"You never part your hair on the left," she said.

"Perhaps it's time for a change, yes?"

She took the brush from my hand and dumped it into her purse. "Whatever."

Chapter 3

JAMIE STOOD WHEN WE ENTERED the coffee shop. Her eyes grew abnormally wide. "Dang, Kael, what happened to you?" Her eyes rested on the blood that stained my shirt, and the holes that ventilated my jeans. It didn't help that she stood a good three inches taller than me. Spartan women rarely topped their men once they were fully grown. When had the world changed so much?

I stood straighter than necessary and raised my chin. It didn't help much. I still had to look up into her green eyes. "I fell off my bike," I replied.

"I'm assuming you're okay?"

"A little bruised, but I'll live," I said.

She glanced over at Elle, who quietly slid into the seat closest to the fireplace.

"What can I get you ladies to drink?" I asked.

Jamie cocked her jaw to the side as if assessing a complicated puzzle. "Um, my usual." She pulled out a five-dollar bill and handed it to me.

"Same here," said Elle, pulling a five-spot from her

wallet.

I filed through Kael's memories, trying to recall the ladies' "usual drinks."

The young man behind the register looked me up and down. "Uh, can I help you?"

I cleared my throat. "Yes, I'll have a black coffee in a mug, a grande decaf peppermint mocha, and a tall spiced chai, please."

The man repeated the order back to me, forcing a smile. "That'll be $12.95."

I pulled a wad of bills from my pocket and paid the man. "Add one of those coffee cakes there, will you?"

The man nodded, then recalculated the total cost.

I returned to the table with the coffees first before going back for my cake. I offered the bills back to the women, and then took my seat across from Elle. Both women looked at me as if I were a stranger about to impose on their quiet time.

"What are you doing?" Elle asked.

I took a sip of coffee and bit off a hefty portion of cake from the neatly cut piece. "Did you want some?" I mumbled.

"You don't drink coffee, Kael, and you never eat anything with flour in it."

Jamie quietly sipped her peppermint mocha and neatly folded the five-dollar bill before tucking it back into her jeans. "Thanks for the treat, Kael."

I smiled, grateful for the distraction. "You're welcome." I looked over at Elle. She continued to eye me suspiciously. "What?" I finally said. "I feel like having something different, that's all."

"Uh huh," she droned, returning the crumpled bill to her wallet.

"So," Jamie chimed, looking over at Elle. "Tell me about your trip to New York. Is your agent cute? Is he married?"

Elle shook her head, looking at Jamie as if the woman had lost her mind. "Yes, my agent is cute. No, he's not married, and no, I'm not interested."

"Listen, Chicka. You can't remain a virgin your whole life. At some point in time you need to find a man and cut loose. Honestly, you're wound tighter than an eight-day clock. A little sex would do you some good."

I smiled, charmed by the sudden pink that colored Elle's cheeks. It brightened even deeper when she looked my way.

She turned the cup on the table, and averted her eyes from mine. "Yes, well, I'm not looking for anyone right now."

"Elle," Jamie chided, "you're thirty-three years old. Unless you want to be a new mother at forty, you'd best get crackin'."

"Well, right now, I have other things to contend with."

"What could be more important than gettin' laid?" asked Jamie.

The color in Elle's cheeks deepened. "For starters, nosy-bit, I need to get my apartment in order."

"Whatever for? Your place is neat as a pin—the epitome of order and all that." She flipped her hand in disgust.

"Not anymore," said Elle. "You remember that book that Kael and I found while geocaching?"

"Yeah," Jamie replied.

"It was stolen while I was gone."

The cake and coffee in my gut felt suddenly heavy. "What book?"

"The one that you and I found in Tahuya last spring."

My eyes narrowed. "The leather-bound one with no name?"

"Yes, exactly."

"Dang!" Jamie exclaimed. "Was anything else taken?"

Elle took a sip of her, and then shook her head. "No, that was it. Odd, huh?"

"Take me to your apartment," I said, starting to stand.

"Now? Can I finish my chai first?"

"No." I started for the door, expecting her to follow. She didn't. Modern women were obviously defiant. No self-respecting Spartan woman would ever think twice about denying a man's wishes.

Mind your temper, Raphael reminded me, though I knew I was the only one hearing his voice.

"Bloody hell," I groaned. This mission was turning into something much more than what I had bargained for. I sat back down and studied the obstinate woman intently, hoping she would feel my impatience. She hardly noticed.

"Do you need help cleaning the place up?" Jamie asked.

Elle took another long slow sip of her cursed tea and tapped the side of her cup with her fingers. "No, thanks. It's not too bad. I should have everything back in order after tonight. It just feels kind of creepy, you know? Just the fact that someone was in my home?"

"Very creepy," Jamie agreed.

When Elle looked over at me, something in her blue-green eyes caused me to look away—I never look away.

"Hmm," she hummed. "Kael, are you feeling all right?"

"I'm fine," I snapped, fighting the annoying impulse to avoid her stare. "I want to see where the book was stolen from, that's all."

"Why? You've never taken an interest in it before. When we found it, you said—"

"That was before," I nearly growled.

"Whoa!" Jamie said, raising her hands. "Down boy. I don't think I've ever seen you so riled, Kael." She leaned over to inspect my head. "Are you sure you didn't hit your noggin too hard?"

I leaned back away from her. "Forget my head. I just want to go, that's all."

"Earlier," Elle started, "you couldn't wait to get to this coffee shop, and now you want to leave?"

"Yes."

Elle picked up her tea and grabbed her purse. "I'll talk to you later, Jamie, okay?"

"Yeah," Jamie said. "Good idea."

I followed Elle out, enduring the cold silence. No words were spoken as we pulled out of the shopping center and merged onto Highway 16.

"I'm sorry," I muttered, though I doubt she heard it past the roar of the wind whipping past our ears.

She continued to drive and sip her tea in silence. Her studio apartment was on Bay Street, right across from the marina in Port Orchard.

She pulled into her carport, parked, stepped out of the car, and then slammed her door shut. I hurried around the car to catch up to her and grabbed her arm. "Hey, I'm sorry."

She rotated her arm up and twisted it down in an attempt to loosen my grip. When her maneuver failed, her eyes widened. Again, I wanted to look away, but held my gaze. Something about her drew me in. Cobras have a similar effect on their prey, I remembered.

For a moment she froze, studying me. "Your eyes," she

murmured.

I blinked and broke the contact.

But she continued to stare. "They're different, more hazel than brown."

I didn't have time to explain about the connection between the eyes and one's soul. Kael McLeod was dead, his spirit gone. When I assumed his body, my spirit took over. My eyes, of course, reflected it. "They change in certain light," I explained.

"Hmm, I've never noticed it before."

Her eyes, too, held a knowing. I knew her as something more than a friend. Her soul was old and familiar. If I stared much longer in those blue-green depths, I feared what I would learn. I released her arm.

It took her a while to look away, but when she did, I was finally able to breathe again.

I followed her up the stairs to the small space tucked between two other apartments. For someone to break in, they would have to be extremely stealthy or risk being heard. The door was unmarred and there didn't seem to be any signs of a forced entry.

"How did they get in?" I asked.

She shrugged. "Either through the front door, or through the slider, if they risked scaling the walls up to my balcony."

The balcony was three stories up with cedar-shake siding; not likely it was scaled. The air in the apartment possessed a heaviness, cold and thick. "Is it always this cold in here?" I asked.

"You've never complained before," she huffed. "I'll turn the heat up." She placed her purse and tea on the kitchen counter then adjusted the thermostat.

I looked around the cramped space. Dust littered the

wooden floors and rugs. Even the furniture had a layer of what looked to be ash. I tasted it—ash indeed, with a hint of salt.

She studied me as I roamed the area looking for clues.

"So, are you a detective now?" she inquired.

The room was spiritually bound by black magic. The taste of it was like copper pennies on my tongue. "You cannot stay here tonight," I said. "The room must be cleaned."

"I stayed here last night, Kael. What are you talking about?"

"Has anyone tried to contact you?"

"Yeah, lots of people. I just released a new book. That's expected."

"What book?"

She lifted a hardcover book from the couch. "Emerald. Jeez, Kael, you practically helped me write it. What is wrong with you?"

I took the book from her hands. From the blurb on the back, it was based on the book she had found in the woods—the one that was stolen.

"Grab some things," I told her. "You're staying with me for a while."

"I'm most certainly not," she countered.

"Your home has been compromised, Elle. I'll explain later, but for now, please just do as I ask."

"Kael, you're scaring me, and that is not an easy feat. Perhaps you should explain now. Ever since you mysteriously rose from that accident, you have not been yourself. I saw your legs, they were severely broken. Your head was bleeding. Now you're walking and acting as if nothing happened?"

I didn't have time for all this. Even if I did explain

everything to her, she would not believe me. "Elle, do you believe in magic?"

I saw her energy shift and retreat as if she were protecting something.

"You know I do."

"The book you found was not a fake. It is real. We need to get it back."

"Why? I don't want it back."

"In the wrong hands, it can be devastating."

She shook her head in disgust as she wiped away the ash from her bedspread. "Where is all this coming from?"

"Black magic," I said. "It leaves a residue of ash and salt."

"Are you saying that someone used black magic to enter my apartment and steal the book?"

"I am."

Her eyes narrowed. "How do you know this, Kael? You don't even believe in magic of any kind, be it black, white, or indifferent."

"I know more than you think I do," I replied with conviction.

She wiped her hand over her armoire. "I just cleaned this."

"The room must be spiritually cleansed and the bond broken."

"How?"

"I need to gather some things."

"What kind of things?"

"Salt, heavy in minerals, white sage, black candles, adders tongue, and a stick made of ash."

"Right," she replied, looking at me as if I had lost my mind. "And how, exactly, do you know about these things?"

"Many years of practice," I replied. It was more like

centuries, but she didn't need to know that. "Do you know where to find these items?"

"The Dragoun's Leir in Belfair will have them."

I grabbed her purse from the counter and handed it to her. "Very well, let's go then."

WE FOUND THE ITEMS I was seeking and returned shortly to the apartment. We discussed the ritual that had to be done during our ride back. Her intuition and preciseness of questions was unnerving. She knew far more than I had anticipated about the art of magic. Her knowledge of herbs and plants was a pleasant surprise as well.

I removed the items from the bag, and shook my head at the adornments littering the simple ash branch. Using my pocket knife, I sliced the beads, ribbons, and rhinestones from the wood.

"What are you doing?" she asked, appalled by my vicious attack on the magical wand.

"I don't need or appreciate this clutter."

"It's enchanted," she exclaimed; "blessed with love and power."

I looked over at her and smirked. "Enchanted?" I scoffed. "You've been reading too many books, my dear. True power comes from the Source and must be called upon by the wielder of the tool. What empowers these tools are the emotions that infuse them."

"What do you mean?" she asked, kneeling beside me. Her curiosity was like that of a child. I found it disturbingly endearing—almost as much as her closeness to me.

"This apartment is filled with emotions. What do you feel?"

Her blush forced me to look away. "There is a side of you, Kael McLeod, that intrigues me suddenly," she boldly stated. Her hand rested on my upper arm.

I gently pulled her hand away, but couldn't bring myself to release it. "Whatever you feel for me, Elle, must be curbed. All that is important right now is finding that book." I looked deep into her eyes, more pale green now than blue. That was a mistake. My heart ached as it did the day Syria took her life. Again, I looked away. "Tell me you understand that."

"I don't," she admitted. "Earlier today, you wanted my attention. Now, you push me away. How am I supposed to understand that? So much about you has changed. It's as if you are no longer Kael McLeod."

I stood and moved away from her. "Is there a place away from here that you can stay for a few days?"

"I thought I was staying with you?"

"No," I said, shaking my head. "That's not possible."

"But you said—"

"No, Elle, you cannot stay with me! Do you have another place to go?"

The hurt in her eyes was crushing. "Yes, I can stay at my parents' summer house in Tahuya."

I gathered the items from the counter and moved them to the center of the room. The ache in her heart added to the myriad of emotions that weighted the small space. I found it nearly suffocating.

I poured a small pile of Himalayan sea salt into my palm, and said a quiet prayer asking the Father to infuse His will into the salt. "Divinus sator sal salis per vestri mos." With deliberation, I sprinkled the salt to the North, to the East, to the South, and then to the West. I held up the ash-wood wand and gathered positive emotions into it that would negate the dark, ominous feel of the room.

The apartment was infused with anger, anxiety, greed, and oddly enough, a bit of jealousy. I countered them with feelings of pleasure, peace, generosity, and trust. I ignored the emotions that poured from Elle at the moment. When my countering emotions were stored and gathered into the wand, I pointed the wand outward and turned clockwise while saying, "Solvo quod contego," releasing the positive emotions into the room and forming a protective shield.

Next, I lit the two black candles, and then the white one. Black, as I had explained to Elle, was used to absorb negativity. The white candle was burned for protection against evil intent. As they burned, I lit a piece of charcoal and waited for it to turn gray. I then sprinkled the dried adders tongue leaves onto the burning coals. The smoke rose and wafted through the room, like hungry dragons looking to gorge on negative emotions. I lit the neatly bundled wand of white sage, let it burn for a moment, then blew out the flame. Smoke wafted up from the bundle. I circled the apartment, clearing out whatever remained of the evil that had invaded this space.

"I need a piece of red cloth," I told her. "Something that has been close to you."

She stood and walked toward the armoire. From the top drawer, she pulled out a pair of red panties and handed them to me.

"These are synthetic." I told her. "Do you have something made of cotton or silk?"

"Picky, picky, picky," she chided, retrieving her intimate wear from my grasp. She pulled out a summer top.

I propped the wand of sage up and allowed it to burn

beside the coal and dried herb. With my knife, I cut her blouse into the shape of a triangle.

"Hey," she protested. "That's one of my favorite tops."

"More the better," I countered. I laid the triangular piece of cloth beside the burning coal, and then added more herbs to the pile, allowing them to burn to ash.

When the ash cooled, I poured them onto the red cloth, closed the tips of the triangle together, and bound them with red thread. "Do you have a shovel?"

"Not here," she said.

"You'll need something to dig with."

She rummaged through her kitchen drawers and retrieved a large metal spoon.

I nodded. "That'll do. Follow me."

We headed down the stairs and toward the front of the building. I pointed to an area that bordered the property. "Dig here."

"Why?"

"You are going to bury the sachet of ash. It will prevent the person from entering this area. He will not be permitted beyond this border." I pointed, indicating a fifty-foot diameter around the building.

"How do you know it's a he?"

"I have a good idea."

I watched as she buried the red bundle and mounded the dirt over it. Her hands were shaking.

"It'll be all right, Elle. I won't let anything happen to you."

Her eyes were dull and filled with pain. "You already have," she said, brushing the dirt from her hands. She stood and walked past me toward the stairs. I had hurt her—that much was clear. The pain was inevitable though. There was clearly something between us, but allowing whatever it was to flourish was pointless. As soon as this mission was over, my body would die and I would return to the Ethereal Kingdom. I had already lost one love. I couldn't stand to lose another.

Elle gathered a few things into a bag and hauled it over her shoulder. I took it from her.

"I can handle it," she said.

"No doubt," I replied, slinging the strap over my shoulder.

"Would you like me to take you home?" Her voice had a cold edge to it.

Common sense warned me to call a cab, but she and I needed to talk. She had to understand the importance of the book and why I needed her help. The Council had given me free rein of the information they had shared. I was instructed to gain her cooperation using any means possible.

"Yes, that would be appreciated."

"Are you going to tell me what happened to the Kael I used to know?"

"He is dead."

She turned and glared at me. "That's not very funny."

"It wasn't meant to be."

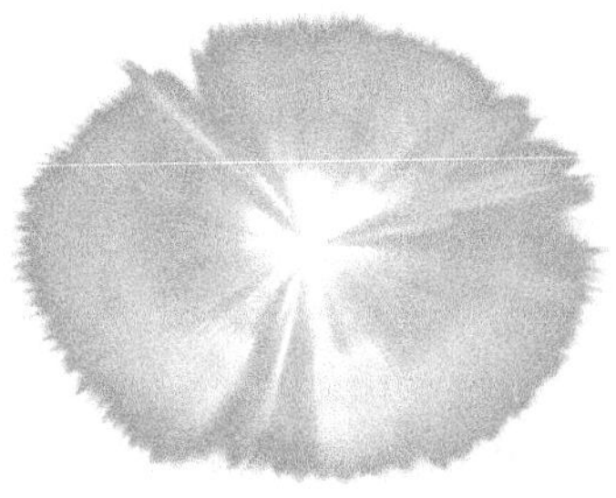

Chapter 4

THE DRIVE BACK TO GIG HARBOR with Elle was another silent one. I was okay with that. I needed time to think things through. If Vincent had the book back, he was no doubt using it to revive deceased acquaintances. Once that happened, all hell would break loose in the literal sense, and it would make getting to him that much harder.

She pulled up to the gate and punched a few numbers on the security pad. The long wrought-iron gates swung open. Kael's parents owned this lot of condominiums and graciously offered a premium unit to their son upon graduation. I supposed I had that to be grateful for. At least I didn't have to worry about having enough money during my brief stay on this Earth.

She pulled into my guest spot and left the car running.

"I would like you to come up if you have a moment," I said, lifting my mangled bike out of the car.

"I'd rather not," she replied.

With a wave of my hand, I killed the engine. "Elle, we

need to talk."

She frowned and turned the key. Nothing happened. "Great. Just perfect." She pulled out her phone and began dialing a number.

"Who are you calling?" I asked.

"Triple-A. In case you haven't noticed, my engine just died and won't restart."

"I'll take a look at it when you're ready to leave."

"I'm ready to leave now."

Part of me wanted to haul her out of the car and march her up to my condo. Another part of me wanted to strangle her for being so bloody difficult. Neither approach would have positive results. I took a deep breath instead.

"Elle, there are some things we need to discuss. Please, give me a chance."

She laughed. "A chance? Why? So you can shoot me down again? No, Kael, I crawled out on that limb and it snapped, stabbing me smack dab in my heart. I'm not about to repeat that mistake."

"Christ, aren't you being just a little too dramatic?"

Wrong choice of words. She jammed her key into the ignition and turned it. Nothing happened. "Ahg!" she screamed, slamming her hands on the steering wheel. "Come on!" She tried it again and again to no avail.

"Come up with me," I offered again. "I'll make us some lunch."

With reserve, she followed me to my condo muttering, "This should be interesting."

I opened the garage, and then leaned my bike against the wall. There were several more bikes in working order, so I wouldn't be out of a ride. There were also two cars in the garage covered by soft black flannel. Based on Kael's memory, one was a red Lamborghini, the other was a silver, more modest Audi TT coupe.

Upstairs, the flat was a cozy one-bedroom suite with a spacious office and a panoramic view of the harbor. The high-tech equipment and indulgent entertainment center would have to go, of course. My tastes diverged greatly from that of my host, Kael. I preferred more of an open space, with an altar, and a hard floor on which to sleep. Yes, changes were definitely in order.

Elle stood by the sliding glass door, looking out at the water. "Why did you say that Kael is dead?" she finally asked.

"Because it is the truth, and I thought that's what you deserved."

"I'm listening," she said hesitantly.

I pulled lettuce and other veggies out of the fridge and set two tilapia fillets to defrost in hot water. Scooting a chair out, I gestured for her to sit.

"What I'm about to tell you, Elle, will be difficult, if not impossible, to comprehend. I do ask, however, that you listen with an open mind. Time is of the essence here and I really don't have the luxury to play mind games."

She took a seat and I poured her a glass of mineral water before continuing.

"When Kael was hit by the car this morning, his life was spent. I took his place. Archangel Raphael healed my wounds."

"Okay," she said apprehensively, "I'll bite. Who are you and why were you sent to take my friend's place?" Her hand shook as she sipped the water.

I drizzled a bit of olive oil in a cast-iron pan, added sage, marjoram and dill with a dash of cayenne pepper and salt. I laid the fish on top and set the heat to medium.

"My name is Avel, son of Hermes Trismegistus. I am

a Spartan warrior who died during the Trojan War. I was sent here by the High Council to retrieve the book that you inadvertently found in the woods, and to destroy Vincent, the dark wizard who adulterated it."

I shredded the lettuce and filled two bowls.

"Hermes Trismegistus," she repeated. "The famous alchemist who created the *Emerald Tablet*?"

"Yes," I confirmed, "and the man who wrote, *The Book of Light*, a reference for healing."

"The book I found?"

I shook my head and added chopped veggies to each of the bowls. "No. Vincent, son of Warducca, a voodoo priest, found my father's book and changed it into its opposite, *The Book of Shadows*. That is the book that was stolen from your apartment."

Her brows furrowed with confusion. "But there were references in that book to the *Emerald Tablet* and the *Sorcerer's Stone*."

"Yes, I'm sure. Somehow, you were able to see past the illusion and read the original text. That explains the jealousy I felt earlier in your apartment."

"Jealousy?" She took another sip of her water.

I turned the fish over and began grating Parmesan cheese into the bowls. "Technically, you should not have been able to open the book without suffering a curse."

"What makes you think I haven't?"

"Those who are cursed are plagued with disease and misfortune. You look well enough to me, and your books are a smashing success—hardly a victim of a curse."

"So what makes me different?"

I placed a fillet into each of the bowls and drizzled a bit of apple-cider vinegar over the top. I added a handful of pumpkin seeds and dried cranberries for color. Elle's eyes widened when I placed her bowl on the table.

"Wow, I'm impressed. Kael's idea of lunch would have been canned soup."

"Yes, well I'm not Kael, and our tastes are obviously different."

Her face turned suddenly somber. "It's odd. He and I were very good friends, yet the loss of him eludes me. I should be mourning."

"The reality of it hasn't hit you yet. I'm standing here in Kael's body, talking to you in his voice, and have access to all of his thoughts and memories. If I hadn't told you what I had, you would think I was Kael."

"No, I wouldn't. You certainly don't act like him."

"Yes, well for now, I must convince others that I am him."

She chuckled. "Good luck with that."

"Jamie was convinced enough."

"She doesn't know you—I mean Kael, like I do. Or did." Her face grew serious again. "I can't believe that he's gone."

We ate in silence for a while. I wanted to give her some time to process all that I had told her. It was human nature to deny anything outside of perceived reality—and this was definitely beyond those bounds.

"You must feel very out of place," she said, turning the glass in her hands. It was a nervous habit of hers, I'd observed.

"I am familiar with this world and the current changes. We are not unaware in the Ethereal Kingdom. Customs have changed, yes, but humans have oddly remained pretty much the same."

"Can you drive and ride a bike?"

I laughed. "I have Kael's knowledge of these things,

yes."

"But you haven't actually done them?" Her pale brow arched in question.

"It will not be an issue," I assured her.

"I'm assuming that once the book is found and Vincent is destroyed, you will be returning to..."

"The Ethereal Kingdom," I supplied. "Yes."

"And what about Kael?"

"His body will perish as it was meant to."

"In a bike accident?"

"Yes," I confirmed.

She lowered her eyes and tried to hide her sadness. I could see it, but she hid it under a veil of mock strength. "Am I in danger?" she asked.

"I'm not sure. Vincent has the book again. He might be satisfied with that."

"But?" she prompted.

"I think you have piqued his interest."

She ate the last of her salad and finished her water. "Why would he be interested in me?"

"You wrote about the *Emerald Tablet* in your book. You revealed information that most humans would not comprehend. That's bound to gain the wizard's notice."

"How do you know he's a wizard?"

"The Council briefed me about him. His parents were killed rather suddenly in a fire. He was unable to save them. I believe he intends to bring them back using the book."

"Is that a bad thing?" she asked, carrying her bowl to the sink.

"Imagine a body without a soul—a being without a conscience."

"Sounds like some of the teenagers I know," she

bantered.

I had to smile. Most humans would be overreacting about now, freaking out, as some might say, but not Elle. Somehow, she found humor in all this—amazing.

"Warducca was a powerful priest in the voodoo arts—not a good man to cross. Imagine a man with such a gift without a soul. Vincent has already fallen to the powers of dark magic. With his father's help, he could cause a wake of destruction that could put a Category-five tornado to shame."

The crease between her brows deepened. "My parents were right," she sighed. "I do seem to attract trouble, don't I?"

I wanted to hold her. The draw she had on me was unnatural. Granted, it had been a long time since I inhabited a human body, and perhaps even longer since I indulged in sexual pleasures. This body was young and I doubt its original owner saw much action in the way of women.

"I'd better go," she finally said. "Thanks for lunch."

Every muscle in my body was tense, including my jaw. She must have noticed and thought I was angry. "Wait," my mouth blurted out, though I couldn't say why.

She stood and studied me with those languid eyes of hers. My heart felt that familiar pang and my stomach grew sour.

"Yeah," I stammered. "It's best that you go. I'll walk you to your car."

She shook her head, obviously confused and grabbed her purse.

"So, what's next?" she said, following me out to her car.

"I'll talk to the Council."

I opened her car's door and watched her gracefully glide inside. My body reacted in kind—cursed physical needs. Being a spiritual being was so much less complicated.

She turned her key and nothing happened. Her eyes closed and her jaw tightened as she pulled her phone out of her bag.

I touched the steering column. "Try it again."

She turned the key and the engine roared to life. "How did you do that?"

I smiled. "Magic."

She smiled back, nearly undoing me. I stepped back and waved goodbye.

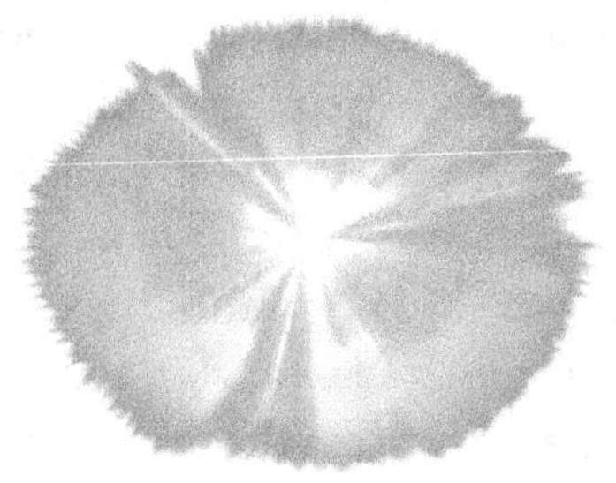

Chapter 5

-Elle-

WHAT HAPPENED TODAY WAS SURREAL, almost like a nightmare but not quite. There was an air of charm to it as well—one that I didn't understand. As I drove to Tahuya toward my parents' cabin, I pondered the information that Kael—Avel revealed to me. Had I lost my mind? I actually sat there and listened to him as if I really understood what he was saying. That was crazy, of course. It didn't make sense, it couldn't.

Spirits don't just take over a body and the memories that come with it. Then again, bodies don't spontaneously heal themselves either. I saw his legs mend and straighten. The gash on his head closed. I saw it, didn't I?

How could I let him talk me into leaving my apartment? Was I daft? How did I know he wasn't part of the whole thing? Maybe he's planning to contact his friend and finish the heist while I'm gone. Great, now I was growing paranoid, I thought.

My hands gripped the steering wheel tightly. They were starting to sweat despite the cold whipping my face. Whoever it was in Kael's body, it definitely wasn't Kael. His eyes had depth now and a wisdom that reflected hundreds of years—and I found myself getting sucked into them far too easily. I was far too attracted to him. Kael had never affected me that way—no man had. I was drawn to Avel, though. Unfortunately, he did not feel the same. He dang near pushed me away like I had typhoid fever or something worse. I frowned, remembering all the men I had pushed away. It was different being on the receiving end of rejection. I didn't like it at all.

I wanted to call him and tell him off—tell him... What? I questioned myself. "Hey, you should be honored to have my attention when no one else ever has?" Yeah, that sounds humble. I would see him tomorrow in karate class. We could talk then.

An hour later, I pulled up to the small cabin nestled in the woods of Tahuya. It had a spectacular view of the Hood Canal and plenty of privacy. Mom and Dad rarely used it anymore. They used to come up from California every summer but since their grandbabies were born, they wanted to stay close to them. Mom hinted that if I were married and blessed with children, they would have a greater excuse to come visit. I guess my relentless charm, success and allure for trouble were not enough for them, I mused. Anyway, I enjoyed more use out of this old cabin than the entire family put together.

I parked under the makeshift shelter constructed of old timber and a low-sloped roof that Dad had made after a particularly harsh winter. It wasn't pretty, but it served well at protecting the car from tree sap and debris. I kind of liked the old pine posts. They looked as rustic as the log cabin. I grabbed my bags from the trunk and hauled them over my shoulder. I hadn't been here for a while and it showed.

Leaves and dirt cluttered the cobblestone path leading to the front door. The garden was overtaken by weeds. The spring grass was long and grew in condensed patches over the rolling mounds my mother mistook as landscaping. Despite my suggestion to plant native, low-maintenance flora, Mother insisted on creating a mock version of California, including citrus trees that begged for a new, more tolerable location. Brown, spotted leaves clung to their branches looking sick next to the new spring growth. I should have pruned them months ago.

I fumbled with the keys and opened the door. A musty scent assaulted me as I stepped through the entrance. I hadn't been here for more than a few months. I must have left a window open or something. The air was cold and damp. I closed the door behind me and carried my bags to my room. Mom and Dad had the master bedroom. I rarely went in there except to clean. The other spare bedroom was used by my siblings perhaps once every five or more years. All of them lived in Dana Point, California.

I plopped my bags on the floor and began removing the sheets from the furniture. Next, I started the pellet stove and noticed that our pellet supplies were low. I would have to pick up some tomorrow. I had enough to last throughout the night and most of tomorrow. The pantry was bare, aside from a few cans of soup and beans. The wine cabinet was stocked, and there were protein bars in the fridge—good thing I stopped for groceries.

The kitchen window was open. I closed it and wiped the dampness from the sill. It took me another two hours to clean the place before I headed out to my sanctuary.

There it stood in all its vinyl glory—my greenhouse. Gardening was the one hobby my father supported. He built this greenhouse for my eighteenth birthday. It was the best gift I had ever received from anyone. It spanned a good quarter acre and was equipped with a circulation fan and an automatic watering system. The double-lined vinyl covering enabled me to keep the environment somewhat stable. Despite all that, many of my plants had not fared well in my absence.

The southern end of the greenhouse butted against a wooden structure where I devised and stored my tinctures, and salves. My sister called it my "Mad Lab." She never had much faith in the power of plants until I concocted a cold and flu tincture for her last fall that worked on her overnight. Now it seemed she was reluctant to be without a good supply.

I brushed the cobwebs aside as I walked through the door. Mason jars littered with dust and cobwebs lined up like sentries along the far wall, while my workbench sported an assortment of burners, glass measuring cups, wooden spoons, and hanging shreds of stained and well-used cheesecloth. Yeah, I need to clean this place up, I thought. It had been too long since I had played with my herbs.

I closed the door behind me and casually inspected my wilting plants. They had sufficient water, but not enough sunlight. I would have to leave the sun lamps on during the day again until the weather became more accommodating. Tomorrow, I sighed. Tonight, I just wanted to settle in, make something simple for dinner, and relax with a good movie and a glass of red wine.

I made my way back to the house, unpacked my bags, and carried the groceries into the kitchen. I opened a bottle of Pinot Noir, pouring a glass to let it breathe. After tearing butter lettuce for my salad, I started cooking the skirt steak that practically screamed my name as I strode past the meat department at QFC. Drizzling a bit of olive oil into another pan, I added a powdered blend of rosemary, sage, thyme, basil, and a bit of salt. The fingerling potatoes were best halved and cooked slowly. I browned them first before adding a bit of water to the pan and allowing them simmer on low heat.

I finished making my salad, adding colorful veggies and a dash of blue cheese dressing. The steak was done in minutes and the potatoes were perfectly tender. I carried my plate and glass of wine to the living room and settled into the lounge chair to select the perfect movie.

My father had a rather extensive selection to choose from. He was a bit of a movie buff—anything from old black-and-white films to recent releases. Every movie he enjoyed was promptly added to his collection, but since he had not been here in quite some time, his "Latest Release" stack contained movies like *Star Wars*, *Tron* and the one I ultimately settled on, *Blazing Saddles*. I needed a light, funny movie with motivating characters tonight, something to take my mind off my apartment, my best friend, Kael, and life in general.

As enjoyable as the meal and movie were, I still couldn't stop thinking about Avel and what he had said. If he truly was the son of Hermes Trismegistus, wouldn't there be something written about him in history? When the movie ended, I quickly cleaned the kitchen and grabbed my laptop. I had become quite adept at researching information and weeding out the garbage that littered the truth like unethical verbal graffiti.

Surprisingly, there was nothing written about the

family of Hermes. I tried looking up the battle of Troy, friends of Achilles, Spartan soldiers, and the like. No mention of Avel. I would think that the son of Hermes would have gained some attention.

I slapped my laptop closed and stood from the couch. I stared at my cell phone lying on the end table. I could call him, I thought. I glanced up at the clock. It was half past ten in the evening—too late to call. No, I remembered, he always stayed up late. At least Kael stayed up late. I knew nothing about Avel.

I grabbed my cell phone and dialed his number. After seven rings, a recording of Kael answered in his familiar jovial voice instructing me to leave a message. "Hi Kael—I mean Avel. This is Elle. Please call me as soon as you get this message. I don't care how late it is. I need to ask you something." I pressed END, and then dialed his cell phone. His voice mailbox was full and I was unable to leave a message.

Part of me wanted to drive back to his place. Another part of me wanted to stay as far from him as possible. He made me feel things I didn't want to feel. I would see him in karate tomorrow, I assured myself. It was best to get some sleep and give my curiosity a rest.

Chapter 6

-Avel-

THROUGH DEEP MEDITATION, I CONTACTED the Council to update them with my findings. Raphael was among them. Raguel, the Head of Council and overseer of peace and harmony, acknowledged me first.

"Avel, son of Hermes, what news do you bring us?"

I lowered my ethereal body to the warm stone floor and bowed my head in respect.

"Vincent has recaptured the book. His magic is strong, and I can feel a shift in the surrounding energy. I believe he is close."

Sophia, the goddess of wisdom, glided toward me. "What of the woman?"

My gut twisted. "I fear she is in danger. Vincent is drawn toward her."

Archangel Michael came forth. "For what purpose?"

"I sensed jealousy and envy from his presence. Perhaps he is curious about Elle's ability to open and read the book without suffering the curse he had placed upon it."

Uriel, the prophet of visions and spiritual understanding, started to say something, but was abruptly stopped by Haniel.

Haniel, after noticing my look of confusion, cleared his throat. "Protect the woman," was all he said.

"Is there something you're not telling me?" I questioned.

Haniel's eyes glowed violet. "There is nothing you need to know right now, Avel. Keep the woman close and safe. Do not allow Vincent to have her."

Raguel nodded his head, as if to say this discussion was over. "You have done well, Avel." There was sadness in his voice. "Stay focused on the task at hand. Destroy the book and deliver Vincent to us. That is all you need to know."

"I would like to keep Elle out of this. I have her staying at her parents' cabin for now. I believe she'll be safe there."

"Stay with her," Haniel warned. "She is not safe."

She is not safe from me either, I thought, forgetting that thoughts were not unheard by the Council.

Haniel laughed, as did the rest of them.

Raphael wrapped his arm around my shoulder. "Time for you to return, my friend."

"I have a very bad feeling about this," I told him.

"As well you should," he admitted. He clapped his massive hands and I immediately returned to Kael's waiting body. Three hours had passed. The room was dark and silent. The phone's red message light blinked in time with the ticking clock.

I pressed play and my heart skipped at the sound of Elle's voice—a distant haunting from a place I had long forgotten.

"Call me as soon as you get this message," she said. "I don't care how late it is. I need to ask you something."

Ask me something? I glanced up at the clock. It was twenty past midnight. I picked up the phone and began dialing her number. My finger hovered over the last digit. I hung up the phone. My hands were shaking.

"Raphael," I called out.

I felt a warmth surround me, and then I watched as his misty form gathered mass and manifested into an impressive image of Gandalf the wizard, cloaked in emerald green. His piercing gray eyes met mine with a knowing softness of compassion. "Avel," he said. "You have something on your mind?"

"I do," I said, standing to greet him. "Who is this woman, Elle?" I asked boldly.

Raphael looked away and tapped his fingertips together as if in thought. "Why does it matter, Avel?"

"She haunts my soul like a ghost from the past. I cannot read her. It's as if a shield has been formed around her to keep me out."

"You have a mission to fulfill, Avel. I suggest you focus on it and be done with this life. Her safety should be your only concern."

"But it's not, is it? There is more."

"More what, dear boy?"

"Raphael, you are many things, but dense is not one of them. Who is Elle?"

Raphael's eyes grew dark as stone as he stared down at me. He unlaced his fingers and placed his hands upon my shoulders. I felt a jolt of energy course through me as if I stood on live wires. It was enough to still my breath.

"Knowing the truth of her will not help with this

mission," he said, his voice as steely as his gaze. "It will only serve to hinder things."

"There are many other souls who can complete this mission. Why was I chosen when I clearly do not merit the consideration of knowing the truth of it all?"

More energy coursed through me, nearly dropping me to my knees. I refused to grant him that satisfaction, bearing the pain without showing it. Stubborn Spartan pride.

He laughed, clearly amused with my efforts. "Impressive, young warrior." He removed his hands and stepped back. "You of all souls should know that there are no accidents. Things are as they should be—always."

"Then please, grant me the courtesy of hearing the truth. All of it."

"When the time comes, you will know the truth. Until then, stay true to your mission."

The finality of his words ensured me that he would not tell me what I wanted to know. Pressing him further would be wasted effort. "Very well, guardian. I respect your position and thank you for your time." I bowed to him.

He raised his chin a notch, knowing that the formality between us was not necessary. The gleam in his eyes held a curiosity as if wondering what I was up to.

"Some things, Avel, are best left unquestioned."

"I honor your wisdom, my friend, but my soul still aches for the truth."

"Souls typically do," he replied, then softly faded from my mortal sight.

I paced the floor, torn between what I wanted to do and my cursed moral values. The Akasha, or universal library, was open to me and easily accessed. Perhaps I could dig into the past of Elle's soul and learn her purpose? And then what? I pondered. The High Council had warned me to concern myself with only my mission and keeping Elle safe, nothing more. The human side of me hungered for something else, something that went far deeper than moral fibers.

Accessing Akashic records would be frowned upon for this purpose, and the Council's warnings were not something to dismiss so quickly. They honored the best interest for all, including mine.

I pushed back the insistent, foolish notion of trying to learn more about this woman placed in my charge. Above all, I was a warrior and obedient to the Lord and his Council—curiosity be damned.

My body felt fatigued, achy and in need of rest. Inhabiting a physical body had drawbacks that I hadn't missed. As a spirit, the only pain I felt was the one in my soul, the piece of me that remained incomplete without my love and mate, Syria. Until my untimely death, I never believed that a soul could ache. I was wrong. Every soul has an equal. When combined, they know the pure power of love—the kind of power that paves the way to your dreams, and gives your spirit wings to fly over the greatest obstacles. Syria and I were blessed with two short years together, though it felt as if we had known each other for more than a lifetime.

I padded my way toward the mattress I had sprawled over the floor and flopped down, suddenly feeling exhausted.

I AWOKE, STARTLED AT THE sound of Big Ben, Kael's annoying idea of a door chime. My entire body ached;

apparently it was unaccustomed to sleeping on a firm foundation. I opened the door and saw Elle standing with her mouth hung open, and her eyes scanning me from head to toe. It was then I realized that I must have stripped my clothes off sometime during the night.

"Hi," I said, "would you like to come in?" Not waiting for an answer, I left the door open and made my way to where my clothes lay on the floor. I pulled my pants on commando, leaving my briefs and shirt where they lay.

Elle came in, closing the door behind her. Mouth still hanging open, she scanned the room, brows high with speculation. She clearly didn't approve of my rearrangement of the furniture.

"Rough night?" she asked, setting her bag down on the kitchen table.

I followed her gaze to the mattress on the floor. "The bed was too soft," I explained, reaching for my shirt.

"I see," she said. "Um, are you planning to go to class this morning?"

She looked far too alluring in that bright pink top and blue jeans that clung to her thighs as if they were molded to them. I pried my focus away while my brain played catch-up to what she was asking.

"Class?" I asked, buying some time.

"Oh," she said, clearly embarrassed. "I forgot. You're not Kael anymore." She reached for her bag as if planning to leave.

I walked over and placed my hand over hers. "Don't leave." The words blurted out of my mouth as if spoken by another being. "Karate? Right?"

"Yes," she said. Her face blushed as she slowly pulled her hand from mine. "Are you going?"

"Are you?"

"Of course," she replied.

"Then, yes, I'm going too."

She stared at me for a moment, as if questioning my motives. "Grab your things," she said. "Let's go."

I followed her toward the door, my hair looking like something the wind had abused. I gripped the bag that Kael had strapped to his bike. The uniform inside would smell like yesterday's spent tuna can and the clothes I wore betrayed my restless night. "Um," I finally said, stopping at the threshold. "Do I have time to clean up?"

She grabbed my hand. "No, we're late as it is."

I tossed my bag in the back of her Miata and hopped into the passenger seat.

"I do have a door," she said, a slight curl wrinkling her mouth.

I didn't reply. My tongue, at the moment, seemed too large for my mouth. Her eyes were sparkling, happy—hypnotizing. Sword of steel, Avel, I chastised myself. Get a hold of yourself.

She turned the key and pulled out of the parking lot. The silence was deafening.

"I got your message," I said, clearing my throat. "You have some questions?"

She glanced over at me. Her expression was pressed between embarrassment and anger. "I waited for your call."

"It was too late to call," I replied.

"I said it didn't matter."

I met her eyes. "It mattered to me."

She looked away. The woman was strong, but not quite confident enough to challenge me. The thought made me smile. She had an endearing quality about her. I closed my eyes and relished the wind against my face. It was an appreciated distraction.

"You said you were a Spartan warrior?" she began.

Keeping my eyes closed, I nodded.

"Did you fight with Achilles?"

"At times."

"There is nothing written about you," she said, her tone laced with disappointment.

When I didn't answer, she continued. "I expected to find something about the great son of Hermes to be documented somewhere."

"Even the recounts of Achilles are inaccurate."

Her eyes widened with wonder. "What do you mean?"

I smiled. "Those who were there during the battles did not keep records. Stories told over evening fires are what you read about now. The true documenters of our times were something akin to your great novelists. They tell a great story, but that is all it is—a story."

Her brows pulled together and she remained silent for some time. "So, what you're saying is that much of our history, as we know it, is nothing but a collection of stories? There is no truth to it?"

"No," I said, shaking my head. "What I'm saying is that the information documented is done so from one or more person's perspective. No one really knows from where their facts had come. One story is rarely told the same way by many people."

"True," she said. "I guess I just never thought about history as being a story."

"That's why it's called 'His-story.' Everything told from the perspective of a person is a story. Only God and His acolytes know the truth of things."

She pulled off the freeway and the deafening wind calmed. It was an unusually sunny day for this time in the morning. The heat of it warmed my skin—definitely something I had missed.

"And what about you?" she asked. "Do you know the truth of things?"

"Some," I answered. My brows furrowed, thinking about the mystery of her and the truth behind my mission. "But not all."

She turned right, and then ventured down the narrow alley that sided with the studio. "Are there some things that are hidden from you, then?" she asked, parking the car and killing the engine.

"No," I answered. "There are some things I choose not to know."

Her expression showed a hint of eloquence, as if she understood my dilemma. We grabbed our bags from behind the seats and headed for the studio.

As we walked in, Master Mac glanced at the clock. There was five minutes to spare. Jamie watched with curious wonder as we bowed before hurrying toward the dressing rooms. I could only imagine what her mind was conjuring, given my rough appearance and Elle's wind-reddened face. Her obvious embarrassment only added to the color of her cheeks.

I took my position near the back of the class, according to Kael's lower rank, just as Elle took hers beside Jamie near the front.

Facing us, Master Mac cleared his throat, then placed his right fist into his left palm and bowed. Kael's body was in decent shape, making the warm-up tolerable. His upper body was not as strong as it could be so doing pushups proved to be more challenging than I cared to admit. My warrior side pressed through the pain and pushed Kael's body beyond anything it may have endured in the past.

My muscles were twitching with fatigue.

Perl paired with me for sparring practice. Her older husband, Jim, paired with Neal.

The sparring bout was entertaining but hardly practical. In a true battle, the maneuvers we were practicing would do nothing short of getting us killed.

"Keep your eyes on mine," I told her. "And keep your elbows in, like this." I positioned her elbows so that they covered more of her body. I then proceeded to demonstrate how to use those powerful elbows in the event of an attack. The smile on her face broadened with renewed understanding as she blocked a previously successful punch to her midsection.

Master Mac was watching from across the room. The weight of his eyes felt heavy against my back.

We moved into some self-defense techniques that would only work if the circumstances were right. In a practical sense, they seemed like a waste of time. Master Mac paired me with Neal, an overly aggressive man who looked like a model marine. His crew-cut hair made his jaw look more chiseled than Brad Pitt's and his chest out-girthed his midsection three-to-one. Compared to Kael's slight frame, the pair of us mirrored David versus Goliath.

After thwarting Neal's first attack with something he did not expect, his aggression spiked to a whole new level. His grips became firmer, his punches quicker. I averted them with ease, leaving him on the floor to reassess his actions. When it became more of a spectacle, earning the attention of the other students, Master Mac stepped in.

"Very impressive, Mr. McLeod. I don't remember seeing these skills demonstrated by you before."

I had to raise my chin to meet his eyes, something I was not used to doing. As Avel, I had always been tall and typically looked down to meet another's eyes.

As if in slow motion, I saw his muscles flex, preparing an attack. My instincts took over and before I fully realized what had happened, Master Mac lay at my feet, eyes wide with confusion and shock, body splayed and pinned beneath my knee strategically placed below his left clavicle. Knowing he had been beat, Master Mac slapped his palm against the floor, indicating surrender.

I stood and offered him a hand-up.

The class ceased their practice and observed the distraction with curious eyes. Jamie's lips turned up into a seductive grin. Elle looked as if she had just witnessed the brutal slaughter of Bambi. Jim and Pearl stood with their mouths held open. I looked away before witnessing a disgusting view of drool. Neal stood, arms crossed with an expression that screamed pure odium.

Master Mac stood, cleared his throat, then bowed. "Very good, Mr. McLeod. Your new found skills surpass your rank. I must admit, I do not recognize the system you employ but its effectiveness was clearly demonstrated. Please keep in mind, however, that this is my class, and my system. I expect you to follow my instructions and practice the techniques that have been demonstrated.

I bowed. "Understood, Sensei. My apologies."

"Neal," Master Mac commanded, "pair with Kael. Pearl and Jim, partner up. Jamie, you pair with Elle."

We ended the class with forms. As a warrior, forms had been an intricate part of training, designed to develop balance, flow, precision and speed. After watching Neal fling his hands as if they dangled on the end of damp rope, I pressed myself to demonstrate the way forms should be practiced.

Master Mac addressed me with curious anticipation.

"Mr. McLeod. Demonstrate five pinion, please."

I stood and positioned myself in the center of the room. I played the moves that resided in Kael's memory of the form, then took a few deep breaths. I bowed, beginning the form. My moves were sharp, purposeful. My eyes focused on invisible foes, while my strikes and kicks packed enough energy to stop an attack, be it real or not. My center was low, and movement was not wasted in setting up my next block and counter-attack. I was pleased with my performance, but Kael's body was not conditioned as a warrior and I felt as if I commanded pudding in place of hard muscle. I ended the form with a slow, respectful Bow. Neal glared at me as if I were a worm he had found in his salad.

A sly smile softened Master Mac's expression. His pale eyes, however, reflected suspicion. "You seem to be full of little surprises today, Mr. McLeod. That was a solid demonstration.

Jamie stood next and performed three kata. Elegant as it was, her moves were hardly effective. Jim and Pearl were slow and methodical as if concentrating more on the moves than on good form. When it was Elle's turn, she offered me a playful look of challenge. She performed five kata with as much grace as Jamie, but the strikes held power. In all honesty, her form put mine to shame.

"Impressive, Ms. Alder," Master Mac commended. He stood and returned to the front of the room to close out the class.

I walked out of the men's locker room to find Master Mac hovering over Elle like a cobra assessing its next meal.

"*True Grit* is playing at the Galaxy tonight. Are you up for having dinner and a show, Ms. Alder?"

I could see Jamie's brows rise as she fumbled with something in her bag, stalling time.

Elle tried to take a step back, but the wall hindered her effort. She looked away from the alluring instructor's gaze. "Um, I'm—"

"Busy," I completed the sentence for her. "She's spending time with me."

Jamie turned away from her bag. The garment she held in her hand fluttered to the floor. Her eyes darted between Elle and me as if she had been edged out of a juicy scandal.

Master Mac slowly turned to face me, enabling Elle to sidle away from the wall. "My apologies." His gaze returned to Elle. "Perhaps another time, then?"

She furrowed her brows. "Yes, I'd like that."

"Perhaps in another lifetime," I added. "For now, Elle belongs to me." The words escaped my mouth before I could stop them. Where was this possession coming from? My time on Earth was temporary and short at best.

As if having an agenda of its own, my body stiffened to emphasize the point I had so carelessly announced.

Elle shot me a questioning stare. "Really?" she said. "Am I aware of this self-appointed ownership?"

I positioned myself between her and Master Mac. "Yes," was all I said, keeping my eyes on Master Mac.

He returned my stare with amusement and challenge. "Well then," he chuckled. "It seems we have quite the situation." He mocked a bow. "I stand down, then." He offered Elle a promising smile before retreating into his office.

"Are you out of your mind?" she seethed.

I grabbed her hand and led her out of the studio. My grip proved stronger than her effort to pull away.

"He is not right for you," I said.

"So," Jamie said, following us out of the studio. "You have been holding out on me." She poked us both in the chest. "You two have a thing going."

"It's no thing," Elle assured her. "It's obvious that Kael hit his head too hard the other day. He's having delusions."

Jamie turned her green eyes back to me. "Uh, huh."

My grip on Elle's hand held firm. She rotated her arm then brought it sharply down to break the hold. Clever girl.

Jamie smiled. "So, are we still having coffee?"

Elle said, "Yes."

I said, "No," at the same time.

Elle forced a smile. "I'm driving," she countered, dangling her keys. "Kael's buying," she added.

"Cool," Jamie said. "I'll see you there."

I forced my smile down as I held the door open for Elle. She offered me a glare in return before sliding into her seat.

Chapter 7

COFFEE WAS BRIEF. I'D MADE sure of that. Jamie was asking too many questions and I didn't want her involved. That woman could make waves that could fill Mother Ocean with envy. Elle was still acting cold toward me and we had yet to discuss what had happened at the studio.

She pulled into the parking space in front of my condo and left the engine running. I assumed she wanted me to exit the car so she could be on her way. With a wave of my hand, I killed the engine.

"Ugh," she roared, turning the key.

"Come inside with me," I said.

"No!" she replied, with indisputable firmness.

I had only known one other woman who would dare stand up to me with such venom. Syria was a rare female—strong, independent to a ruddy fault, and stubborn as the wind. This woman was her equal.

"We need to talk, Elle. There isn't much time. In case you have forgotten, I have a mission to fulfill and you are an intricate part of it."

"Despite whom you think you are, I'm not part of your mission, nor do I want to be. Now please, get out of my car."

"I cannot leave you alone."

"Funny, you had no qualms about it last night." She turned her key again with no results, then slammed her hand on the steering wheel. "Damn it!"

"The Council has instructed me to stay by your side until the end of this mission."

She turned to scowl at me. "To hell with your Council, your mission, and you. I do not belong to you, nor will I ever."

"My apologies," I said, my voice lowered with honest regret. "I overstepped my bounds. If it would help, I would return to the studio and apologize to Master Mac."

She studied my eyes. "I like him, you know."

The change in my expression caused her to look away.

"But only on the surface," she added. "He's a player and will always be chasing his next challenge. I was curious to get to know him better, that's all."

I took a deep breath and pushed down the feeling of violence that begged for release on the pompous sensei. "Understood."

Elle tried her key again with no effect. "I need to call Triple-A."

"There is nothing wrong with your car," I said. "Come inside and we'll talk."

"What do you mean there is nothing wrong with my car? I can't get it to start." She pulled her key out of the ignition.

I pointed to the steering column and the car roared to life. I waved my hand and the engine purred to a stop.

"Your car is fine," I said, stepping out of the car.

She looked at the keys in her hand, then back at me. "How did you do that?"

"Come," I said, growing impatient. "We have much to do."

She followed me up to my condo. "Why were you instructed to not leave my side?"

"Vincent has an interest in you," I said, over my shoulder.

"Why?"

I opened the door with my will and we stepped inside.

"You're telekinetic," she replied.

"Among other things," I said. "Are you hungry?"

She nodded. "You haven't answered my question. Why is Vincent interested in me?"

"You have a gift that intrigues him."

"A gift?" she inquired.

I pulled eggs, sausage and vegetables from the fridge and placed them on the counter. "The book you found has a curse placed upon it. That curse didn't affect you. I'm sure he wants to know why."

"Yes," she said, sitting at the table. "You mentioned that before. I just don't know what it all means."

I poured us both a glass of iced tea and set hers on the table. "It means you're in danger."

"Will he try to kill me?"

"No," I said. "Knowing Vincent, he will want to use you for his own gain."

Her eyes widened. "Use me?"

"He sees a power in you. If he can harness it, combine it with his own, that power can be tripled."

She stood and started to pace the room. "Combine it," she muttered. "What exactly does that mean?"

"Couple with you and—"

She held her hand up, "Never mind. I don't want to know." Her lower lip trembled a bit, but she tried not to show it.

I wanted to reach for her, place my hands upon her delicate shoulders and offer comfort, but held back. I turned and concentrated on cooking breakfast instead. I had overstepped our friendship once and did not want to repeat the error.

She rubbed her arms, pacing the hard oak floors, her thoughts blurred as she played out images of possible horrors that lay ahead. Her mind was quick, imaginative, and intuitively accurate. I fought the urge to tell her. Too much knowledge and confirmation were often dangerous allies.

Her hands shook as she took a sip of her tea.

"I will keep you safe," I assured her.

She nodded in acceptance of that bold claim, but doubt still etched her eyes. "My parents always said I had a flair for trouble." She stifled a laugh. "I guess they're right."

"Another's opinion is only right if you give it the power to be so," I said. I turned the heat down and allowed the omelet to cook slowly under cover. I joined her, setting my tea on the thick and heavy glass table. The sound of the impact jolted her from her thoughts.

"I wish I'd never found that blasted book," she muttered.

"But you did, and fate cannot be changed."

"I don't believe in fate," she said.

"Fate, God, Angels, and even demons, do not require your belief to exist."

She looked at me with sullen eyes. The blue of her

irises looked ashen now, and sadly dull. "My life will never be the same, will it?"

"Life is ever changing, Elle. Every ending gives birth to new beginnings. It is a journey with only one destination—death."

She smiled. "That's cheery."

I shrugged. "It's life."

"What's it like to die?" she asked.

"Everyone's experience is different. For some, it's peaceful. For others, it's torturous."

"And the afterlife?"

"Not what you would expect," I said.

Her eyes sparkled with curiosity. "In what way?"

I met her gaze. "You feel things more deeply," I said. "Love, joy, sadness. Your physical sensations are lost, but your emotions are enhanced. Energetically, you are connected to everything around you. Words are not necessary. Your thoughts are felt by all."

"Is there coffee there?" she mused.

I smiled. "Physically, no. Energetically, all is available and can be brought forth by will."

"So, I could conjure piles of chocolate, enjoy it, but not gain a single pound?"

I laughed. "Yes. Since you no longer have a physical body, weight is irrelevant."

"Death doesn't sound so bad," she said.

"For some," I clarified, "death is perpetual."

Her delicate, blonde brows furrowed in confusion. "What do you mean?"

"If you take your own life, or are killed unjustly, you must return to this Earth to fulfill your obligations."

The creases between her brows deepened with fear and worry.

"Your death," I explained, "Must be part of your destiny—your life contract."

She stood and started to pace again. "I don't ever want to come back," she said. "Never."

"Understood," I said, standing to check on the omelet.

We ate our breakfast in silence and finished the dishes together, both lost in our own thoughts.

"So, what's next?" she said, lifting her chin and straightening her shoulders. She looked ready to take on the world with a shaky heart.

"We retrieve the book, find Vincent, and deliver him to the Council."

"Sounds simple enough."

"We must stay together," I added. "Either here or at your place."

Her thoughts assessed the situation and fear laced her mind. Both of our places sported only one room. Though the thought of it excited her, the reality froze her heart. "The cabin has three bedrooms," she offered. "I think it would be best."

"I'll gather my things."

IT DIDN'T TAKE LONG FOR us to get settled. Elle had wandered out the back, claiming she needed some time to think things over. I searched for her several hours later, finding her in the massive greenhouse that occupied most of the rear property. I quietly observed as she sang to the plants while tenderly caring for their needs. Those she had harvested were formally thanked and offered her gratitude before she crushed the leaves, seeds, and roots. She then added them into a brew on a hotplate. Some of the crushed leaves and roots were added to a jar filled with clear liquid. She secured the lids then shook them vigorously before placing them on a shelf.

I smiled, remembering how Syria used to tend to plants in much the same way. She had a gift for making medicine like her mother, Demeter, Angel of protection and plants. Syria once said that there was no plant on this Earth that didn't have medicinal purposes, even those that could kill when used unwisely. The sound of her strong but delicate voice rang in my memory like a favored song that could never be forgotten. My heart ached and grew heavy with longing for her. I had stopped wondering if I would ever hold her in my arms again.

"Avel," Elle said, slightly startled. "I didn't hear you come in."

"I didn't want you to."

She looked away, her face flushed with embarrassment. "Welcome to my sanctuary," she said.

I walked closer to glance over her shoulder at the thick liquid on the hotplate. "What are you brewing there?"

She slowly stirred the concoction with a set of cheap chopsticks. "Pain salve. Pearl and Jim like to use it to ease their arthritis."

I breathed in, trying to identify the ingredients, but couldn't. "What's in it?"

"A heated base of extra-virgin olive oil with powdered comfrey leaves and root, calendula flowers, feverfew, catnip, meadowsweet and white-willow bark. I allow it to cook at 200 degrees for three hours, then drain the mixture. After that, I add some shea butter and a bit of beeswax. As it cools, I fold in peppermint, wintergreen, rosemary and lavender essential oils. Then, I leave it to solidify."

I laughed, amazed at the alchemy of it all. "Where did

you learn such things?"

She shrugged, "Books, mostly. I've always been intrigued with the healing properties of plants. I've played with them since before I could remember. My father built this place for me in hopes that someday I would become a doctor of some sort."

"That sounds fitting," I said. "Why did you not pursue it?"

"Too many restrictions," she said. "When you have a license, you are closely governed and controlled." Her eyes met mine. "I don't like being controlled."

"Yes," I laughed, "I sense that."

She skirted around me and retrieved a few more jars from a box on the floor. I watched as she added more foul-smelling liquid to the herbs in the jars.

"What is that awful stuff?" I asked.

She laughed, obviously enjoying my sour expression. "Everclear alcohol. I use it to make my tinctures."

"People actually drink that?"

She smiled. "Yes."

When I didn't reply, she fetched a small dropper bottle from the shelf. The label read "Mellow Fellow."

"And that is?" I questioned.

"For you," she said. "Tonight, you will have the best sleep ever."

I wasn't sure if I should be pleased or concerned. I needed to have my wits about me.

"Don't worry," she said, as if reading my thoughts. "It won't dull your senses. It's a mild calmative with powerful results, that's all." She slipped the bottle into her pocket.

I helped her in the greenhouse for another hour before we retired inside. I built a fire in the hearth while she prepared chili and cornbread for dinner. We shared a bottle of Zinfandel, then settled on the couch to watch *Troy*.

After I pointed out the numerous inaccuracies in the film, Elle walked over and turned the movie off.

"You know that movies are purely meant for entertainment purposes, don't you?"

"Hardly entertaining when the facts are scrambled beyond recognition," I said in disgust.

She headed for the kitchen and retrieved the bottle she had brought in earlier. I was curious how she was going to prepare such a concoction that would be tolerated by my mouth. After she put water on the stove to boil, she placed a dropper full of the tincture, the juice of a lemon and bit of honey into each cup. The boiled water was added next. After about five minutes, she handed one cup to me.

"Sip it slowly," she said.

Cautiously I sipped the brew, expecting a foul taste to invade my mouth. I was pleasantly surprised. "Hmm, this is good," I exclaimed, taking another sip.

"When prepared properly, tinctures can be quite pleasing."

We took our tea to the living room. I added another log to the dwindling fire, and then joined her on the couch.

"So, if Vincent succeeds in restoring his dead parents, what are we facing?" she asked.

"The bowels of hell," I replied.

"How do we stop something that is already dead?" She sipped her tea, blue-green eyes gazing at me with child-like curiosity.

"We sever their heads," I replied.

"Sounds simple enough." She forced her tea down through a restricting lump in her throat, betraying her discomfort with the idea.

"Providing they don't kill us first. We are talking about dark, magical beings, Elle."

"So what's your plan?"

"Vincent will wait for the full moon to cast his spell. That gives us ten days to find the book before he has a chance to resurrect his father."

Elle looked more at ease. "Can he use the book when the moon is nearly full?"

I thought for a moment. "Yes, it is possible; however, the full power of his intentions may not be achieved. What are you thinking?"

"What if Vincent resurrects others as practice before he tries the spell on his father and mother?"

"You suggest he's building an army of half-baked minions?"

"It's possible," she said, taking another sip of her tea.

"If that's the case, we have an even larger problem at hand."

"Do minions have magical powers?" she asked.

I shook my head. "No, they would mimic simple-minded thugs without a conscience."

"So, how would Vincent use them?"

"To do his petty work," I said, "so he could remain in the shadows, undetected."

Elle sipped in silence, mulling things over. She had a fascinating mind, one that rivaled old Aristotle. While she played out various scenarios in her head, she tapped her pinky finger against the side of her cup, an odd gesture that Syria often employed when trying to solve difficult situations.

"What are you thinking?" she said, smiling over at me.

Lord, that smile could undo me. I stared out the

window into the darkness. "You remind me of someone I once knew."

"Someone nice, I hope," she jested.

The need to tell her about Syria closed my throat nearly to the point of suffocation. I thought I was finally over that woman. For a long while, I had not felt for her with such pain.

"Avel?" she said, moving closer. "You look like you've swallowed a bitter pill and it's still stuck in your throat." She studied me with concern. Then, with a softness that only a dove could mimic, she touched my hand.

I fought the urge to pull back as the energy of her coursed through my body like liquid lightning. At that moment, her face changed and I saw her soul.

"Syria," I murmured.

She pulled back, frowning.

I gripped her face in my hands and forced her to look at me. Fear widened her eyes as mine looked into hers. Then suddenly her pupils softened with recognition. I let her go. My hands started to shake.

"No," I growled. "This cannot be." I released her, stood from the couch, then started to pace. The Council would not do this to me.

"Avel," she said, her voice shaky. "I feel funny." She, too, was shaking. It was a common reaction to soul recognition, especially when the emotions attached to them were so deeply rooted. "Who am I to you?" she said. "Who is Syria?"

I continued to pace, refusing to acknowledge this feeling of betrayal. "My wife," I said, my voice barely audible.

She curled her legs beneath her on the couch and held them close to her body as if seeking comfort. "That's impossible," she said, her voice distant. "All of this is impossible," she added, her eyes shifting like a woman played a fool.

She looked at me with such intensity I felt the sting of her pain. "You shouldn't be here. None of this is real, not you, not Vincent." She started to cry. "God, I am cursed. I wished I had never found that blasted book."

"It is not the book that curses you," I said, trying to keep the anger from my voice. Part of me wanted to comfort her, another wanted to confront the Council for placing me in this situation. They knew—they had to have known. The thought of it pierced my soul like a scabbard laced with pepper. I wanted to call Raphael, but given my current state of emotions, that would not be wise.

"It never fails," said Elle, her voice shaky and distant. "Every time I am attracted to a man, the mistake of it all becomes sickeningly apparent."

"The mistake of it all," I repeated. "Explain."

She flinched at the sharp edge of my words. "I avoid relationships. They make me uncomfortable."

I remained silent, prompting her to continue on her own accord. I wasn't sure if I should reveal Syria's past or not. The ramifications could be devastating.

Elle bit her lower lip. "Is everyone reincarnated?"

"No," I answered.

"Why me?"

I continued to pace. "I need a moment," I said. "Alone."

Confused and disappointed, she stood wearing a concerning frown. "I'll be in the greenhouse."

I waited for her to leave before calling Raphael. He arrived with a solemn look on his face. I didn't have to ask him if he knew the truth of it all; he did, and so did the other Council members.

"Have I done something wrong?" I asked, staring into his silver-gray eyes.

"No," he said.

"Then why? It pains me to see her. The Council knows this and yet they assign me here with her." My voice grew hard and I had to silence my thoughts or risk showing unforgivable disrespect. Archangels were patient, but not even God would help the soul who dared to show them any contempt.

"Would you like us to assign another?" he calmly asked.

The thought of another soul protecting Syria—Elle—made my gut ache. What if he failed to defend her? I would know it. Syria would return to life on Earth as another being, plagued with the same heartache, and depression that caused her to repeatedly take her life. She never understood the cause of that depression or heartache, but she felt it and lived it. That was why relationships made her uncomfortable. In a sense, she lived in her own personal hell with no recourse but to live through it without understanding or reason to ease the edge of it all.

"No," I said, "it's too late for that."

"Help her," Raphael's voice was suggestive, but guarded.

I stopped pacing. "And how, pray tell, do you suggest I do that? My tongue is tied. She cannot know the truth of her past. Already her questions rise, only to be avoided." I tried to keep the seething anger from my voice, but my emotions were too raw to conceal or control. If the powerful Archangel struck me down right now, I would almost welcome the blow.

"The Council understands your predicament."

"Am I to remain silent, then?"

Raphael tapped his fingertips together as if considering a dangerous move on a chessboard. "You may tell her what you must with no restrictions."

"And the ramifications?"

"Her future is already altered, Avel. Her time has drawn to a close. This will be her final lifetime."

My belly felt pummeled with the impact of those words. If Elle chose to end her life, or another took it from her, she would not return. Her soul would be lost with many others who failed to complete their life contract. I would never see her again. As it was, she had been granted many opportunities to fill her purpose—more than was typical. She was special, however, and her integrity was pure. Now, she was being given the gift of knowing, a warning of sorts. The Council was giving her an opportunity that few received in a lifetime. The thought of it melted my anger into a puddle of guilt and shame.

Raphael must have noticed the change. It made him smile. "Sometimes," he said, "exceptions are made for extraordinary circumstances. Elle did not find that book by chance, Avel, nor is she immune to its curse. You may thank Archangel Jeremeil for her protection thus far."

Jeremiel was the Archangel of visions and soul retrievals. He and I rarely saw things on the same level and the distance he maintained between us left me rather perplexed at this unexpected act of kindness. "Why?"

"You have served our Father well, Avel. He has felt your pain and is not without mercy. The chance Syria has before her is because of the love you once shared. It is a powerful emotion and one that is worth investing in.

Your time here is short," he reminded me. "Use it wisely." With that, he faded away leaving a wake of warmth and the scent of sandalwood behind.

My mission, I realized, had little to do with Vincent and his abuse of magic. The Council had the power to annihilate the young necromancer with little effort. This mission was about something larger, more substantial.

Suddenly, a coldness gripped the air. From the window, I saw the light in the greenhouse go out. I ran out the back door and tried to enter the clear vinyl dome but the door was secured shut. "Elle?" I called out, then forced the door open. Splinters of wood scattered onto the dirt floor. I listened but heard nothing. The coldness grew sharp, and the scent of rotting flesh was apparent. I ran back toward the small shack. The door was locked. I willed it open and found Elle with a beefy arm holding her in a neck lock, eyes wide with her feet barely touching the floor.

The thug who held her looked like something out of a horror movie. His flesh was raw like a three-day-aged corpse. The red-flannel shirt hung on his body, tucked loosely in blue jeans littered with dirt and holes.

"Let her go," I warned.

The corpse laughed and tightened his hold.

Elle gurgled and tried to struggle free.

I willed a tincture bottle from the shelf and directed it at the thug's head. The bottle exploded and the pungent smell of comfrey and alcohol drowned the stench. The thug wavered for a moment, released his hold, then collapsed into a heap on the floor. Elle fell back, banging her head against the wall. I had to get her out but did not want to leave the corpse intact. He had to be dismembered and burned or else he would reassemble himself and grow stronger as a result.

"Elle," I said, shaking her, "wake up!"

She mumbled something incoherent, then opened

her eyes. When they regained their focus on the hideous thug, she scrambled to her feet with terror.

"Easy," I growled. "I need to take care of him. Get back to the house and lock the doors."

Without a word, she did as I asked. It was not at all what I had expected of her. Elle was frightened, yes, but she was stubborn to a fault and not one to miss out on the action.

Rotting flesh is not as easy to pull apart as one might think. I used my will and a sturdy shovel to sever the head, and then carried it and the body outside where they could be burned.

Elle came back with a gun clutched in her hand, aimed at the corpse's body. Her hands were shaking.

"He's dead," I assured her.

"For some time, by the looks of him," she added, still aiming her gun.

I smiled and shook my head, then willed a flame around the body. "Add some wood," I instructed her.

Keeping her eye on the body, she added fallen pine branches to the flame. She didn't seem at all surprised by the sudden flames, nor did she question my intentions.

We stood in silence, watching the fire devour the body and severed head, the stench of it filling the air. When the flames died down, all that was left was aged bone. With a wave of my hand, they were crushed to powder and carried away with a gust of wind.

Elle dropped the gun and fell to her knees, the impact of what happened finally hitting home. I retrieved the gun and carried her inside.

Chapter 8

PER ELLE'S INSTRUCTION, I MADE us a cup of tea, using a calming blend of linden, chamomile and lavender flowers. I had to admit, the brew was surprisingly good with just enough flavor to keep my interest.

We sat on the couch, sipping our tea in silence. Elle, dressed in pale-gray sweats, had her feet tucked under her and a soft blanket cradled in her arms. She resembled a young child recovering from a nightmare. I fought the urge to comfort her, knowing it would only lead to something far more dangerous and irreversible.

I felt compelled to apologize for her involvement, but the feeling was not heartfelt. In truth, I was relieved to know the veracity of it all, and the fact that she was given a standing chance at redemption. Would my involvement help or hinder her, I wondered?

"Why did that—thing try to kill me?" she said.

"He wasn't trying to kill you. I believe he wanted to take you back to Vincent. When I entered the shed, he used you as a threat."

"A threat?"

My thoughts swirled, feebly attempting to piece together a puzzle in the wind. "Vincent knows I'm here. The minion he sent was a warning. If he wanted you, he would have sent more."

"Will there be more?" she asked, her eyes wide and glistening.

"No doubt," I said. "Not tonight, though. I have placed wards around the premises. Anyone with ill intent will be destroyed if they enter. Tomorrow, we will stay at my place."

"Do we have to?"

"It is best, Elle. This place can be breached in time. My place is more secure and difficult to enter without notice."

She started to rock again, and fell silent for some time. I understood now why the Council was so concerned for her safety. They were right, as usual. And, as much as I hated to admit it, if they had been up front with me about who Elle was, I would have rejected the mission. Now, it was too late, something they also counted on, I was sure.

"Sometimes I feel like life itself is hell," she finally stated.

"Why?"

She looked at me with such emptiness in her clear blue-green eyes that my soul spilled with compassion.

"You mentioned that not all souls are reincarnated to live on this Earth. Clearly, I am, though I'm not sure why. As I think about it, I see the patterns of punishment. My family looks down on me, my love life is non-existent, and I often think of—"

I waited, but she didn't continue. "What?" I prompted.

"Death," she said. As the words fell from her mouth,

her eyes dilated to a near-perfect blackness. "I really don't have much to live for."

I sipped my tea, trying to push down the lump clogging my throat. "Life is a gift that should never be taken lightly, by anyone." My eyes fixed on hers.

"You don't understand," she said.

"Yet, I do understand. You feel you have nothing to live for. Ironic, isn't it? There are those who are sick and facing only days of life and wanting years, and then there are those like yourself who are young, beautiful, and healthy yet wishing for death. We always crave what we cannot have."

I stood and retrieved the gun from the table. I checked the ammunition, before handing the weapon to her. "You want to end your miserable life, Elle. I won't stop you—I never could."

She inspected the gun. "What do you mean, you never could?"

I sat next to her, held her hand with the gun and cocked the hammer. "You say you feel as if you're living in hell," I recounted. "Well, in a sense, you are. Unfortunately, taking your own life does not release you from its binds. You return, feeling the same emptiness you felt before you died. That never changes." My voice was harsh and my hands shook as I released hers. "I spent centuries trying to save you. I can't do it anymore. You either need to save yourself, or live eternity in this hell that you have created. I will not ask you to make this choice again. Make it now and stick with it. I am tired of waiting for you."

I stood and walked toward my bedroom. It was the hardest thing I had ever done. If she pulled the trigger, those harsh words would be the last I would ever say to her. I would have to let her go forever and never speak her name again. The choice had to be hers.

The silence that followed was both assuring and disturbing. Sleep was not an option. I tried meditating, pacing, then eventually lost my thoughts in a Tom Clancy novel. A soft knock rattled my door.

"Avel?"

"Come in," I said.

She did. Her eyes were red and swollen. "May I sit?" she asked, gesturing to the spot on the bed beside me.

I nodded.

She snagged a tissue from a box on the wicker end table and blew her nose. "Tell me about her," she said. "Syria."

"Have you made your decision?" I asked.

"For now."

"No," I roared. "That is not good enough. I will not live through your lifetime again with my heart against your dagger's bitter edge. Give me your word that you will see this life through, may it be good, bad, or indifferent."

Her eyes widened. "You want my word?"

I laid the book down between us. "I do."

Her eyes roamed to my bare chest then suddenly looked away. Sensing her discomfort, I swung my legs from the bed and retrieved my shirt from the chair in the corner of the small room.

She took a deep breath, and then another. I knew what I asked of her was difficult if not improbable. I also knew that the Syria I had grown to know and love would not be able to give her word and break it. I prayed her aged and battered soul retained that integrity even if at a worn degree.

"I give you my word," she said, her voice barely audible.

"Speak the words," I said, my voice much more harsh

than I intended. It was a struggle to rein in the raw emotions threatening to explode.

Her eyes narrowed and her lips grew firm. "I promise to live my life to the end," she said with conviction.

I opened the drawer beside the bed and grabbed a pad of paper and a pen that I had placed there earlier. I wrote a proper promise down, then handed her the paper. "Speak these words aloud, three times."

She read the words then shook her head and rolled her eyes. "Are you always this demanding?"

"Yes."

The paper in her hand crinkled as her fists tightened. She took another deep breath and closed her eyes for a moment. "What if I can't keep my promise?"

"If you cannot keep it, the words will not flow from your lips. Once spoken three times, the vow is sealed."

She read the words again, biting her lower lip. "I, Elle Alder, promise Avel, son of Hermes, to live my life to its full capacity without falter, so help me God."

"Again," I roared.

"I, Elle Alder, promise Avel, son of Hermes, to live my life to its full capacity without falter, so help me God."

"Once more."

A smile softened her delicate features. "I, Elle Alder, promise Avel, son of Hermes, to live my life to its full capacity without falter, so help me God."

I folded the paper and stuffed it into my pocket. "Be it so," I added. "As above, so below." I held out my hand and spat in the center of it. "Spit," I told her.

She wrinkled her nose then added her spittle to mine. With a thought, I set the liquid to fire until a blue ash was all that was left. "Press your hand to mine."

She did, her eyes wide with wonderment. She reminded

me of a child in the midst of something magical.

I led her from the room. “Come, we must wash our hands together.

“How did you do that?” she asked, as I handed her a towel.

I looked at her, puzzled.

“How did you burn that spit in your hand without burning yourself?”

“Magic.” I smiled.

She moved to swat me with the towel. I spun, caught it, and then wrenched it from her hands. Her feeble attempt to counter the attack only landed her on her backside with my knee upon her chest.

She struggled, groaned, tried to kick and pinch me, and then finally fell still.

I raised a brow, waiting for her complete surrender. With a loud groan, she slapped her hand against the floor, indicating defeat. I stood and lifted her up.

“If you were Kael,” she said, “it would be you lying on that floor.”

“Clearly I am not Kael.”

“Clearly,” she affirmed, brushing her hair from her eyes and straightening her sweatshirt. “Well, since you don’t seem to be giving me any answers tonight, I’m heading off to bed.”

I watched her walk toward her bedroom, rubbing her right hip. “We’ll talk in the morning,” I said.

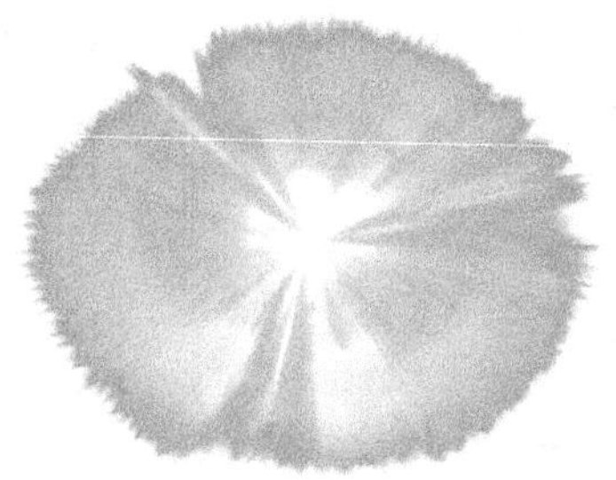

Chapter 9

I AWOKE EARLY THE NEXT morning to the appetizing aroma of spicy sausage and sweet biscuits, laced with pungent coffee brewing in a French press.

Elle stood in the kitchen beating eggs in a red plastic bowl. Her thin blonde hair mocked the braid that attempted to hold it together. Fine wisps haloed her head as she hummed the tune to the song playing on the radio.

I quietly slid the stool out on the opposite side of the counter and took a seat.

Elle turned and nearly dropped the bowl from her hands as she saw me there. She placed the bowl down and covered her heaving chest with her hand. "Jeez, Avel, do you always sneak up on people like that?"

My eyes settled on her chest. "I would apologize, but it wouldn't be heartfelt," I smiled.

She dropped her hand, her face visibly redder. She retrieved the bowl from the counter, turned her back to me and began beating the eggs again. "I hope you're hungry."

"I am." I studied her for a bit, trying to determine what she was thinking. When she turned to face me again, her brows were furrowed into a deep frown, while her lips remained taut.

"You seem talkative this morning," she commented, sliding a cup of black coffee before me. "Cream or sugar?"

"Neither, I like it black."

I watched as she doctored her own coffee with half-and-half and maple syrup.

"What," she said, stirring the concoction with a wooden spoon that was long and slender.

"Interesting mixture," I said.

She put the milk and syrup back in the fridge then checked the eggs.

"Did you sleep well?" I asked.

"No. Not at all, and you?"

"Quite well, thank you."

I saw her back stiffen.

"Care to tell me what's on your mind?" I asked, sipping my coffee. It had a nutty flavor that confused my palate. I wasn't sure if I liked it or not.

"I need some answers," she finally said.

"What kind of coffee is this?" I asked, the after-flavor clinging to my tongue like a sappy glue.

"Hazelnut."

"Hmm," I said, pushing it away.

Her frown deepened. "You don't like it?"

She resembled a puppy that had just been reprimanded. I pulled the cup back and held it in my hand.

"It's good," I choked out.

She narrowed her eyes and pulled the cup from my hands. After filling her cup with what was left in the press, she made another pot using unflavored grounds.

"I'm assuming Columbian is acceptable?"

"Yes," I said. "Thank you."

While she waited for the kettle to boil, she rinsed my cup, and then stirred the eggs with slow, even strokes. She checked on the biscuits and turned the oven off, sliding the plate of sausage into the oven to keep warm.

The kettle was boiling so I stood and removed it from the stove to pour water into the press.

Elle didn't seem to notice.

I helped set the breakfast counter with utensils, napkins, and plates. After that was accomplished, I carried the press over to fill my cup.

Silence was something I was very comfortable with, so I didn't press her for conversation.

Elle served breakfast onto each of our plates, her jaw held tight and her eyes fixed on her task. I was curious to see how long the silence would last.

She started eating, while my hands hovered over the meal. "Father, thank you for this meal and the loving hands that prepared it."

"Amen," she said, her mouth full of food. She swallowed prematurely before adding, "Sorry. I never got into the habit of praying."

I started eating.

"What, no comment?" she said

"This food is very good. It smells great."

"I meant about my praying, or lack thereof."

"No," I replied. It didn't matter to me one way or the other.

"No lectures about heaven and hell?"

"What do you want to know about them?"

She scuffed then shook her head. "Absolutely nothing," she said. "I get an earful of that stuff from my family."

"I take it you're not close to them?" I nearly bit my tongue the moment the words escaped my mouth. I really didn't want to know more about her. In truth, I wanted to keep my distance and not get involved. I figured if I remained cold and aloof toward her, she would do the same. It was best that way.

"Not at all, really," she said. "They are all very religious and have a strong idea about family morals."

"And you don't?"

"I don't know what I believe in anymore. My brother and sister are both happily married. My parents seem happy enough." She shrugged.

I continued to eat, wondering if she would expand on the matter.

"I, however," she finally continued, "can't seem to find anyone to love."

Don't get involved, I reminded myself. I continued to eat.

"How about you?" she asked.

I finished my sausage, then slid my plate back. I looked at her, trying hard not to get lost in those familiar eyes. They were not the same dark color as Syria's, but the spirit in their depths was the same. In this life, they were colored with the most vivid shade of blue speckled with green.

"Avel?" she asked, her eyes widening with concern.

"Yes," I said, clearing my throat. "I loved someone."

"Syria?"

I nodded then tried to drown my thoughts and feelings in my coffee as I gulped it down.

Elle stood to fill the press with more hot water. "Last night, you said I was her. What does that mean?"

I growled, trying to rein in the wave of emotions that

urged me to bolt from the house and get away from her. I took a deep breath, instead.

"What I'm about to tell you will seem so far-fetched, Elle, that you won't believe it anyway."

She filled my cup, then hers before she sat. She folded her tiny hands and rested her chin upon them. "Try me."

I took a sip of coffee and gathered my thoughts. "Several hundred years ago, you and I were married. Your name was Syria. We had known each other for years, but were married for only two before I died in battle. You carried our son, due to give birth in only four moons." I swallowed, trying to release the constricting lump in my chest. "One moon after my death, you took your life and the life of our young."

She sat back, the pain that etched her face was genuine. "Oh God."

"Since then, you had to come back to this Earth and live out your contract. The pain that caused you to take your life the first time stayed with you, causing you to..." I couldn't finish. The memory of it all was too unbearable.

"It all makes sense now," she said, her gaze lost in distant thought. "When people get too close to me, I panic as if losing them will tear my heart to pieces. I even hold my family at a distance. My heart is empty inside. I've always felt empty."

I nodded. "Yes, it is the epitome of hell. You wanted to know about it, but ironically, you have been living it for hundreds of years."

She stood and walked toward the sliding glass door that opened to the back yard. She stood there, looking out at the gardens before asking, "Is it perpetual?"

"No," I said. "Only you can make it so."

She turned to face me. "How is that possible?"

"The Father gives us free will. Before we are gifted with life on this Earth, we agree to a contract. That contract must be fulfilled before we return to his Kingdom."

"What is my contract?"

"That is between you and the Father."

The crease between her brows deepened. "What if I don't know what it is?"

"You pray for guidance and trust in what you receive."

She retrieved her mug and took a long, slow sip. "I don't believe in religion."

"You don't have to. Religion has nothing to do with God or his creations."

"Him?" she inquired. "How do you know he's not female?"

"Actually, he's neither male nor female. The energetic force that he emits is male in nature, while the manifestations that are born from that energy are female, hence Mother Earth and her children."

She scoffed. "Seriously? You believe in that crap?"

I raised a brow. "Do you believe you are drinking from a cup?" I asked.

"Yeah, it's solid. I can hold it in my hand."

I waved my hand and caused the cup to vanish. Her eyes widened.

"How did you do that?"

"The cup is something that was manifested. It is as real as all life on this Earth. It is also an illusion."

I waved my hand and brought the cup back to her hand.

"The cup never left. I just made you believe that it did." I stood and walked toward her. "Your beliefs are powerful, Elle. They define your reality. You may not believe in the Father and His truths, but He believes in you. In this life, you are given the chance to return to me in the Ethereal Kingdom." I gripped her arms. "It will be your last chance."

She looked away from me and took a deep breath. "That's why you made me promise last night, isn't it?"

"Yes," I growled. "Now you understand."

She set her cup down and began clearing the dishes. "I guess I should start going to church or something, right?"

"Your church is all around you, Elle. It is not something you must attend. The Father lives in your heart, He always has. Just talk to Him and be silent. He will answer you."

I scraped the food off the plates, and then set them to soak in the sink.

"He never has before," she said.

"Is that why you have been given more chances than most souls to make things right?"

When she didn't answer, I expanded my point. "If He didn't listen to you, I would not be here and you would have been cursed by The Book of Shadows. It is only by His mercy that you are given this chance."

She stopped scrubbing the dishes for a moment pondering that thought.

We finished the dishes in silence, each lost in our own thoughts. Mine was on the days ahead of us. I was to find Vincent and destroy him and the book. Something the Angels could do with minimal effort. Why, then, was I sent here?

Elle played a big part in all this I was sure of it, but in what capacity? I wondered. Vincent was interested in her, of course, but his interest was misconceived by believing she had thwarted his curse. The Angels would have known that.

"So what's next?" asked Elle, hanging up the towel.

"We leave this house and I pull you into a world where only nightmares exist."

"Is this a one-way ticket sort of thing?" she asked.

"Yes and no," I replied. "Your life as you've known it will change forever."

Her lips curled slightly. "That doesn't sound so bad."

Her eyes sparkled the way Syria's did before facing new adventures. To Syria, the thrill of the unknown was what drove her forward. She had never backed down from any danger and that inner strength was what I had loved the most. If I wasn't careful, this woman would breach my fragile control and open a wound I was not sure she could ever heal.

Chapter 10

WE RETURNED TO MY CONDO only to find it in shambles. Vincent's minions had torn it apart.

"Why?" Elle questioned, looking at the debris of glass, broken ceramics and wood littering the floor. "What were they looking for?"

"Nothing," I said, kicking away a piece of wood. "They were making a statement."

"Let me guess," she said. "We know who you are and we want you dead?"

I had to smile at the calmness with which she spoke those words. "Something like that. Vincent knows I'm here. This is his way of communicating that knowledge as well as his distaste for my wards. He used his minions to break through and deliver his message."

"Now what?"

"I call on Raphael."

She pointed her thumb to the front door. "Do you need me to leave?"

I shook my head. "No. If he doesn't want you to see

him, he will remain hidden from you."

She brushed the broken lamp from the couch and took a seat, apparently eager to see what would soon transpire.

"Raphael," I called. "I need your counsel."

He manifested before me in a blue mist until he stood complete. This time, he looked like an old-timer who had just been called in from a week-long fishing trip. His waders were still wet and reeked of salt water. I glanced over at Elle. Her jaw was open and her eyes were wide with wonder.

"Great impression," I told him.

He glanced down at his attire. "I was in the middle of something when you called," he said.

"Fishing, no doubt," I observed. The vest with various hooks and lures was a solid clue.

"They are far more challenging to catch than I thought," he said. "Those slippery little buggers were playing with me I'm sure of it."

I gestured to Elle. "Archangel Raphael, I would like you to meet Elle Alder." I then gestured to the old man standing before me. "Elle, Archangel Raphael in all his glory."

"Miss Alder," Raphael purred. It's always a pleasure to see you again." His voice was young and silky.

Elle forced her mouth to close.

"Elle, you look like Alice after falling down the rabbit hole," I commented.

Raphael walked over and touched Elle's hand. She, no doubt, felt the sting of his energy but couldn't bring herself to pull back.

"Always a spirit of beauty," he said. "I see what Avel loves in yo—."

"Okay," I interrupted him. "As you can see, we are in a

bit of a bind. Vincent knows I'm here." I gestured to the mess littering the floor. "His message is clear."

Raphael released Elle's hand, and then pulled at his beard as if pondering the situation. "So much for our element of surprise."

"In nine days, he will try to resurrect his parents, I'm sure of it. The Council must end this madness before it's too late."

"If we could, would we have sent you here?"

I had wondered about that myself.

"The Council has boundaries, Avel."

"But it was the Council who sent me here. They are already involved."

"And the plan would have worked so long as your identity remained intact. Now that Vincent knows who you are, the Council is suspect."

"Meaning?"

"We tried to shift the odds in our favor. It backfired. The fallen will counter the assault, I assure you."

"The fallen?" Elle asked.

"Dark Angels," I explained. "You know, the original battle between good and evil?"

"Like God and the devil?" she queried, disbelief in her tone.

"Yes," Raphael and I answered in unison.

Raphael looked at me with cold gray eyes. "I must take you back."

"No," I said, "Elle is still in danger. So long as Vincent has the book, he will want to use her."

Raphael shook his head. "Even the most innocent of intentions become distorted in the shadows," he murmured.

"What about the Spirians," I offered.

The silver in his eyes sparkled with renewed hope. "Yes, perhaps they can help in this matter."

"Who are the Spirians?" asked Elle.

"Human Angels; gifted beings," I said. "They often live undetected by humans even though they live among them."

"Their vow not to interfere with human issues will be a problem," said Raphael.

"Necromancy is hardly a human issue," I argued. "Vincent crossed that line when he entered the realm of black magic."

The old Angel pursed his lips and paced the littered floor as if nothing hindered his path. "You will need to contact Khalen; he governs this region. His clan is strong. Gain his cooperation and we might stand a chance at disarming the dark ones."

He projected an image into my mind, showing me how and where to contact this man named, Khalen.

"You cannot die by Vincent's hands," Raphael warned me.

"Understood." I nodded.

Raphael faded into the light, leaving only a scent of sandalwood in his place.

"Wow," said Elle, standing and wringing her hands together. "I feel as if I've walked directly into the twilight zone and everything I thought was real has morphed into a never-ending nightmare."

"Exactly," I agreed. "This is, indeed, a nightmare."

"So how do we find this Spiritan character?"

I laughed. "Spirian," I corrected. "According to Raphael's images, he lives on Harstine Island."

"Let's go," she said.

"It's not that easy," I countered. "You and I are human.

You don't just waltz into a Spirian camp looking to talk to the leader."

"Why not?"

"Grab your keys." I took her hand and led her out of the condo and back to her car. "Move quickly, we haven't much time."

"Where are we going?" she huffed, trying to keep pace.

"To The Wellness Center in Belfair," I said. "Khalen owns it. Since it is a public location, we stand a better chance at contacting him there.

"How do you know this?"

"Raphael sent me images."

"Images?"

"Yes," I explained, "a way of communicating without words. Whales and dolphins have used it for centuries."

"Right," she said, firing the engine. "I know that center. I sold them some herbs, tinctures, and salves a while back. I don't remember a man named Khalen, though."

"Spirians are a different breed of humans," I said. You don't want to cross them. They read your mind, and can manipulate your thoughts."

"Perfect," she sighed. "Why do I feel as if we're walking into a tiger's cage?"

We drove west on Highway 16 in silence for several miles before she spoke again. "So, are we surrounded by super-people all the time and don't even know it?"

"For the most part," I replied. "Humans live a very sheltered life. They give power to their governments and follow rules that often lead them astray from the truth."

"You speak of humans as if you are not one of them."

"I am a spirit, Elle, living in a human body that doesn't belong to me."

"Like a Spirian?"

"No," I corrected. "Spirians are born to this Earth. Aside from having very large and highly-developed pineal glands, they are essentially human."

Their powers and gifts grow with time. Mine, however, will fade with each passing day. In a sense, I become more human.

"So, you won't be able to sabotage my car or set spit on fire?"

"No, I will be completely human in a couple more days, having only the power of simple magic."

"That's too bad. I kind of liked that about you."

"Then perhaps it's a good thing my powers will fade."

She frowned and changed the subject. "How are these Spirians going to help us with Vincent?"

She pulled left onto Highway 3 heading toward the small town of Belfair.

"Spirians are gifted and live for a very long time. They govern the balance of good and evil here on Earth."

"Are they a threat to us?"

"Those known as Shadows are. The people we seek are called the Protected. They honor the Father's law."

A train overpass welcomed us into the town of Belfair. Elle slowed down. "Will they know what you are—a spirit?"

"Yes," I said. "It will make them leery about our intentions."

"Hmm, leery Spirians. This should be interesting."

She pulled left into The Wellness Center parking lot and parked in front of the small gray building. With a deep breath, she removed the key and we headed for the front door.

A tall, blonde-haired woman looked up from behind the long counter. "Elle?"

"Hi Ro," Elle replied. "This is my friend, Av—Kael," she choked.

Ro glanced at me speculatively, then looked back at Elle. "Are you delivering more product?" she asked. "We ran out of your pain and healing salve quite some time ago."

A slightly older man walked around the corner. "Hey, Elle. Long time no see, stranger." He offered her a lingering hug, causing my nerves to react in kind.

Elle grunted under the weight of the man's affection. "Hi Gregg."

He stepped back and offered me the same untrusting look the woman did. "Who's your friend?"

"This is Kael, a friend of mine from karate class."

Gregg extended his hand. "Good to meet you, Kael."

I matched his strength with my own, meeting his eyes. Having to look up to him was a bit disconcerting, and he wasn't even wearing shoes! Next time, I would have to remember to request a taller body. I shuddered, praying there wouldn't ever be a next time.

"What brings you here?" he asked.

Elle nudged me. "Kael needs to speak with someone," she said.

Both Ro and Gregg pierced me with a stare I could almost feel. I cleared my throat, and then said with forced confidence, "I understand Khalen owns this center?"

Gregg nodded. "He does."

"I would like to speak with him."

"We don't see much of him these days," said Ro. "Is there something we can help you with?"

"I seek counsel," I said, knowing the formal word would grant us some kind of an in. The two before us were not Spirian, but there was an uncanny vibration about them that marked them as something different than human.

"What is this regarding?" asked Gregg. His tone more tense now.

"It's personal," I countered, maintaining eye contact. I was told, with Spirians, it was one way to earn their trust. Gregg was not Spirian, but he was connected to them, that much was obvious.

"Do you have a way for him to contact you?" Ro asked.

Elle wrote down her cell phone number. "Have him call this number," she said.

"Can I speak with you for a moment?" Ro asked her.

Elle glanced at me, and then nodded. "Sure." She followed Ro to a room in the back, while Gregg hovered around me, offering small talk.

I noticed that Ro was also barefoot and wondered if either of them could afford shoes.

- Elle -

RO PLACED HER HAND ON my shoulder. "It's nice to see you again, Elle. Your friend seems nice."

She was fishing, I knew. I decided to give her as little as possible, not really knowing how she fit into the grand scheme of things. This whole metaphysical warfare was new to me and I didn't want to get Avel into any more trouble.

"How long have you known him?" she asked.

"Seven years," I replied. "He's a good friend."

"Nothing more than that?"

I frowned. "No, why?"

Ro smiled. "Judging by the way he wanted to behead

my husband for hugging you, I would venture to say he was more than just a friend."

I wasn't about to inform her that he was my husband several hundred years ago. That probably wouldn't go over real well, and it certainly wouldn't help our situation. "Kael is a bit—intense is all," I said, twisting my hands.

"What is this about, Elle?" she finally said. "You have never met Khalen. What does this friend of yours want with him?"

"He just wants to talk to him, Ro. Honestly, I don't see the concern in that."

"About what?"

I started to pace, clearly perplexed about how to explain our position. "Like he said, it's personal." I shrugged, indicating I knew nothing more than that.

"How does he know Khalen?"

"I don't know. He said he owned this center and needed to speak with him. I don't get involved in his business."

Ro's expression softened. "I'm sorry," she said, touching my shoulder. "I feel like I'm interrogating you."

I met her eyes. "He's a good man and I trust him."

She smiled. "Okay." She opened the door and I followed her back to the lobby.

I saw the vet from across the street coming toward the center. As he got closer, I recognized him as Ian, the younger of the two brothers who owned Belfair Veterinary Clinic. He had purchased some tinctures from me several months back.

He opened the door and smiled over at me. His flirtatious grin did not escape Avel's notice. Before he could lift me into a bone-crushing hug, Avel stepped between us.

"Kael," I said, slightly embarrassed by his sudden

show of jealousy. "This is Doctor Ian."

Kael held out his hand. Ian took it with a smile as if accepting some silent challenge.

"Aye," said Ian, "Yer finally spoken for, lass. It's about time." His light Irish accent was always attractive to me, but his playboy tendencies were a real deterrent.

"Kael is a friend," I confirmed.

Ian winked at me. "I'd say he's much more than that."

Ro and Gregg looked on with amplified curiosity.

I winced as Avel grabbed my hand and pulled me close to his side. "We apologize for taking your time. Please give Khalen our number. Inform him that time is of the essence."

Ian stepped between us and the door. "Perhaps I can offer some assistance. Khalen is a good friend of mine."

"Good," said Avel, staring up at the tall man of six foot four. "Then perhaps you can give him a message. We will be in town for the next hour. It is imperative that we speak with him very soon."

Avel was small compared to the handsome vet, but he held an air of confidence that drew my appreciation.

Ro must have noticed me staring and smiled in response.

Ian offered me a nod then stepped aside. "I will let him know."

Avel pulled me toward the car. My head pounded as if my skull was pressed between a vice-grip.

"Where to?" I asked, rather enjoying this little adventure.

"Coffee," he said, holding his head.

"There is a Starbucks on the next corner. Do you have a headache too?"

"Yes, it's from that damn Spirian."

"What do you mean?"

"Ian. He's a Spirian, probably sent to scent us out."

"Ian? The flirtatious vet is a Spirian?"

"Could you not feel the hum in the room?"

I frowned, remembering feeling something, but not really equating it to anything particular, let alone a hum. "Maybe."

We walked into Starbucks and ordered two coffees. "You know," I said. "You don't have to act so jealous around me. People are going to think we're an item," I jested.

I saw him stiffen and had to smile. "You looked very formidable against Ian," I said.

We got our coffees and sat in the corner facing each other.

"Spirians are not something I would pit myself against," he said, turning the cup in his hand. "I was merely matching his intensity to ensure him that my intentions were solid. If I were a Shadow, he would have sensed it immediately. His confusion comes with my association with you."

"A mere human?" I offered, feeling slightly inadequate.

Avel laughed. "Hardly mere, Elle. Your gift with herbs is known and appreciated, even by the Spirians."

I felt my face grow warm then hot as he reached for my hand.

"And just for the record," he added, "we are much more than friends."

"That was another lifetime ago," I reminded him. "I'm a different person now."

"Perhaps, but you are still my wife in spirit. So long as I am here on this Earth, I will treat you as such."

His words both frightened and thrilled me. In one

sense, I didn't want to feel owned. In another, I like the dominant nature of his statement.

"And what if I say I don't want to be your wife."

He arched a brow in question as if doubting my proclamation. "Then look me in the eyes, woman, and make such a statement."

I met his gaze, confident in my ability to do so. When I opened my mouth, however, nothing came out.

He laughed. "You never could speak a lie," he said, overly pleased with himself.

Ian came in and walked toward us with a serious expression that nearly caused me alarm. I knew that man. He was never serious about anything.

"Come," he said. "I will take you to Khalen."

We stood and followed him out to a large Jeep that looked old and ready to retire. I hesitated when Kael grabbed our bags from the back of my Miata and opened the door for me.

"What about my car?" I asked.

"Leave it," he said, tossing our bags to the back and sliding in beside me.

Chapter 11

IAN PRESSED HIS LEG AGAINST mine as he started the engine. Avel noticed, which made Ian smile.

I moved my leg away and scooted closer to Avel, hoping to disarm the tension in the car. I felt funny, as if my entire body was tingling like a limb that had fallen to sleep. The scenery looked unfamiliar, even though I had traveled this highway multiple times. My sense of direction was scrambled. Was this even Belfair anymore?

Avel nudged me. "He has us in an illusion."

"An illusion?"

"It's his gift. An illusionist makes you see and experience anything of his choice. He doesn't want us to know where he takes us."

I held Avel's hand mostly for security and to ensure that my illusion was not separate from his own.

"It is difficult to control a human mind for long," Avel explained. "The fact he can do it at all demonstrates his power."

"You almost sound impressed," I said.

"I am."

The tingling ceased. It took a moment before I realized we were parked beneath a thick canopy of trees. I looked around at a campsite littered with yurts, cabins, and tents. Small groups of people gathered around fires, talking and looking in our direction.

"Where are we?" I asked.

"Harstine Island," Avel replied. "Smack dab in the middle of it, to be exact."

Ian looked at him with genuine shock on his face. "You seem very perceptive for a human." He drew out the word, human, as if doubting Avel was one.

Again, I felt inadequate. I had been alive for thirty-three years and had never heard of a race of Spirians in the area. Nor had I encountered a spirit in human form. Alice in Wonderland had nothing on me at this point, I was sure.

We exited the car. Avel gripped my hand and held me protectively by his side. If things did go wrong, I wondered if he would be able to protect me.

"Come," said Ian, leading us toward a large yurt in the center of the yard. "Khalen waits for you inside."

My instincts screamed in warning. I felt like a prisoner walking the long and dismal Green Mile to my painful execution. Avel must have felt it as well. His body looked tight and ready for battle. Small as he was, I knew firsthand how formidable he could be when pressed.

We walked up a short flight of stairs and followed Ian into the spacious yurt. I had never seen one inside. It was much larger than I could have ever expected and furnished far more elegantly than most mansions.

The bright lights irritated my eyes and they took a while to adjust to the room's intensity. A comfortable fire crackled in the center hearth, offering an inviting atmosphere. My nerves began to ease a bit.

Avel spied the leader of the clan immediately and lowered his head to him. “Thank you for your counsel,” he said, meeting the man’s golden eyes.

“Sit,” the man said. His voice was low and commanding. There were others with him; an older man and a woman sitting on the floor by a large dog that resembled a wolf.

“I am Avel, son of Hermes. This is Elle Alder, my mate.”

“Your what?” I questioned.

“I thought you said his name was Kael,” Ian questioned, clearly not happy about the deception.

I started to open my mouth, but Avel’s level stare warned me to stay quiet.

The woman petting the dog, glanced over at the leader, then stood and walked toward me.

“Hi, Elle. I’m Skye, Khalen’s mate. Let’s take a walk.”

I looked over at Avel. He nodded. The woman seemed friendly enough and I did look forward to leaving this meeting and Ian’s harsh glare.

“He’s angry with me,” I said, as I followed her from the yurt.

“Ian, yes. He does not appreciate being lied to.”

She walked a little different and I noticed how she held onto the collar of the large dog. When she turned toward me, her eyes did not focus. The woman was blind.

“Yes,” she confirmed. “I am.”

“Am what?” I inquired, knowing full well that she couldn’t possibly know what I was thinking.

The woman smiled. “Your thoughts are open to me,” she said. “You are very perceptive and noticed the fact that I’m blind. I was merely confirming your suspicions.”

"Where are we going?" I asked, following her down a path she seemed very familiar with.

"To a log by the lake, where we can talk."

The fact that she was blind was slightly comforting, but the strength I sensed from her was still unnerving.

"Don't be alarmed," she said, reading my thoughts as if I had spoken them. "I won't harm you. I just noticed how uncomfortable you were among the men and thought you might like to talk to me instead."

"You're very perceptive yourself," I offered.

She sat, then patted the spot beside her. "Have a seat."

Her dog nuzzled my hand. Her fur was soft and clean, her eyes warm with trust. I scratched under her ears.

"That is Maiyun," the woman said. She pointed to the ground and the dog immediately laid by her feet. "In the yurt," she said, "you did not like your man calling you his mate. Why?"

"Because I'm not," I said. I opened my mouth to explain, then quickly shut it, not really knowing how much I should reveal.

The woman frowned. "Your spirit is a mate to his spirit, but you have been separated by several lifetimes," she summarized.

I looked at her with disbelief. "Good Lord, how did you know that?"

She smiled. "Spirians read thoughts," she explained. "Humans are more difficult to understand, but your thoughts are quite clear to me."

"Then why ask the question if you already know the answer?"

She laughed. "I can't read your life story, Elle, only your thoughts. I asked the question to bring the thought to your mind where I could access it."

"Oh," I said, feeling suddenly vulnerable. I pressed my hand against my head, fighting the wave of nausea threatening to purge my breakfast.

Skye placed her hand over my head. The headache and nausea faded. When they were gone, she removed her hand.

"That will help for a while, but the feeling will return so long as you're here."

"How did you do that?"

"I am a healer. It is one of my gifts."

I laughed. "Nifty gift," I said, grateful for the brief reprieve. "Avel said it was the hum that surrounds Spirians that causes the headaches."

"Yes, that is correct. He knows much about us. I'm curious about his story. He is not completely human. There is something about him that is unfamiliar."

"He calls himself a spirit in a borrowed body."

Skye shook her head and stared out toward the lake where two herons vied over a fish. "Explain."

I told her about Kael and how Avel took over his body. Seeing that she could easily read my mind and we did come here to gain their trust and help, I felt compelled to tell her all that I knew about the situation.

"You seem oddly at ease with all this," she observed.

"I'm really not," I laughed nervously. "I keep expecting to wake up."

"But you really don't want to, right?" she guessed correctly.

I smiled, knowing the truth of it. "No, not really."

"It seems odd that you and Avel's souls were separated. Is this common for humans?"

I frowned. "I'm not sure. Avel said that I took my life shortly after he died in battle. I was pregnant with our son at the time. He said that I had to return to Earth until my contract was satisfied."

Skye nodded as if understanding. "I feel the pain in your heart."

"Feel free to remove it," I said. "I wouldn't miss it."

The woman sadly shook her head. "I'm afraid I can't do that, Elle. There are some things I cannot heal."

I shrugged, partly knowing the request was feeble at best. "You said that you were Khalen's mate? That sounds kind of barbaric."

Skye laughed. "Yes, I thought so too when I first learned I was a Spirian. Now I know the meaning behind it. Mates are united for life, and sometimes beyond life if the souls are willing. A marriage between a husband and wife can be severed. Unions between mates can only end in death."

I shuddered. "That sounds awful."

"Does it?" she questioned. "You were bound to Avel hundreds of years ago, yet you still feel bound to him. That is why you won't give your heart to another."

It made sense. "That was another lifetime ago," I said, the words flowing from my mouth as if it were not me who was speaking them. "In this lifetime, I'm nobody's mate." I emphasized the last word.

Skye laughed, again amused by my ignorance. "Avel called you his mate to ensure Khalen that you were not available to others. Avel must have known that Khalen would force you to leave the camp if you were not spoken for."

"That's absurd. Why would I have to leave?"

"An unclaimed human female is a danger to the clan and is forbidden to stay."

I started to ask why such a stupid law existed, then

shook my head and decided to let that thought go. "I'm not claimed," I declared with some conviction.

"It doesn't matter what you think," she said. "If Avel verbally claims you, it is his responsibility to keep you safe during your stay."

I groaned, knowing I had lost this battle.

~Avel~

CLEVER MAN, KHALEN. HE SENT his mate to talk to Elle so that our stories could be compared. Spirian mates could telecommunicate over any distance. He, no doubt, already knew Elle's side of the story, having read his mate's thoughts. It was a handy gift to have, I remembered. My own ability to read thoughts had faded somewhat.

Ian had left shortly after the women. I was relieved to have him gone. The hum in the room was rough enough with the other two Spirians.

The man Khalen introduced as Case, his father, was the leader of the clans in Europe. He was a man of few words and intense power. My head felt ready to explode. It was no wonder why these Spirians lived so far from humans. How they managed to mingle with them at all was a mystery.

Only after I explained my situation and request for help, Case spoke his first words.

"Why should we get involved? This is a matter of the Angels, is it not?" Another Brit. Bloody perfect, I thought.

Khalen, too, had a British accent with a hint of Scotts. Though, unlike his father, Khalen's accent was more muted.

"Technically, yes," I verbally danced. "However, when Vincent practiced necromancy to create his minion army, he overstepped that boundary."

"That is a rather weak argument," said Khalen; just as arrogant as his father. "The Council made a bad gamble and is looking for an out."

"With due respect, sir, the Spirians have also made poor choices."

Khalen nodded, acknowledging that fact. "Aye, my grandfather, Shanuk, always said that mistakes rarely happen without intent."

"I understand that Spirians relish a good challenge," I chanced, hoping to spark an interest. "From what I hear, things have been rather dull in your realm."

Case and Khalen exchanged glances, barely smiling.

"Your sources are correct," said Khalen.

No matter how tall I tried to sit, the men across from me dwarfed my height by a good foot. Were all Spirians this bloody tall, I wondered?

My thoughts made Khalen smile. "Tell me, Spirit, what is your role in this?"

"I was to retrieve the book before it could be used. It was taken from the female in my charge. She can link me to Vincent." Knowing how impatient Spirians can be, I kept my verbiage short and to the point. They could fill in the rest by tapping my thoughts.

"Among other things," Khalen stated.

I pressed my jaw, willing my mouth to stay shut. Tapping my thoughts was one thing, but accessing my emotions was unforgivable. Angering these men, however, would not serve my purpose.

His eyes narrowed. "This angers you? Why? I'm curious."

I closed my thoughts to him and that seemed to surprise him. Instead, he gained his knowledge from his mate. I could see it in his eyes.

"I understand," was all he said, dropping the subject as if it were a plague.

The man obviously had a story of his own he wasn't willing to share. Judging by his body language, he understood my position far too intimately.

Case seemed disinterested in my personal matters and still pondered the issue of getting involved in a matter that defined the gray line. His wisdom and strength surpassed those of his son; but Khalen was cunning in ways I couldn't comprehend.

"Vincent is human, is he not?" asked the older man. His dark gray hair and obsidian eyes defied his age. I knew that Spirians could live for several hundred years, but it was rare. Their looks offered little in the tale of their age.

"He is the son of Warducca, an old v—"

"Voodoo priest," Case announced.

"You know him?" I asked.

"Oh, Aye. I know him. He's the bastard son of Javin, an old Shadow I once knew."

"Is Warducca a Spirian?"

"He's a halfling," Case explained.

"Then how can he have a son?" asked Khalen.

Case tapped his fingertips together. "Exactly," he exclaimed.

"I'm not following you," I said. Conversing with Spirians was akin to reading a book with missing pages. They communicated with one another through images so often that words seem to elude them at times.

The eyes that peered back at me were laced with frustration.

"Halflings," Khalen explained, "are children born of a Spirian father and a human mother. They cannot have children. They are sterile and have very short lifespans, lest they live with Spirians."

"So, you're saying that Warducca could not have sired Vincent?"

"It's impossible," said Case. "What is known about Vincent's mother?"

"Her name was Madrona. She was born in Brazil, grew up in Spain, met Warducca at age seventeen, they married a year later. She died in the same fire that killed Warducca," I said.

"Interesting," Case muttered. "Who were her parents?"

"I'm not sure, but I can find out," I said.

"Does Vincent have a mate and children?" asked Khalen.

I shook my head. "No, he never married. From what I know, he's a bit of a recluse."

"Impossible," Case retorted. "How old is this man?"

Shrugging, I guessed, "Late thirties, early forties. Why?"

Case pinched his brows in deep thought. "If he's the son of a Spirian, he would need to live with other Spirians or die. His mother would have known that and would have surrounded him with others of his kind."

A thought sent chills down my spine. "Is it possible to revive a Spirian?"

Case straightened, following my thought path. "It is."

"The results would be disastrous," Khalen explained. "No Spirian, not even a deranged Shadow, would attempt such a feat."

"Unless Vincent's mother kept her race a secret," I

said.

"To have Vincent," said Khalen, "his mother would have to unite with another Spirian. She would not want to reveal this to her husband."

Case stood and added another log to the fire. "If Vincent does not know the truth of his race, he may inadvertently revive his Spirian friends without knowing the consequences."

I shifted on the couch, suddenly feeling beyond my realm of comfort. "If Spirians mate for life," I reasoned, "why would Vincent's mother be allowed to live with Warducca? Wouldn't her mate want Madrona with him?"

"Shadows are an odd lot," said Khalen. "During that time, they often took multiple mates." He stood and poured three cups of coffee, handing one of them to me.

Case stared into the flames, lost in thought. "We will need the Angels' help on this matter," he said, almost to himself.

My skin shimmied as if a strong wind brushed against it. "That is highly unorthodox," I said, stating the obvious. "The Angels do not govern the physical dimensions."

"No," said Case, "but they do govern the higher ones."

"If the Shadows are involved," Khalen stated, "they will not know what hit them."

"They wouldn't expect the Angels," I concluded aloud. "Brilliant." Gaining the Angels' cooperation, on the other hand, would be far more challenging.

"You have a connection with Archangel Raphael," said Case. "Perhaps you can persuade him?"

I choked a laugh. "Convincing a tiger to live in the ocean would be more achievable," I said, "but I will try."

Chapter 12

I FOLLOWED THE MEN OUTSIDE and smiled at the sight of Elle playing with the large dog belonging to Khalen's mate.

Elle smiled up at me. "Look, Avel, she likes to shake hands."

"I see that."

"Skye has invited us to stay here," she said.

Khalen looked surprised at his mate. "Has she now?"

"We have a spare cabin," Skye added, "and they need a safe place to stay. Elle is claimed by this man, so there is no danger to the clan."

I watched Elle's reaction to Skye's words. There was none. Odd. I half-expected her to balk at what she earlier considered a demeaning statement. When her eyes met mine, I smiled. She quickly looked away and my smile broadened.

The woman had feelings for me, but chain-it-all, she wouldn't show it. As much as I enjoyed a good challenge, this one was out of my reach. Getting involved with her was a mistake, I reminded myself. My time here was short. Her heart was not something I wanted to tether at this time. For the sake of the clan, however, I would maintain the facade.

"She cares for you more than you think," said Skye, in a voice meant only for my ears.

Damn Spirians. I would have to remember to close my thoughts more diligently in the future.

"My mate is right," Khalen admitted. "Please stay for as long as you like." His eyes glowed like gold with the statement.

A lovely woman with long gray hair and luminous eyes hurried toward us. She resembled an older lady who had been granted a new lease on life. Her smile was bright and matched the lively bounce in her steps.

Case greeted her with a fierce hug. "Ah, my beautiful mate, just in time to meet some new friends."

She looked ready to burst with excitement. I doubted it was due to meeting new guests.

"Logan took his first step," she blurted, bouncing up and down. She had a delightful British accent that seemed more refined than her mate's.

Case laughed and hugged the woman he obviously loved. "Forgive my mate," he said. "Logan is our youngest of four children and Eve still insists on celebrating every one of their milestones." He pulled her against him and squeezed, indicating that her little quirk was not only tolerated, but adored.

"It seems tonight offers much to celebrate," he said. "Eve, darling, I'd like you to meet Avel and Elle. They will be staying here for some time."

"Oh," she said, covering her self-conscious grin. "You must think me horribly rude." She extended her hand to

Elle first, and then to me. "Elle, Avel. What a pleasure it is to have you here. I'm Eve, Case's mate."

"Delighted to meet you," I said.

"Come," said Skye, "I'll show you to the cabin. I'm sure you'll want to freshen up a bit before the evening meal."

She led us to the back end of the camp, near the lake. It was evident that she was blind, but she got around rather well with the help of her dog.

"It's a simple cabin," she said, leading us through the door. "But you have a bed, your own kitchen and a roomy hearth. Wood is stored in there." She pointed to a small pine door that was built into the stone hearth.

She walked over to a cabinet just to the right of the kitchen, then opened the door. "There is some wine and liquor in here, if you want." She closed the door. "The fridge is not stocked, but if you need something, just let me know and we will get it for you. There is plenty of fresh milk, eggs, and bread every morning. Coffee and tea are in the cupboard just left of the sink."

"This is very generous of you," I said, taking her hands. I thought I saw her blush. She was a rather plain-looking woman, but stunning just the same. There was something about her that demanded attention— her stature, perhaps?

"Khalen and I would love to have you for breakfast come morning. We eat at around nine."

I released her hands. "Thank you."

"I will have one of the children bring you fresh milk for your coffee. It will be left on your doorstep."

"Your hospitality is appreciated."

"Well," she said, smiling. "It isn't every day we are visited by a spirit and his human mate."

This time, it was Elle's turn to blush. She pressed her fist to her mouth and turned away from me.

"I'm sure," I said, lost for other words. I walked her and her dog to the door. "Thank you, again."

"Oh," she blurted and suddenly turned, nearly causing me to run into her. "I almost forgot. If you would like to shower or use the privy, they are not far." She pointed to a round dark-green building with tan support posts. "Dinner is served just before sunset. Tonight, we eat outside. The weather is good."

"Sounds great," I said. "Again, thank you."

I watched her leave. Kids played soccer in the distance, while a horse grazed in a nearby meadow. The camp was humming with activity. It seemed every member had a task of some sort.

Ian, the man who brought us here, worked in the pasture now, digging some sort of trench. He worked beside another man, slightly taller, but similar in looks.

When I turned, I noticed Elle looking around the room as if strategizing a play on a chessboard.

"You okay?" I asked.

She started wringing her hands together, a nervous gesture she often employed when she had something to say but the words were caught in her throat.

I chuckled. "I'll sleep on the floor, if that's what worries you."

"It looks pretty hard," she commented.

"Yes, I prefer it that way. I'll get our bags from the car."

"Avel?"

I turned toward her. "Hmm?"

"How long do we plan to stay here?"

"Not long," I replied sadly. In truth, I didn't have long.

In nine more days, the moon would be full and Vincent would try resurrecting his parents. Once that happened, life on Earth would never be the same. The humans would not survive.

NEEDING SOME ALONE TIME, I headed toward the lake to find some privacy. The camp stretched for miles. I followed a path around the lake; it had been well used. When I was sure to be alone, I called on Raphael.

He appeared in a blue smoke before manifesting into a young man wearing khaki shorts, hiking boots, and a billowing shirt with baggy pockets. As an Angel, he had an identifying look that rivaled the highest-paid GQ model, though he frequently changed that look to suit his needs and desires. I wondered if his manifestations were part of some deep inner need of his to live in the physical world.

"Heavens no," he replied, having read my thoughts. "Don't be absurd. I'm merely biding my time here until our mission is fulfilled. Speaking of which, how are things progressing?"

"The Spirians are willing to help, provided the Angels participate."

Raphael seemed to grow several inches taller. His eyes widened with surprise. "Highly unlikely. We don't deal with physical matters. You know that."

"Yes," I confirmed, "I do know that. The Spirians believe the situation may be more dire than we had anticipated, however, and full cooperation from the Angels is required."

Raphael scowled. "Dire? In what way?"

I told him about the possibility of Vincent being a Spirian Shadow, and about his mother. There was also the unknown variable of Vincent's true father. As I revealed this information, Raphael sat and pondered the information.

"Interesting, indeed," he admitted. "The Council must be informed immediately."

"We must know more about Vincent's mother and the man who sired her son. Can we check the hall of records?"

"We would have to approach the High Council of the Spirians for that information. This collaboration of forces is highly unorthodox; however, I do see the beauty of it." His silver eyes flashed with a hint of excitement. "I will contact you later this eve." In a rush of a breeze, he was gone.

I left to get our things from the car feeling much lighter in step and fueled in a way that I had not felt for many centuries.

On the way to the car, I noticed Elle speaking with Ian. My gut wrenched at the sight of it. Ian looked down on her like an eagle admiring its prey. The man had looks, brawn, and gifts that would tantalize any female. I should be happy for her. In truth, though, I felt a pang in my heart that equaled the bite of a dull blade.

"Don't worry," Khalen said, observing my reaction. "He cannot have her, nor would he try. His heart belongs to another."

"I wasn't worried," I lied, a feeble attempt in the company of a Spirian.

He laughed. "You love her, but won't allow yourself to take her in fear of having to leave her alone."

"That is an annoying gift you have," I said, continuing my way toward the car.

He followed me. "I felt the same way toward my mate," he said. "I was stubborn and foolish to think she needed my protection."

"Our situation is different," I growled, wanting to drop the subject. I lifted a bag from the back of the Jeep.

Khalen grabbed the other one with little effort, and then proceeded to walk with me back to our cabin.

I appreciated his help, but not the conversation. "I spoke with Raphael."

"Yes, I'm aware of that."

"Of course you are," I said. "Is there anything that escapes your notice?"

He raised a brow, accentuating his arrogance. "If it did escape my notice, I would hardly know about it, correct?"

I looked at him. His height nearly caused my neck to cramp. "Touché."

We walked in silence for a moment before he spoke again.

"If your time is short on this Earth, my friend, do you not think it should be spent in full course?"

"Meaning?"

"Make the most of it. Take that woman and make her your own."

I shook my head, the mere thought of his words churning my gut. "You don't understand. Things between Elle and I are complicated."

"She was your mate in another lifetime. Your death caused her to take her life and now she is stuck in perpetual hell. I think I understand."

His gain of knowledge disturbed me. Typical of Spirians to break up a complicated matter and turn it into a single sentence.

"I will be leaving this life soon. To get involved with her would only end in disaster. It is best to leave her heart untouched and receptive to another man."

"One who will not leave her?"

"Exactly."

He followed me into the cabin, set the bags on the bed, then walked over to the liquor cabinet to pour us a drink.

I accepted the glass and enjoyed a healthy swig. Fine Scotch goes down too smoothly to disclose its subtle threat.

"Everyone dies, Avel. We cannot predict when it will happen. The woman will not love another, her heart won't allow it. She does, however, love you. It would be a shame not to indulge her while you can, would it not?"

"And what happens when I leave? I'm setting her up for the same heartache that caused her to take her life. I can't do that."

"From what I understand, she has repeated that act in every lifetime since—without your involvement. A life without love is hard to endure, Avel."

I took another sip of my drink. The man's words were acid, burning as they sank deeper into my flesh of reason.

"When I do leave," I said, my voice sounding distant, "will you keep her safe?"

"She cannot live here," he said. "But rest assured, my dear mate will keep her close. She is quite fond of her."

"Skye is an amazing woman."

Khalen raised his glass and smiled with pride. "That she is. Elle, too, is extraordinary."

"She has a gift with herbs, you know."

"Yes, I'm aware of that. It is something Eve can help foster."

I finished my drink and set the glass on the table. "I'd best find Elle. She will want to get cleaned up before dinner."

Khalen downed his drink then set his glass beside mine. “It is good to have you here, Spirit.”

I nodded, and then headed out the door. It was odd being addressed as Spirit, but in truth, I was a spirit, nothing more. I had been given another brief moment of life, and with it, a torrent of emotions that would linger forever.

The Angels said that emotions were a gift from the Father and should be treated as such. Unfortunately, emotional gifts cannot be exchanged or forgotten. Raphael once told me that he longed for emotions, but Angels were spared them. In exchange, they had wisdom and power. I found it ironic how we tend to crave what we cannot have.

Elle glanced up at me and smiled as I approached her and the young veterinarian. He was teaching Elle how to milk a goat. She had milk on her shirt and a few speckles on her face.

“Look,” she said. “I’m actually milking a goat.”

“Yes,” I laughed. “I see that. Did you get any of it into the bucket?”

She glared. “Yes, some.” She tipped the bucket to show me. “It’s not as easy as it looks. Want to try?”

She had obviously forgotten that we raised goats in our life together. “Sure,” I said, not wanting to pass up a chance to impress her.

She stood away from the stool and gestured for me to take her place. I did, and effortlessly finished the task of milking the goat.

“You’ve done this before,” Ian acknowledged.

“Many times,” I smiled, noticing the surprised look on Elle’s face. I aimed the goat’s teat toward her.

“Don’t you dare,” she warned, her eyes narrowed and

stern. The deep blue of them grew icy cold. I squeezed the teat and projected a stream of milk directly at her face.

Her resulting expression of shock, disbelief, anger, and the promise of vengeance was worth the risk.

Ian raised his hands and led the goat away from the area. “Come on girl. We’re stayin’ outta this one.”

Elle wrapped her arms around my waist and wiped the milk from her face on my shirt.

“That’s it,” I said, lifting her over my shoulder.

She slapped my back and kicked her feet. “Where are you taking me?”

“The showers,” I said, with a smile in my voice.

“Avel!” she shouted, slapping me harder. “Put me down, right now!”

I ignored her request. The spectacle earned the attention of the camp. Khalen smiled and clapped his hands together. Skye slapped his arm as we passed, obviously not pleased with his approval of the situation.

I carried Elle to the women’s showers. The hut was empty. In the corner, I saw where Khalen had placed a stack of clean clothes and towels for our use. Sending thoughts to him was proving to be quite useful.

I set Elle down and began undressing her.

“Please don’t,” she said, looking down.

I lifted her chin. “Look me in the eyes and tell me you don’t want this, Elle, and I will leave.”

Her vibrant blue eyes met mine. Her lips were trembling. The desire was there along with fear and apprehension. Her mouth opened, but no words came out.

Slowly, I lowered my lips to hers. In my mind, I was back in time when she was my wife. The kiss felt full, willing, and familiar in a way that only a spirit could recognize. When I started to pull away, she stopped me, gripping the back of my head as if I would disappear if she relinquished her hold.

After what felt like eternity, we parted, both out of breath and stunned with paralyzing desire.

"Wow," she finally said. "I wasn't expecting that."

Again, I started unbuttoning her blouse, now stained with a dribble of milk. I let it fall off her shoulders and pool to the ground. As I started releasing her jeans, she fumbled with the buttons of my shirt.

I took my time with her in the shower, bathing her, but not allowing it to go too far.

"I want you," she moaned. "All of you."

"Be careful what you ask for, love. You just may get more than you bargained for." I kissed her then, tasting her need. The time, however, was not right. "I won't take you here," I growled. "Not like this."

Her eyes widened. "Why?"

"Have you been with a man before?"

She lowered her head as if ashamed and shook it. "I never met anyone who made me feel like this."

I continued to wash her hair. "Our time together is short."

"Yes," she said. "I know."

"If another man wants to court you, I want you to be open to it."

"I won't promise that," she said with conviction.

I walked her out of the shower and covered her with a soft towel that smelled like white sage.

"I will promise, however, to live the remainder of my life thinking of you. You will leave this Earth, but your spirit will remain in my heart, always.

I pulled her close and buried my face in her hair. My soul rejoiced at the sound of that promise, but my heart ached for the love she may never know. "A lifetime without sharing affections with another being is a long time," I reasoned, but my argument was half baked. In truth, the thought of another man in her arms made my blood boil.

"The bridge is there for me to cross. If the need arises," she said, "I will use it. Until then, take comfort in knowing it is there and acknowledged."

I pulled back from her, smiling. "Now you sound like the wife of a Spartan warrior."

"I am," she said.

By nightfall the camp was alive with fires and gathering people. The smell of roasting meat permeated the air. As we drew closer, aromas of fresh dark bread, basted potatoes and corn teased my ravenous appetite. Large bowls of fresh greens dominated a small table with smaller bowls of fruit and various condiments.

"Welcome," said Eve, meeting us with a beaming smile. For an older woman, she had a bounce in her step and the energy of most women in their prime. Her happiness shone through her expressions like a light from within. Even her dark eyes sparkled.

"This is quite the spread," I said.

Eve looked back, as if I had seen something she hadn't. "If I had known we would be celebrating new guests, it would have been more impressive. This, however, is a typical dinner for the clan."

Elle's eyes widened. "You eat like this every night?"

"When the weather is nice," she clarified. "During poor weather, we typically eat indoors with our immediate family."

She led us to an area where we could find plates and utensils. "Please, help yourselves to whatever you want, and then join us at the main fire." She pointed toward a bonfire near the edge of camp between two large yurts.

We filled our plates before joining the others at the fire.

"Come," said Khalen, "sit." He gestured to a low bench constructed of two stumps and a cedar slab that had been sanded smooth. "Can I pour you some wine?"

"Yes," I said, sitting beside Elle, "thank you."

He handed me two glasses, and I passed one to Elle.

I recognized most of the people; Case and his mate Eve, Ian, Khalen and his mate Skye, and two others.

The man I had seen with Ian earlier this afternoon stood and offered his hand. "Hi, I'm Aidan," he said with a firm shake. "This is my mate, Sunjia."

The delicate woman beside him stood and held my hand with both of hers. She was of dark complexion and exotic looking, with dark-framed eyes and jet-black hair.

"Pleasure to meet you," I said, following with a gesture toward Elle. "This is my mate, Elle."

Aidan offered Elle a hug. Sunjia followed suit.

"Welcome," Aidan said, taking a seat beside his mate.

"I didn't know that spirits could mate with humans," said Sunjia.

"They were mated in another lifetime," Khalen explained, completing the picture telepathically.

Sunjia and Aidan's eyes showed a hint of understanding and confusion.

I sipped my wine and allowed it to linger on my tongue. I hadn't had juice this fine for hundreds of years. I closed my eyes and swallowed.

Khalen and Skye laughed.

"It's one of our favorites," she said. "Borolo, from Italy."

Elle also savored her first sip before commenting, "Camping at a five-star resort. I like it."

It was obvious that money was not an issue with this clan. They seemed well-stocked in both food and drink and were generous with both.

The meat was tender, sweet, and wonderfully flavorful. I wondered what it was, knowing it hadn't come from any store.

Having read my thoughts, Skye said, "We are fortunate not to have to buy meat from the store. Khalen and Aidan went hunting last week. It's elk. Do you like it?"

"Very much," I replied.

Elle sampled a bite, then frowned. "It's very different."

We all laughed. "Game meat," Khalen explained, "can take some time to get used to."

"Any word from the Angels?" Case asked.

"Raphael said he would get back to me this evening. He is contacting the High Council of the Spirians."

Case smiled. "That should be interesting."

"Yeah," I remarked. "He didn't seem too enthused about it either."

The Angels and Spirians were members of the same realm, but they were as different as tigers to brontosauruses. Where Spirians excelled in physical matters, the Angels were adept at the more subtle aspects of life.

"Do the Angels and Spirians get along?" Elle asked.

"Can lions and gazelles roam the same prairie?" Khalen replied.

"Yes," she said, clearly confused.

I held her hand. "Imagine trying to convince the two

to hunt together."

"That's ridiculous," she said. "One is a hunter, the other forages. A gazelle wouldn't know the first thing about hunting."

"Exactly," Case and Khalen said together.

"Why do we need the Angel's help?" she asked.

"We are hunting a Spirian necromancer who may resurrect something that could destroy all that is good on Earth." I explained. "He may or may not know who and what he truly is."

Aidan tossed a twig he had been twisting into the fire. "How can he not know what he is?"

"I didn't know who I was," said Skye. "Not until I met Khalen."

Aidan and the others could have easily been filled in through telepathy, but Case and Khalen used verbal communication for the sake of Elle and me. It was important for her to know the truth of the situation.

"Vincent," Case explained, "our necromancer, is a bit of a mystery. His father is unknown."

Elle looked confused. "I thought Warducca was his father."

"Vincent may believe the same," said Khalen, pouring each of us more wine. "Warducca was a halfling and was incapable of siring children."

The creases between Elle's brows deepened. "Halfling?"

"There was a time," Khalen explained, "when Spirian males were forced to mate with human females. The offspring were neither human nor Spirian. They were halflings, ungifted for the most part, and sterile."

She mused for a bit, trying to fit the pieces together. "So, you think Vincent's mom had a bit of a fling and got pregnant?"

"Spirian women who get pregnant do not do so just for a fling," Case said. Judging by his regretful expression, his voice was a bit harsher than he had intended. He took a deep breath and continued. "Spirians mate for life, Elle. Before a male Spirian can sire a child, he must unite with the female. It is a bond that can only be severed by death."

I could almost see her process the information as she stared into the flames. She sipped her wine, eyes distant in thought.

"We don't know who her mate was," I said, hoping to clarify the situation. "It seems rather odd that both Warducca and Madrona died in an inexplicable fire."

"Or," Khalen added, "why they were allowed to stay together after Vincent was conceived. Her mate would not have allowed that unless he had ulterior motives."

"What of Madrona?" asked Elle. "Why would she mate with another man when she knew the consequences?"

"When a Shadow claims a soul," Khalen seethed, "the soul no longer recognizes discernment."

I could see Elle's confusion building. She sipped her wine and frowned.

"The man who claimed her," I clarified, "may have compromised her ability to recognize right from wrong."

Elle shook her head as if giving up the notion of understanding this odd realm of reality. She took another sip of her wine.

"Hey," I said, "you might want to slow down on that stuff."

A horde of young children ran toward us. One of them was crying.

Skye stood and faced the young. She held out her hands to the small boy who was crying. "Zhentu, what's wrong?" Her hands instinctively moved to the boy's arm. Large blisters covered the top of it. In a moment, they were gone and the boy calmed in his mother's arms. "How did this happen?" she asked an older boy that obviously belonged to Khalen.

He looked more like his father with dark hair, golden eyes and an air of leadership about him. Pointing to an older girl with blonde curls, he said, "Shaiya did it."

All eyes turned toward the two identical-looking girls. Shaiya was slightly taller than her twin. Both had green eyes that equaled the brilliance of flawless emeralds.

"Forgive us," Khalen interrupted. "These are our children." He started with the oldest twins, and ended with the youngest in Skye's arms. "Shaiya, Kaili, Gabrihen, and Zhentu."

Each of the children nodded as their names were announced. The youngest, Zhentu, had sandy-blonde hair and blue eyes. He resembled both parents but lacked the confidence of his older siblings.

I nodded back.

"Shaiya," Khalen commanded. The sound of his voice sent chills down my back. I could only imagine what it felt like to that young child of six years.

The young girl stepped before her father then glared over at her brother, Gabrihen. The look was immediately reprimanded with a sharp look from her father. The girl gasped and dropped to her knees.

"What happened?" Khalen asked, his voice low and demanding.

Shaiya kept her eyes down and her hands respectfully folded before her. "Kaili and I were playing with our marbles. Zhentu kept trying to take them, even after we asked him to stop."

"Did you burn him?" asked Skye?

The girl nodded. "Tria said I had that ability."

Sunjia's eyes widened. "Why would she do that?" She glanced over to where a young woman sat with other teens at a nearby fire. The girl glanced over at her mother, rolled her eyes, then grudgingly sauntered toward us.

I assumed the girl was Sunjia's daughter. They shared the same exotic features, with dark-lined eyes the color of coal and silky black hair.

"Mother," the girl said, her voice inflected with irritation from having been summoned.

Sunjia addressed her daughter. "Tria, why would you tell Shaiya about her ability to inflict harm on others?"

Tria glared at her mother. "I got that gift from you," she nearly seethed.

Sunjia stood. "Come with me," she told her daughter."

"I'm kind of busy right—"

When Aidan stood, Tria's eyes immediately lowered. "Yes, mother." She stood and started to follow the woman.

"Tria," Aidan called.

The young lady turned, her face visibly paler. "Yes, father."

"If you ever use that tone again, with anyone, I will make sure you never do it again. Understood?"

She nodded then followed her mother to their yurt.

Aidan poured himself another glass of wine, and then sat beside Khalen. "I apologize for my daughter."

Khalen nodded. "She is at a difficult age." He turned his attention back to his daughter. "Shaiya, you must never use your gifts to inflict harm on others. I will not warn you again. Understood?"

The little girl's eyes teared over. "Yes, father."

"Apologize to your brother."

Shaiya stood and offered her baby brother a hug. “Sorry for hurting you, Zhentu.”

“Zhentu,” Khalen called.

The young boy turned his eyes toward that commanding summon.

“You must not take something that is not given to you. Apologize to your sisters for interrupting their game.”

The little boy sniffed. “Sorry for inpting your game,” he struggled to say.

Skye set him down. “Off you go now. Find someone else to play with.”

The children ran off, grateful to be gone from the tension that was building.

Raising children was difficult enough. Raising children with gifts must be more so, I thought.

“We have a level of discipline in this camp that must be maintained,” Khalen explained. “The children are taught to respect others early on in life. There are no exceptions.”

“It must be challenging,” I said, trying to divert some of the tension oppressing the air.

Khalen’s eyes seemed to glow. “Only for the children,” he added.

Skye’s attention was drawn toward the children. She stood. “Excuse me for a moment.”

Maiyun, her dog, moved to her side and expertly led her toward the children. Watching the woman walk, however, made me wonder if she really needed the dog’s help.

“Maiyun takes her job very seriously,” Khalen said. “She is getting old, but she still insists on helping Skye whenever she can.”

“How old is she?” Elle asked.

"Nearly ten, now, but she has some years left in her."

The dog's gray and white markings clearly showed of Husky blood, but she was larger than most Huskies. Perhaps she was part wolf?

"Malamute," Khalen clarified.

I looked over at Elle, who had polished off her third glass of wine. When Aidan leaned over to offer her a refill, I shook my head.

"She is not Spirian," I said.

"What is that supposed to mean?" she slurred.

I took the glass from her hand. "It means, my dear, that you do not have the same tolerance for alcohol."

"And you do?"

"I do, yes, but this body does not." I felt the shimmy in the air. Raphael was near.

I stood. "Wait here," I told Elle. "I'll come back for you."

Chapter 13

I FELT RAPHAEL'S PRESENCE, BUT he was not manifesting before me. There was another presence with him.

"Avel," Raphael said, his voice distant but clear. "Gather the Spirian leaders. I will talk to them."

I walked back to where the group sat talking by the fire. "Archangel Raphael would like to speak to you," I said to Khalen and Case."

Both men stood. Khalen turned to Aidan and Ian. "Come," he said.

I turned to Elle. "Stay with the women," I told her. "I'll come back for you."

"I'm a part of this," she said. "I want to be included."

"I think we all should be," Skye added.

This earned a look of warning from Khalen. Skye matched his challenge with one of her own. She was either a very brave woman, or an incredibly careless one.

"Very well," said Khalen. "Perhaps we could use a bit of female insight on this matter."

Skye stood and steadied Elle as she stumbled away

from the log. "I guess you're not used to drinking."

"I didn't think I had that much," said Elle.

"Borolo is very potent," said Skye. "It must be sipped slowly."

"Good to know," said Elle, allowing the blind woman to lead her toward the large yurt. "Your mate doesn't seem too happy about having us women join the party."

"He believes that war is a matter for men, and nurturing the family is the woman's job."

"How very chauvinistic of him," said Elle.

I had to smile at that one. Even as a Spartan woman, she had a hard time staying out of the mens' business.

"In time," said Skye, "he will learn how truly valuable a woman's insight could be in such matters."

Khalen turned to face his mate. "I already do, love." He smiled.

Elle nodded toward him. "You seem to have a knack for melting that harsh exterior of his."

"Only on the surface," claimed Skye. "Inside, he is all leader, I assure you. Once he digs his heels in on something, only the Father, Himself, can budge that man."

Elle glanced back at me. "I know someone like that."

I smiled at her. She had no idea just how stubborn I could be.

We settled into Skye and Khalen's yurt while Eve made us all some tea. She had a heart that yearned to serve, that much was obvious. She also felt great joy when many were gathered around her. The warmth of that joy radiated like the summer sun at high noon.

I sat beside Elle, then called out to the Archangel. He manifested as his formal self in the center of the room and nodded toward me. In this form, he appeared young, dark-haired and fit. His eyes were a rich brown with copper flecks. Massive golden wings covered his back, neatly tucked. He called this manifestation his true self.

He turned toward Khalen and Case and knelt. I had never seen the Archangel kneel to anyone save God and members of the Council. Then again, Raphael was known to show great respect when he deemed it was earned. Perhaps he viewed the Spirian leaders as something akin to his level?

Just as shocking, Case, Khalen, Ian and Aidan returned the gesture, on their knees and bowing their heads.

"Spirian leaders, thank you for your audience."

"Archangel Raphael, it is an honor to be in your presence," Khalen replied.

The formality of it all looked well-rehearsed as if they met this way frequently. Then again, I thought, Angels and Spirians communicate on an entirely different level. As a spirit, I understood that level to a degree, but not completely.

I looked over at Elle, who sat mouth open, staring at the image of the young man before her. He looked real enough and resembled an airbrushed model— flawless, masculine, and appealing in every way.

Skye also stared at him like a child looking at a stunning rainbow. I knew she couldn't see his form, but his aura shown like no other. Having observed Skye, I assumed she could see such auras. They vibrated at a level that could be sensed with the pineal gland, also known as the third eye. Because Spirians had highly developed pineal glands, it was possible that she could detect the Angel before her.

Eve sat next to her mate, keeping her eyes soft and fixed on Raphael. There was a low hum in the room as if a thousand voices resounded in a single note. I could feel the vibration in my bones.

Elle reached over and held my hand. I squeezed hers in return, assuring her that all was right.

"Raphael," I said, "I'd like to introduce you to Khalen, leader of this clan; his mate, Skye; father, Case; mother, Eve; and good friends, Ian and Aidan."

As I introduced each person, Raphael nodded and smiled. "It is rare, indeed, to meet the infamous Spirians," he said.

"I'm pretty sure none of them have met an Archangel either," I countered, amused with his odd formality. It was unlike Raphael, a free-spirited gypsy-type, to act like a stuffy diplomat. "Were you able to convince the Archangels to join us in this venture?"

"They were adamant to stay out of it until a very convincing Spirian joined the conversation. He seemed to hold a high standing with the Spirian High Council, though he was not a formal member. His argument was strong enough to gain full cooperation."

Case frowned. "What did this man look like?"

Raphael shrugged. "Silver hair, blue eyes, tall, solid build and stunning white teeth."

"Shanuk," Case and Khalen said in sync.

"Yes, I believe that was his name. He was an odd bird, frequently talking in parables and philosophical phrases."

Skye laughed. "That sounds right. Frustrating, isn't it?"

Raphael smiled and nodded as if remembering something humorous. "In the end, he said something like: 'Together, the sun and the moon can move oceans.' I thought it quite strange, but the simple phrase was enough to gain the Angels' cooperation in this matter." He scoffed. "I must admit, they are all quite excited about it."

Case refreshed his cup of tea, and then took a long, slow sip. "What about Madrona and her mate? Were you able to learn more about their union?"

Raphael shook his head. "That's a strange one. According to the records, Madrona doesn't exist."

Case lowered his cup to the tray. "How is that possible?"

"I didn't exist either, before Shanuk revealed my true identity," said Skye.

Khalen remained deep in thought, staring into the flames of the circular hearth, eyes blurred in trance. "She is the perfect pawn," he stated in a low, calculated tone.

Case's eyes widened as if peering through a telescope at an approaching tsunami. "Of course—to mate a woman who doesn't exist would easily hide their numbers."

"In English, please," Elle retorted, "for us, simple humans."

"Shadows are a tricky lot," Raphael commented. "Cunning as a hungry fox."

"Hungry and desperate," Case added.

Elle stood and started to pace, holding her temples. "I shouldn't be here. This is a nightmare I want no part of."

"Run if you must, my dear," said the Angel, "but the nightmare will certainly find you."

"Vincent still hunts for her?" I asked, already knowing the answer. The young necromancer was intrigued with Elle. The scent of him in her apartment made that apparent. He thought she was charmed, being able to handle the book and avoiding its curse. Elle had become his next conquest.

"Why?" she said.

"Your existence is rare," Raphael stated, earning the

interest of everyone in the room, including me.

"Explain," I said, not even trying to hide anger from my voice. My gut wrenched with the thought of having been placed in this predicament unaware of certain truths.

Raphael met my eyes with a subtle warning to remain respectful. My gaze did not soften.

"As you are well aware," he stated, "Syria's soul has been given many more chances to fulfill her life contract—more than any other soul in history."

Elle focused on me, her eyes pleading for an explanation.

"Go on," I said, already knowing that fact.

"In doing so, we have created a soul with certain—gifts."

"Gifts," I repeated. "I was told her ability to handle the cursed book was at the hands of Archangel Jeremeil."

Raphael nodded. "That is correct. But you also know that each time a soul is touched by an Angel, the soul becomes gifted. When a soul is touched by an Archangel, the gifts are—more intense."

"Gifts?" Elle questioned. "What gifts? I'm as ordinary as a bar of soap, I assure you," she scoffed.

Raphael turned to Khalen. "If you please, attempt to reprimand this woman." He pointed toward Elle.

Her eyes widened as she stared at Khalen. She had seen a bit of his power displayed upon his children, I was sure.

Khalen fixed his attention on Elle. Nothing happened.

"She is temporarily immune to your powers," said Raphael. "She is protected from external harm, to a degree."

Elle started breathing again, then plopped down on the couch beside Eve, who gently patted her hand.

"To a degree?" Khalen questioned.

"The protection she now has will fade in time. She will have a strong shield, but she will not be able to defend herself against strong Spirians. The Shadows will certainly want her. Without the protection of a clan, she is vulnerable."

"If Vincent has his way with her, their offspring will be something akin to a Spirian on steroids."

"But she is human," said Case.

"A human who has been touched by an Archangel is no longer human. She is an Angel in physical form."

Elle's face turned pale. "I don't want to be an Angel in physical form."

"Did Jeremeil know this before he touched her?" I asked.

Raphael nodded. "He did."

I stood and walked across the room toward him. "You know what this means," I growled.

"What?" said Elle. "What does it mean?"

"He had no choice," Raphael growled back. "She was about to open the book. Her death would have quickly followed."

"Great Father in Heaven," Case muttered. "What a bloody mess."

Elle stood and started rubbing her temples again. "Okay," she said, pacing the room. "Let's just pretend that I'm a simple human with no gifts and absolutely no clue as to what is going on. Do you think it possible that you can step your consciousnesses down a few pegs and explain to me what is happening?"

I turned to face her, edging the anger from my tongue before I spoke. "You are no longer human, Elle. That is what this means."

"What am I?"

"A physical Angel," Raphael answered. "People will be unusually attracted to you. Gifts will start to manifest, and age is no longer a factor."

She sat down again next to Eve, eyes distant in thought.

"Basically," I added. "Life as you once knew it is about to change—drastically."

"What do you mean, age is no longer a factor?" asked Elle, her eyes starting to tear over.

"You won't age," I said gently. You won't experience disease, and you cannot be harmed."

Her eyes darted as if fitting the multitude of pieces together on a very complicated puzzle. "If I cannot age, get sick, or be harmed, how long will I live?"

Raphael shrugged.

"This is not right," I growled. "Why her?" My fist grew tight, aching to pound into something hard. "The Father cannot ask this of her."

"He can," Raphael said. "Everything has a price, my friend. Life doesn't come cheaply."

"This is my punishment, then?" asked Elle. "For taking my life, this is my payment?"

"No," Raphael answered, his image wavering. "The Father does not punish, ever. You have been given a chance to live, a chance to redeem your soul. I suggest you make the best of it."

I could see his image starting to fade. Remaining in this physical realm took a great deal of energy for celestial beings. Raphael was strong, but his time with us was spent.

"Avel," he said. "I must go. The Angels will do what they can to learn more about Madrona and her son. Call upon me when you have something to share."

With that, the room brightened and his image faded into a sandalwood-scented mist.

The room remained quiet as each person reflected on his or her own thoughts.

"I don't want to live forever," Elle murmured. Her eyes glistened with tears.

Skye moved over and took her hands. "You won't be alone," she said. "You can stay here, with us."

Khalen growled. "Skye."

"What?" his mate retorted. "You heard Raphael. She is no longer human."

"Nor is she Spirian."

"I'm nobody," Elle chimed in, her voice defeated.

Skye glared at her mate. "No, you're not."

"Enough," Case roared. "We have more important matters to tend.

Eve stood and took Elle's hand. "Come, dear. Let's take a walk."

"Good idea," said Skye, casting a look of disappointment toward the men.

Khalen growled again as he watched the women go. I could feel the tension in the room increase and wondered what things would be like if he and his mate ever got into a heated debate. I would not want to be around for that one, I was sure.

Chapter 14

-Elle-

I **FOLLOWED THE WOMEN DOWN A** trail that bordered a small lake. There was no small talk, or even shallow condolences shot my way, just blissful silence, almost as if they sensed I needed some space.

We rounded a corner shaded by large maples and Douglas firs before Skye led us to a long, smooth log edging the lake. Her dog, Maiyun, stayed by her side. When we sat down, the large animal laid her head upon my lap. I was never much of a dog-lover, but this intelligent animal was quickly stealing my heart with those soft, brown eyes.

I scratched behind her ears and took a semblance of comfort from the softness of her fur. "What am I going to do?" I murmured, to myself rather than to anyone around me.

"Well," said Skye, "Shanuk always said that there are no accidents, only possible outcomes."

I glanced over at her, my brow suspended in confusion.

"And that means?"

Skye smiled. "My interpretation is that you cherish what you have today, because tomorrow is uncertain."

I laughed. "How, pray tell, did you ever conclude that meaning?"

"After many hours of sitting before a fire, contemplating Shanuk's wisdom, that's what finally made sense."

"Okay," I laughed. "This Shanuk character sounds like a piece of work."

"You might say that." Skye smiled, her gaze turning distant. "He was my grandfather, and a good friend."

"Hmm," I replied, not really knowing what else to say. My mind was so caught up in my own disaster that I couldn't seem to muster any compassion for anyone else. It was pitiful, really, and horrible.

Another bout of silence followed. Both women seemed quite comfortable with it. I, however, suddenly felt uncomfortable.

Maiyun soon grew tired of my affections and lay beside her mistress' bare feet with a groan. Skye lazily rubbed the dog's belly with her toes. Looking at the roughened condition of those feet, I concluded that the woman walked barefoot quite often.

"Thank you," I said, desperately trying to break the silence.

Skye smiled. "You're welcome."

"How do you know what I'm thanking you for?" I asked.

"Considering your thoughts," she said, "I assume you are thanking me for suggesting that you stay with us."

I pursed my lips. "Partly, but mostly, I wanted to thank you for being with me now, even though I'm not the best company."

Eve tossed a pebble into the water, causing two ducks to skitter away to the opposite side of the lake. She hadn't said a word since we the left the yurt, but her face displayed utter contentment with life. Her eyes were bright, skin relaxed and a half smile played upon her mouth. I wondered what it would be like to be that happy.

"Well," Skye admitted, "Eve and I kind of know what you're going through."

I glanced over at the two women, wondering how in the world they could possibly know the full weight of my circumstance.

"I was a human once," said Eve. "Case turned me into a Spirian only six short years ago. As far as I know, I'm the only human to make that transition."

Skye patted my arm. "I was raised as a human. I met Shanuk when I was forty-five years old. Until that time, I lived as a human, never knowing why I just didn't fit in." She shook her head in quiet remembrance and smiled. "For years, I felt like a square peg that had been shoved into a round hole. When I met Khalen, my life started making sense but not right away. It took some time to adjust. It will take you time as well."

The woman looked much younger than forty-five. "How old are you now?"

"Fifty-two."

I sat back and took another long look at the simple, but beautiful woman beside me. Her silver eyes sparkled against the moonlight reflected in the lake. "Honestly, you look to be in your twenties."

She smiled. "Being a Spirian has its advantages."

"You two seem so happy," I said. "I don't think I've ever known that feeling." Now I was sounding even more pathetic than I was acting. God, I wanted to crawl out of my own skin and sink into the cool, concealing earth.

"You are happy around Avel," Eve commented.

"Yes," I smiled. "I am—strangely enough. I've never been attracted to anyone like I am to him. It's weird, really. I avoid relationships. They're confusing and unpredictable."

"Men are confusing and unpredictable," Skye commented.

"And we aren't?" asked Eve with a smile.

"We're women," Skye retorted. "It is expected of us."

We laughed, recognizing the irony of that statement.

"You should join with him," Skye said. "He's good for you."

"His time here is short," I sadly admitted, "and mine is eternal." Acknowledging that fact made my stomach twist and threaten to purge my dinner. Living with this eternal emptiness was hard enough. Living with it forever was unfathomable.

"Wouldn't some time with him be better than no time?" asked Eve.

"Losing something you never had is far easier than losing something you want to keep," I explained.

Skye chuckled. "Lord, now you sound like my stubborn mate. He fought the urge to make me his own for the same silly reasons. He was afraid to lose me, so he nearly tossed me aside to spare himself that awful emptiness."

"How did you change his mind?"

Skye frowned. "We nearly killed each other."

"It doesn't matter," Eve intervened. "What matters is making the best of the time you do have together, right?"

The conversation grew silent and I figured there was much more to Skye's story than she was willing to reveal. None of my business, I concluded. It was time to change the subject.

"I'm going to have to leave camp tomorrow."

Skye looked worried. "Will you be back?"

I had to smile at the sadness in her voice. In time, I could grow to like this woman. It was an odd feeling for me. I rarely got close to anyone. Jamie and Kael were the closest people I had to friends, and I only practiced Kempo with them, shared coffee, and took in an occasional movie. Other than that, we did very little together. Kael and I did some geocaching, and I did go shopping with Jamie once, but that was a stretch for me. I was pretty sure that was uncommon for most people.

"Yes," I said. "I just have a martial arts test I need to take this Saturday in Gig Harbor."

"I'm not sure Avel will like you leaving. Does he know?" said Eve.

"Avel doesn't own me, and certainly has no right to tell me what I can and cannot do."

There was an odd sparkle in Skye's eyes. "Can you teach me?"

"What?" I asked.

"Martial arts."

Eve raised her hand. "Oh no. Don't even think about it, Skye. Khal—"

Skye covered Eve's mouth. "Khalen won't mind."

I looked between Eve and Skye. "Does Khalen have something against martial arts?"

"No," they both said in unison.

"Khalen does not want Skye to learn how to fight," Eve explained.

"I don't want to fight," Skye admitted. "I just want to know how to defend myself."

"Sounds reasonable to me," I admitted.

Eve rolled her eyes. "Well, I'm not going to be around when he finds out." With that, she stood and walked away.

"Is he really going to be that mad?" I asked.

Skye scrunched her nose. "He's a little over-protective at times, but he did agree to teach me. He just hasn't gotten around to it yet."

"Why is it so bad to learn martial arts to protect yourself?"

Skye stood and started leading us back to camp, her dog immediately jumped to her side. "He's afraid it will make me overconfident."

"And that's a bad thing?"

She smiled. "Not from where I stand." Her eyes brightened. "Hey, you want to meet a good friend of mine?"

"Sure," I replied, though I wasn't really ready to return to the bustle of the camp. It was dark outside, but the waxing moon shone bright. Skye didn't seem to notice.

She led me toward the pasture where several animals were kept. If there was ever a Garden of Eden for animals, this certainly was it. Pastures rich and green spread across many acres of land, separated by barely visible fences. Shelters were scattered in each one, providing protection from the cold and rain. Some contained goats, while others had chickens, turkeys, and small cows that looked more like dwarfed buffalo.

We entered one of the pastures and Skye released a shrill whistle that sounded like a hawk announcing its presence. The ground rumbled and I heard a distant nicker. From the right came a copper-colored horse with a blaze down her nose that made virgin snow look dirty.

The mare nuzzled Skye's hand, looking for a treat.

"This is Belle," Skye said.

I allowed the horse to sniff my hand, then rubbed her large jowl. "She's beautiful."

Skye grabbed a handful of mane and easily swung up onto the mare's back. "Come, I want to show you something." She held her hand down to me.

"You want me to ride with you?"

She nodded.

"I can't swing up like that."

"Stand on that log," she said, pointing to the one we had been sitting on. "I'll come get you."

"You have no reins," I said, stating the obvious.

"I don't need them." She guided the horse to the log and waited for me to climb up. "Have you ridden before?"

"A few times," I said, "but it's been awhile." I raised my leg over the mare's back and allowed Skye to pull me up. The warmth of the mare's body felt good and strangely familiar.

Skye urged the mare forward and onto the path we were on. The gentle sway of the horse lulled me into my thoughts. A dangerous necromancer was after me and my life was in turmoil, yet in this space, this moment, I felt complete, safe, and in utter bliss. I smiled. "This feels good," I said.

"Yes, I understand. I often find peace on the back of this horse. I think she likes it as well."

We wound our way through old-growth trees where only the sounds of nature could be heard. The smell of moss and evergreens was prevalent and offered a sense of freshness to my scrambled mind.

Toward the end of the lake, Skye veered the mare left through a thicket of ferns. The soft feather-like leaves brushed our feet as we ventured through.

Then we came to a clearing. A meadow of blue, yellow,

red and orange greeted us like a loving family. I was sure this place resembled paradise in the bright sun. Tonight, under the light of the moon, it looked almost surreal.

"Oh," I said, not really believing any of this could possibly be real. "This is amazing."

Skye led the horse to the center of the meadow, then swung her leg over the horse's neck and gently slid to the ground. The mare bent her neck down to graze on the tender grass. I followed Skye and slid to the ground.

"This is my thinking place."

"I like it."

She turned to look at me and smiled. "I thought you would." She walked silently toward a large boulder beneath a huge majestic willow tree. With little effort, she climbed on top and patted the space to her right.

Maiyun chased after critters, content to leave her mistress unattended for now.

"You certainly don't act like you're blind," I said, scrambling up the rock beside her.

"And how do blind people act?"

"Well, the few that I have encountered use a cane or a dog to get around, and they certainly don't ride horses with no leads and climb boulders with such ease in pitch darkness."

Skye laughed. "Then you haven't been around them much." Her expression fell serious. "It doesn't take sight to see what's around you. We have other senses that are often ignored."

She held up her hand. "Place your hand close to mine but don't touch it."

I did as she asked.

"Now, close your eyes."

"Okay."

"Tell me when my hand is one inch from touching yours."

I felt the heat of her hand, and then something else. Like a magnet, I felt a resistance, almost pushing my hand away. It came closer, then something inside my belly shifted. "Now," I said, without much thought.

"Open your eyes."

Skye's hand was just a little over an inch away from my own.

"Wow," I said, "that was weird."

"Your instincts are strong. You should develop them."

I looked down at my hand. It still tingled. "I actually felt you get closer."

Skye smiled. "It works with objects as well, like tables, rocks, and trees. That's how I get around so well."

I remembered how I felt that same shift in my belly when making tinctures and salves for specific people. I inherently knew what they needed to get better.

"Yes," she said, reading my thoughts. "You have a gift with medicine."

I frowned. "Archangel Raphael said that my gifts would be strong after being touched by that other Angel."

Skye looked at me, waiting for me to continue.

"I haven't noticed anything different."

She shrugged. "Perhaps it takes time. Spirians need to learn to use their gifts before they become stronger." Then her eyes grew wide. "Sunjia will be able to see your gifts," she said excitedly. "She's a seer."

She grabbed my hand and slid from the rock. "Come, we must see her before she leaves."

I followed her, nearly losing my footing as we hurried toward the mare. "Where's she going?"

"She and Aidan are leaving with Ian this evening to fly

to Brazil."

"Brazil?"

"Yes. Khalen wants them to investigate Madrona's family. They will be gone for a few days." She swung up easily onto Belle's back. I found a rock to stand on and waited for her to pick me up.

After I found my seat and balance, she looked over her shoulder. "Hold on."

She urged the mare into a trot, then into a smooth canter. I held onto Skye's waist marveling at how easy it was for her to stay balanced. I felt myself shifting over the mare's back like a bag of marbles. The mare didn't seem to notice, though I was sure she had.

Maiyun ran beside us, tongue hanging out of her mouth, and easily keeping pace. For an older dog, she moved with impressive grace and ease.

Skye stopped the mare at the edge of camp before sliding to the ground. I did the same.

"Go back to the pasture, Belle," she said, then lovingly patted the mare's rump. The horse tossed her head, spun around then ran toward her pasture at the far end of the camp.

The beautiful, exotic woman who was Aidan's mate, loaded a bag into the old Jeep and looked toward us. "Skye, Elle," she said in greeting.

"Do you have time?" asked Skye.

Sunjia looked back toward her yurt. "Some," she said. "Aidan is eager to leave. Khalen wants him back in three days. Aidan says that's hardly enough time and is feeling edgy."

"This can wait," I said, feeling odd for asking the kind woman to stop what she was doing.

She and Skye exchanged looks. Sunjia's expression

turned to one of concern. “Look at me, Elle,” she said. Her eyes began to glow like obsidian with a yellow halo. “You have a strong connection with plants,” she said. “And you have good intuition.”

That, I already knew. “Anything else?”

Sunjia shook her head, then frowned. “No. That is all I see clearly, but there is more. It’s shielded from me now.” Her eyes dimmed.

Part of me felt deflated. “Thank you.”

“Do you need help with anything?” Skye asked her friend.

“No. Aidan is loading the rest of the bags. Ian is ready to go. He is eager to see his female, Erika.”

“It has been nearly three months. I’m sure he is.”

Aidan tossed two more bags into the Jeep. He smiled at the three of us as he approached. “Ah, what a lovely sight you three make.”

Skye smiled and shook her head. “Always the charmer.”

He wrapped his arm around Sunjia. “Ian is chompin’ to go, love. Are ye ready?”

“Let me say goodbye to the children.”

He snatched her hand. “Crimy, lass, you said goodbye to them twice now. Leave ‘em be.”

Sunjia hugged Skye. “Take care of them.”

“I will. Stay safe. “ Skye returned the hug.

We watched as the three of them drove away.

“I didn’t think it was possible to get plane tickets so fast to Brazil.”

“Ian has his own jet,” Skye explained. “My Uncle Arcadie has special privileges that enable him and his family to travel worldwide without complications.”

“Arcadie must be an important man.”

“If he were a human, he would be akin to the Pope.”

I shook my head. Until this week, I never knew Spirians existed. How does this race of people live so far off the grid where they remain unnoticed, I wondered?

We made our way through camp. Avel and Khalen stood talking over a pile of smoldering coals where a rack of meat was being cured.

Skye offered her mate a bone-crushing hug, which was returned with equal fervor. Witnessing it both warmed and embarrassed me, much to my surprise.

Avel smiled, noticing my visible discomfort. He moved closer to my side, then sniffed a few times. "Have you been around horses?"

Khalen laughed. "Don't worry, lad, you'll get used to that smell soon enough." He pulled his mate tight into his arms. She gave him a mock glare.

Avel smiled. "It smells good on you."

I nudged him hard in the ribs, making him huff and bend forward. It did little to soften his sense of humor, though.

He burst out into a laugh. "Hey, what was that for?"

"Are you saying that smelling like a horse is better than how I typically smell?"

"Ooo," Khalen warned. "Time to find a few more pieces of petrified wood." He held his hand out to his mate. "Care to join me?"

Skye looked at me and Avel. "Yes, that's a great idea."

Avel watched them go, looking like a dog that had just been abandoned.

I tried pulling away from him but his grip was unyielding. "I need to get cleaned up, Avel. Let me go."

"Did you need some help?"

"No," I practically shouted. He started to follow me back to the cabin. I turned to face him. "Don't you have something to do?"

"Absolutely," he said, smiling.

"Honestly, Avel, what has gotten into you?"

His face softened. "I believe you have, my dear."

I couldn't tear my eyes from his hypnotic gaze. There were years etched in those hazel irises that felt familiar and welcoming as a warm fire on a cold evening. My stomach felt hollow. I swallowed, trying to regain my senses.

"Avel, do you really think this is a good idea?"

"What would make it not so?"

"The fact that you must leave me soon. I'm a target for a crazy necromancer, and I have been recently blessed with an immortality gift that I don't want. You might guess that I'm in a really bad mood."

He stepped closer to me and wrapped his arms around my waist. "And if we don't do this, will any of that change?"

I looked down and shook my head.

"Then what do we have to lose?"

"Each other," I quietly said.

He crooked a finger under my chin and forced me to stare into those will-swaying eyes. "Elle, it has been hundreds of years since we last made love. If those years have not separated our hearts, what makes you think that anything else will?"

"I don't think I can lose you again."

"You have never lost me, love, ever." He released his hold and stepped back. "Go. Take your shower. But," he added with great authority, "tonight, you are mine."

I walked away from him feeling both thrilled and terrified. Some primal part of me wanted him in the most animalistic way, while another part of me knew I had no idea how to love a man. It was hardly modish to claim one's virginity at thirty-three years old. Most people would consider that a tragedy, especially a man looking for an equally skilled lover.

Avel obviously had no idea what he was getting himself into.

Chapter 15

AFTER SOME QUIET TIME, READING a book, checking my email, and answering Jamie's endless questions, I showered, changed into clean clothes that Skye had lent me, and then made my way back to the main fire where everyone gathered.

I still felt as if I were camping at some elaborate resort with a charming rustic flair. I thought my parents' cabin in Tahuya was roughing it. Khalen did have electricity available and an internet connection, which I thought was odd, so things weren't too bad. There was not a TV in sight, but I certainly didn't miss it. There was so much going on around camp, that the days flew by in a blink.

Avel stood and greeted me with a smile and a bright red glass of wine.

"I believe I have grown to love these people," he said.

"So now I know; endless wine and food is what it takes to earn your heart."

"Not to mention useful gifts, unbound intelligence, a sense of community, and phenomenal accommodations."

Khalen approached us with his arm draped around Skye. His other hand held a glass of wine. She held her youngest, Zhentu. His steel-blue eyes would rob some woman's heart someday, I was sure.

Khalen focused on Avel. "Aidan and the others will touch down at Arcadie's place in eight hours," he said.

"Arcadie's place?" I questioned.

"He has his own airfield," Skye explained. "He has a magnificent home. We'll have to show it to you some day."

I laughed. "Me go to Brazil? Yeah, right."

Skye frowned. "Why not?" Then her mind shifted gears as if a sudden thought flashed through her. "Khalen, have you thought to ask Tetris about Vincent's father?"

Khalen looked confused for a moment, then brightened with revelation. "Of course!" He kissed her full on the mouth, then stepped away. "You're brilliant," he said, rushing off toward Case's yurt.

Avel and I must have resembled two cartoon characters who had just been slammed with an iron pan. Skye smiled, her silver eyes sparkling with amusement.

"Tetris is in charge of the camp in England in Case's absence."

Our confusion didn't dissipate one iota.

"He's a wizard—a third-generation wizard."

I pursed my lips.

Skye exhaled, clearly exasperated by our lack of knowledge. Spirians are very impatient, I noticed.

"A wizard is a Protected form of Spirian—the good guys," she clarified. "The Shadow side of a wizard, or bad guy, is called a necromancer. They hold a very tight circle and not much goes unnoticed by one or the other."

"So," I started, hoping to clear my confusion, "a wizard would most likely know about the son of a necromancer?"

Skye's smile brightened. "Exactly."

"Clear as mud," Avel groaned.

I jostled him. "Don't worry about it. This Tetris guy may have some answers for us. That's all you need to know."

"Right," he said, taking a long pull from his wine.

"I need to get this young man cleaned up," said Skye. "I'll see you two later."

-Avel-

I LED ELLE TO THE FIRE where Eve and some other women were chatting. I recognized one of them as Ro at The Wellness Center. The other two were unfamiliar.

Eve greeted us with a smile. "Avel, Elle, I want you to meet Ro, Ember, and her sister, Jade."

"We've met," said Ro. "Welcome to the camp."

The two sisters looked at us and smiled. Ember looked slightly older than Jade, but not by much. Both of them had auburn hair and green eyes. I wouldn't call them stunning, but they were pleasant to the eye. By the looks of them, they had spent the afternoon in the garden with Eve.

"Hi," Ember said. "Eve has told us about you."

"You seem to have the upper hand on us then," I said. The charm in my voice must have been evident, because I felt Elle stiffen. Ah, jealousy. It was a beautiful confirmation of her feelings for me. I tightened my hold on her to ease her worry.

Jade stood and offered her hand. "I'm Jade," she nearly purred. Her eyes roamed over me as if I were a shiny pair of shoes at Nordstrom. I shook her hand then quickly released it.

Elle stuck out her hand. "I'm Elle."

Jade shook it lightly before sitting beside her sister.

"So," said Jade, her sea-green eyes fixed on me. "How long are you planning to visit?"

I felt Elle stare at me, probably harboring the same interest in that inquiry. Her body remained stiff as we took a seat across from the ladies. The log on which we sat was hard but strangely comfortable.

"Nine days," I said, knowing that if this issue with Vincent was not resolved by then, there would be no use for me here. The Council would call me home.

"That's great," Jade exclaimed. "My sister and I are staying for a few days. Perhaps we can get better acquainted?"

"He's taken, Jade dear," Eve blurted.

The woman actually pouted and sighed. "All the good ones are."

Ember rolled her eyes. "Actually, we're leaving tonight, Jade. You know that."

Jade sipped her wine. "Spirian laws, and all that. I know."

Elle remained uncomfortably quiet, sipping her wine and staring into the flames. She allowed her hand to drop from mine. I scooted closer and wrapped my arm around her shoulders. I was pleased to feel her lean into me.

I knew the answer I had given the flirtatious woman was what had made her suddenly distant. The thought of leaving was hard on me as well. There was no skirting the fact, however. Facing it was the only way to ease the pain of it all. The Angels called it "facing the dragon." In all their wisdom, it was the only way to conquer fear.

I squeezed her, hoping to ensure her that she was mine

and no other could take her place. Khalen had been right. Loving this woman during my time here would leave my mark on her and would help to reclaim the joining of our souls. I had little time left and wanted to make the best of it. The next few days would be the calm before the storm. When Aidan and his brother returned, our attack on Vincent would be quick and strategic. Still, the danger of it lingered and the outcome was unpredictable.

With the Spirians and the Angels banding together, the results would be nothing short of spectacular.

"I need to leave early tomorrow," Elle said between sips.

"Leave?" I questioned.

She looked at me as if I should have known her reasons. "My test is tomorrow, Avel. I can't miss it. It's bad enough that I have not shown up for the past two workouts."

"Your test?" My mind was occupied with strategies for taking Vincent down.

"Yes, Avel. I test for my brown belt tomorrow. You know that."

"Elle, it's not a good idea."

"I won't miss this test," she said, her jaw stubbornly set.

I had to determine Vincent's whereabouts. If he was anywhere near Port Orchard, Elle would be stuck here whether she liked it or not. I set my empty glass down beside her. "I'll be back." As I stood to leave, she reached for my hand.

"Where are you going?"

"Back to our cabin. I need to find Vincent and know that he won't be anywhere near you tomorrow."

"I'll be in the studio. What could happen there with five black belts around?"

"A lot," I said over my shoulder.

I hurried back to our cabin. Once there, I found a worn shirt of Elle's, my container of salt, three white candles, and a common stone I had imbued with Vincent's energy in Elle's apartment.

I cleared a spot in the center of the room, lit the candles; one placed at the north point, the other two in the southwest and southeast corners forming a triangle. I sprinkled salt along the inside perimeter and quietly sat in the center holding the stone in my hand. I slowed my breath and focused on Vincent.

His image blurred in the back of my mind as my intention gathered strength. A handsome black man, tall, well-proportioned and sharply dressed, stared back at me, his dark eyes bright with hope and menace. He was standing in front of Elle's cabin in Tahuya, sensing the wards I had placed along the perimeters.

He was looking for her. It would not take him long to find her at the karate studio. He would know about the test. The man smiled, as if reading my mind. I dropped the stone.

Was it possible? Could he have known I was tapped into him? I had to talk to Khalen.

When I returned to the fire, Elle sat with the others. Khalen and Skye sat across from her engaged in what appeared to be a humorous conversation.

I nodded to Case, Eve, Khalen and Skye, then to the sisters I had met earlier. Jade returned my greeting with a seductive grin.

Elle smiled as I took a seat beside her. My glass of wine had been refilled. I took a long pull of its tannic offerings.

"What's wrong?" she leaned over and whispered. "You

look like you've seen an evil spirit."

"I need you to stay here tomorrow," I answered.

She shook her head. "No."

"Elle, I saw him. He knows where you are."

"Who? Vincent?"

"Yes," I seethed.

"Come with me then."

"It's too dangerous."

Our conversation drew the attention of the others. Khalen had already started reading my thoughts, as well as Elle's. The crease between his brows indicated his concern. He moved to sit closer to us.

His mate was not too far behind. As if anticipating the need for discussion, Case and his mate rolled their logs closer to form a tight circle. Case used his telekinetic gift to move Skye and Khalen's logs. The display was quite impressive, given the control he exhibited. My own gifts had faded, leaving me too much like a human for my comfort.

The sisters, Ember and Jade, remained where they were. Khalen must have warned them to find another fire to join for now; they both stood, cast me a worried look, then left to join the younger crowd's fire.

"Elle," Khalen began. "It is not a good idea for you to leave the safety of the camp."

"I have a test that I will not miss," she said. "It is a commitment that I had made some time ago and I will not break it."

Skye placed a hand on her mate's arm. I could feel the hum around the circle increase in intensity and knew the leader's authority had been challenged.

"Elle," I said, "Khalen is leader of this clan. His advice is not ill-given, nor should it be ignored."

"As a leader then," she countered, her chin held much too high for a woman who should be showing respect, "you certainly understand the importance of keeping a commitment."

Khalen started to open his mouth, then stopped when Skye squeezed his arm.

"Elle is not of this clan, my love. She does not understand our customs."

The hum eased a bit and Khalen's sharp, golden stare focused down on me. "Come, we must talk." His voice had an edge to it that could easily cut my throat if I had refused.

I stood and followed him out of the circle.

"Tell me what you know," he said, once we were out of the others' earshot. I had quickly learned to keep my thoughts to myself and it clearly annoyed this leader.

"Vincent is looking for Elle. It will not take him long to track her if she leaves this place." I opened my thoughts to Khalen to inform him of the upcoming test and why it was so important to Elle. The hardness in his jaw seemed to soften a bit.

"Where is Vincent now?"

"I saw him standing outside of Elle's home. He couldn't pass through my wards. But if he tracked her there, he will have no issues with finding her in town."

"Aidan and the others are returning home. Arcadie and Tetris are coming as well."

"What are you thinking?" I asked.

The deep creases between his brows deepened. Only a man who thought too deeply could develop such defined lines. "Perhaps we could use her as a decoy for young Vincent."

"No," I answered, much too quickly. "I will not allow

Elle to be used as bait."

Khalen's dark brow arched with curiosity. "Can you stop her from leaving?"

"She has no car. Where is she going to go?"

Khalen laughed. "A woman like that will find a way, dear boy, believe me."

I studied him. His expression held a hint of knowing, which I found disturbing. "You are a clan leader. Can you not bind her to this camp?"

"She is not Spirian, nor is she a member of this clan. My binding on her would be weak—too weak to hold the likes of that woman."

"Surely no female would thwart your demands, Khalen."

A smile softened his features. "Convince my mate of that fact and I will deem you leader of this clan."

I glanced over at Skye. The woman had a strength about her that even I would not challenge. I sadly shook my head. "My time here is short as it is, my friend. I do not wish to end it prematurely."

He laughed. "Wise choice."

We returned to the circle, choosing to drop the subject. If Elle did find some way into town, we would be prepared. Of course, it was best if she didn't know that plan.

She watched us as we took our seats. "Is it settled, then?"

"It is," I said, offering no other information. Skye looked at me, then toward her mate who was just as stubborn at keeping our plan secret.

"I will take you into town, tomorrow," said Skye.

I nearly choked on my wine. "Good Lord, tell me you don't drive."

She looked convincingly shocked at my statement. "I do."

"But you won't be doing any driving tomorrow," Khalen added.

Skye's eyes narrowed. "Why?"

"You bloody well know why. It is in Elle's best interest to stay in this camp."

"And you would bind me to this camp?"

He matched her look of defiance with one that even I would not dispute. "I would."

Skye growled.

Case and Eve seemed amused with the argument. They listened, quietly holding hands. Case had a suggestive grin on his face as if knowing how this would all play out. Eve had a sparkle in her eye, evidently finding pride in her son's ability to command a situation and stick with it.

I, on the other hand, felt the hum increase to alarming levels as the two mates battled wits. Maiyun growled almost imperceptibly, displaying her vexation. Neither Khalen nor Skye seemed to notice.

"Skye," Elle finally broke in, "it's all right. If these men are so adamant about me missing my commitment, then let them have their way."

"I'm sorry," Skye said. "Men can be so stubborn sometimes."

"You of all people should know the danger Elle is facing," said Khalen.

"I also know the frustration of imprisonment due to fear," she retorted. "The clan could escort her, Khalen. They could keep her safe."

"The clan?" Elle choked. "I'm not about to show up for my brown-belt test with the entire clan in tow."

Skye rolled her eyes. "Not the entire clan, just Khalen,

myself and Case should be sufficient. Avel will come along, too, I'm sure."

She added me as an afterthought. I wasn't sure if I should be insulted or flattered.

"No," said Khalen, "and that is the end of this discussion." His expression backed his statement.

Skye studied him for a moment, then quietly sipped her wine.

"Anyone want dessert?" Eve asked, hopeful to have an excuse to leave the sudden discomfort of silence.

"I'll help you," said Skye.

"Me too," Elle chimed in.

Typical females. They stir the mud then leave the pool until the soot settles around the men left standing in the midst of it all.

"Skye," Khalen called out, then waited for her to turn to face him. When she did, he smiled up at her. "Be a dear and bring a bottle of brandy out with you."

"Of course, my love," she seethed.

Khalen must have telekinetically zapped her on the backside because she released a squeal and jumped as if something had bitten her. She then glared at him over her shoulder.

When he raised a brow, she turned and followed the other women back to Eve's yurt.

"She's a challenge," said Case, taking a sip of his wine.

"Yes," said Khalen. "I wouldn't want her any other way. But, there are times when she pushes the line too far."

"Don't all women?" I queried, remembering how challenging Syria always was and how Elle mimicked her old soul perfectly.

"Not Spirians," Khalen growled.

After a moment of silence and few more sips of wine,

I finally had to ask, "Does she really drive?"

"Only when she can get away with it," said Khalen.

"I take it you don't approve?"

His quizzical expression was answer enough. "Would you?"

I shrugged. "It would be interesting to see how she does it without being able to see."

"Sometimes, I think she sees too much," Khalen grumbled.

"How does she do it?" I asked.

"She sees the energy in all things," he explained. "She describes it as a sort of halo that shimmers around things, including rocks."

I nodded slowly, "Uh, huh."

"Like the halo that shines around your friend, Archangel Raphael," Case clarified, "only not quite as colorful."

It was difficult not to notice that brilliant halo. I thought only the Angels had it, not all things.

"It is the signature of the Spirit, our Father," Case continued. "Since we are all touched by His spirit, we shine with His essence."

Again, I nodded, this time with deeper understanding. I had never thought about it, but it made sense.

The women came back from the yurt with their hands full. Eve carried a platter of truffles while Elle had several snifters dangling between her fingers. Skye followed with a bottle of brandy and napkins.

Case moved a short log to the center of the circle where the truffles could be placed.

Gabrihen, Khalen's oldest son, came running toward us. "Father," he said so formally it sounded as if it should have come from a boy nearly three times his tender age of four years.

"Yes, Gabrihen."

"Seth is going to tell stories soon. Is it okay if we stay up and listen?" The boy eyed the dark-chocolate balls decoratively placed around a sprinkling of cacao powder.

Khalen smiled. Soon after, Seth came as if being silently summoned.

"Khalen," he said, acknowledging his leader. He then bowed to Case, and added another greeting to him.

Case nodded back. "Seth."

"Gabrihen tells me you are about to tell stories to the lot?"

"I am."

"I trust these stories will be appropriate for young ears?"

Gabrihen walked over and gave his mother a long and lingering hug. She reciprocated with tender kisses on his soft head of hair. It was odd to see that woman be tough as steel when pitted against her mate, yet show such tenderness to their young.

"Yes, Sir," Seth replied. "They will all be appropriate." He too eyed the decadent balls.

"There's dessert in the kitchen for you young," Eve said, noticing the hungry looks on both boys' faces, "and hot cocoa on the stove."

Seth eagerly headed in that direction, then stopped short. "Do I have your permission, Sir?"

Khalen looked over at Skye, still hugging their son. "With all those sweets, the kids aren't going to be able to sleep a wink," she said.

"Just a little for everyone, Seth, okay?" Khalen said.

"I'll have them in bed in an hour."

Khalen smiled and nodded. "Thank you, Seth."

The young man ran toward Eve's kitchen with two teens in his wake.

"It has been a long time since I have seen young children show such admirable respect," I said, truly impressed.

"Disrespect is swiftly addressed," said Khalen, looking directly at his mate.

She stopped mid-sip, then set her glass and the youngster down. "Go back to your fire, Gabrihen. You don't want to miss Seth's story."

The youngster kissed his mum and then his dad before darting back to the other fire.

She playfully scooted away from her mate, then giggled uncontrollably when he gripped her waist and pulled her back to him, covering her face with kisses.

"Khalen, stop," she laughed. "Please, you're crazy."

Maiyun groaned then trotted back to the couple's yurt. Apparently she had enough for tonight and was eager to retire.

Case reached for the brandy. "Well, if you two are too busy, I believe I will serve the brandy." He lifted the bottle toward me and raised a brow.

"Yes, please," I said. He served each of us a drink before taking a truffle and handing it to his mate.

Khalen lifted Skye into his arms, then carried her back to their yurt.

"Good night," Case called after them.

Khalen waved his hand.

"Save me a truffle," Skye called out, giggling.

Chapter 16

I WAS TEMPTED TO CARRY my little vixen back to our cabin as well, but her deep thoughts and obvious distance deterred that idea.

Instead, we talked to Case and Eve until the fire dimmed to embers. After helping clean up the leftover food and dishes, Elle and I sauntered back to our cabin in silence.

"What weighs down your thoughts?" I asked her, as we made our way past the smaller yurts, smoldering fire pits and gardens. Our cabin was on the far side of the camp, offering a semblance of seclusion and privacy.

The large trees rustled as the wind blew past them. It was a clear night. Stars dappled the sky. The salty scent of the Case Inlet clung to the breeze, potent with algae and minerals.

"Nothing," she replied.

"Right." Typical female response when the world rested upon her shoulders.

When we reached the cabin, I stoked the fire and lit

candles for light. "Would you like some tea?" I asked her.

"Sure," she replied, settling on the couch with her computer.

I started the water boiling and watched as her fingers danced over the keyboard. "What are you working on?"

"Another book," she replied.

This conversation was like pulling a hot pig out of a cool bed of mud. "What's it about?"

"A Spartan warrior who teams together with Angels and a gifted race of beings to bring down an evil force that threatens the balance of the Earth."

I pulled the tins of tea that were stashed in the cupboards and combined some of the leaves into a relaxing blend of chamomile, lemon balm and hop flowers. I added a pinch of peppermint for flavor.

"That story sounds familiar. How does it end?"

She continued typing for a moment before pausing to answer. "The Spartan falls in love, the battle is fought, and balance is restored."

"Well, that sounds good."

"Then," she continued, "the Spartan dies, leaving his true love behind with only the shattered remains of what is now lost."

"People and feelings are never truly lost, Elle, unless they are forgotten."

"It is difficult to remember someone you can no longer hold."

"The physical is temporary, the spirit is eternal. What you feel in your heart cannot be removed unless you choose to starve the emotion that keeps it alive."

She continued to write. I poured some boiling water into the teapot, swirled it around, and then poured it out into the sink. After adding more hot water to the preheated teapot, I added the herbs. While it steeped, I pulled two cups down and carried them over to the table in front of the couch. It was a rustic table assembled from an old maple root that had been cut three inches thick. The finish was simple, sealed but not polished.

Elle continued to type without looking up. I returned to the kitchen for the pot of tea and some shortbread cookies that Eve had left for us. The woman had a knack for baking, and she seemed to enjoy it as well.

"Can I pour you some tea?"

"Yes, thank you," she said, continuing to type.

I had the sinking feeling that the comment I had made earlier about making her mine was the core of her distance from me. She was nervous, I could smell it.

"Elle," I said, trying to keep my voice gentle. She did not look at me. "If you do not want to make love to me, I understand."

She stopped typing. "What gives you that idea?"

I reached over and closed her computer, picked it up and set it aside. "Call it a poor observation, but you have been acting rather distant all evening."

She lifted her cup and took a long sip. "Mmm, this is good." She reached for a cookie and took a bite.

I waited in silence, hoping she would choose to open up to me. The fire crackled in the background. The candles flickered, casting a warm glow over her tanned face. This outdoor living agreed nicely with her. She had color and her eyes seemed to sparkle more, except for tonight.

"Are you going to talk to me?" I asked.

She continued to nibble on her cookie. In truth, I wanted to pitch the plate of cookies, the tea and her computer against the log wall until they shattered into a hundred pieces. I wanted her to talk to me, or at least acknowledge that I was here.

"Very well," I said, gathering my blankets and pillow and laying them on the floor. I didn't bother undressing before sliding under the covers.

"Are you mad?" she asked.

Mad was an understatement. "Why would I be mad, Elle? I share my feelings for you, bare my soul, only to have you freeze it with your blizzard heart. No, I'm not mad. I'm hurt, disappointed, and void of hoping I'll ever be with you again." With that, I turned my back to her and closed my eyes.

"We are destined to be eternally apart," she said. "Sometimes I think what we once had was cursed from the start."

"Yes," I countered, "that certainly explains why the Angels broke every ethereal law to give you a chance to redeem yourself."

"It was an Angel who cursed me with eternal life," she spat.

"So that you could have a life," I retorted. "God, how can you be so damn blind!"

She stormed over to the bed against the far wall and flopped herself down. We both fell asleep to the sound of her sobs.

THE NEXT MORNING, I AWOKE to an empty cabin. Her bed was made and her clothes were gone. The hollow feeling in my gut was a black hole, beckoning my soul to follow it into its lifeless vortex.

I went to her bed and searched for anything I could use to track her—a hair, a piece of clothing, anything that would link me to her spirit. The pillow and blankets smelled like her, lilac and vanilla. A long, blonde shaft of hair tangled around my fingers. I held it to my lips. “God, thank you.”

I gathered my salt, candles and objects to prepare my meditation. Concentrating was difficult. I had to find her. My hands shook as I held the strand of hair and closed my eyes.

I did some breathing exercises to calm my thoughts and still my body. The ethereal vibrations began humming through me. It was a familiar feeling and one that my spirit hungered for. The pain of emotions faded along with the bounds of my physical body. Once again I was pure spirit, whole and complete with all that is.

I thought of Elle and Vincent. They were connected and he knew where to find her. There was another entity with him, one that was unfamiliar to me, yet I knew was significant. He’s protected, I thought, but not by an Angel. There was someone else.

A knock pounded against my door, snapping me back to the physical realm with dizzying swiftness. The headache that followed was nauseating.

The door opened and Khalen stepped inside. “Aidan and the others are back.”

I shook my head, trying to regain my senses.

“Where’s Elle?” he said.

I stood, then stumbled trying to find my balance.

“What the hell’s the matter with you?” roared Khalen.

I grabbed his impeccably pressed shirt. “I was in deep meditation when you pounded my door, dear friend. The feeling of being wrenched back to this plane is akin to having your balls sucked through a straw. Give me a moment to recover, for God’s sake.”

I released his shirt then walked into the kitchen to wet my face with cold water. When the headache started to fade, my vision cleared and my body felt solid again.

"Elle is gone," I seethed. "No doubt on her way to Gig Harbor."

"Then our time is short. We'll talk in the car."

I threw on some clean clothes and met Khalen and the others out in front of his yurt. His Escalade was running.

"Stay alert," Khalen told Skye.

She nodded. "Stay safe," she replied.

An older man with stunning blue eyes sat shotgun next to Case. In the back, I sat behind Aidan, Ian and another old man who looked like a hippie from the sixties. His long gray hair was tied in the back by multiple thongs, decorated with crystals and tiny bells that annoyingly tinkled with every move. He wore elaborate jewelry that would make Mister T envious.

Khalen drove us out of the camp and onto the main road of Harstine Island. He gestured to the man sitting next to his father. "Avel, this is Arcadie, and sitting just in front of you is Tetris."

The old man turned to me and smiled. Arcadie raised his hand in greeting.

"Raphael, are you with us?" I said.

"I am," came a voice. "The Archangels are standing by."

"There is another who protects Vincent," I explained.

"We did not detect another," said Raphael. "Are you sure, Avel?"

"Yes," I said, trying to keep the edge from my voice. "I felt him when trying to connect with Elle and Vincent. It's as if a veil has been placed around him."

Khalen looked over at Aidan and Arcadie. "What do

we know about his father?"

He drove left onto the bridge leading off the island. It felt as if we were moving at a snail's pace. My nerves were raw. Elle was in danger and our plan to save her was risky.

Arcadie spoke for the first time since we met just a short time ago. "Madrona herself seems to be a bit of a mystery." He had an accent similar to Khalen's, only there was another dialect there that was difficult to discern. It was clear to see his resemblance to Case, his brother. Both of them had very strong jawlines, height, and similar features. Unlike Case's dark hair, however, Arcadie's hair was silver and tucked neatly into a short queue.

"Yes," Aidan added, "she doesn't seem to have a Spirian family."

"How is that possible?" Case questioned.

Khalen was the one to answer. "Skye did not have a Spirian family, either, until Shanuk found her."

"Yes," Case interjected, "but the Council knew of her existence.

"Only because Shanuk revealed it to them."

"True," Arcadie said. "So, the question is, why didn't her parents want the Council to know about her?"

The men in the car were silent for a moment as Khalen turned right onto Highway 3 toward Belfair.

"How did Madrona meet Warducca?" asked Tetris. His British accent was more like that of Case, refined and smooth.

Arcadie shrugged.

Archangel Raphael was the one to answer. "Warducca's father introduced them."

"Now how would Javin know about Madrona, an undocumented orphan?" asked Case.

Khalen followed with, "And why would he want to

pair a Spirian woman with his halfling son?"

"Maybe he didn't know she was a Spirian." I said.

Khalen pulled onto Highway 16 before replying. "Spirians know other Spirians, just as you would recognize another spirit."

Tetris tapped his long forefinger nail against the door frame. He looked deep in thought. "Who is Javin's father?"

Case glanced back at him. "Tecal, why?"

"Because that makes Javin a half-brother to Baru."

Listening to this conversation was like watching a spider weave an intricate, multidimensional web in which I did not want to get trapped.

Raphael chimed in. "If Baru were to mate with Madrona, their child would be intricately linked to the Shadows in a very powerful way."

"Yes," Arcadie agreed, "but why would Madrona mate with a Spirian? She would have known about the commitment."

"Not if the Spirian resembled her husband," said Tetris.

I leaned forward, finally putting some of the pieces together. "So Madrona believed she carried Warducca's son, not knowing he was a halfling?"

"Yes," said Tetris. "She was a Spirian who was raised outside of the grid. There would be no way of knowing about halflings."

"But I thought Khalen said that Spirians would be able to recognize other Spirians. Wouldn't Madrona inherently know that the man she mated with was not her husband?"

"She was young and untrained," he explained. "Baru would have been convincing enough to fool her, despite the difference."

"Why deceive her in the first place?" I asked.

"Maybe Javin wanted his line to continue. Since his own son was sterile, the next best thing was for his half-brother to mate with Madrona," Case guessed.

"No," said Tetris. "I believe Baru acted on his own accord."

"Take the next exit," I told Khalen.

We pulled up to the karate studio. There were three cars in the lot; none of them was Elle's. I climbed out of the SUV, walked up to the studio and leaned into the door to push it open. It was locked. Master Mac recognized me looking through the small window and walked toward the door.

He opened it and frowned. "Kael, we are in the middle of a test."

"Yes, I know that. I'm looking for Elle."

"She's here."

"May I speak with her?"

Master Mac looked over his shoulder. I saw Elle shake her head. Master Mac smiled, looking like a cat who had just cornered his mouse. "She doesn't want to talk to you now, Kael. I suggest you return in three hours." He then closed the door and relocked it.

There was magic in the air, I could feel it. I looked around me but saw nothing.

"What is it?" Khalen asked, always perceptive.

"Vincent's here, I can feel him."

Everyone piled out of the car. Given the size of them all, I was surprised we all fit. I felt like a dwarf or a young child. Compared to them, I was young. At 33 years, I was akin to a teenager, albeit a very mature one.

Tetris turned sharply, and then disappeared. Just poof and he was gone. My breath caught in my throat. "Where did he go?"

Case laughed. "Don't bother yourself, boy. Tetris is notorious for transferring."

"Transferring?"

"Similar to time-warping. He can travel through space with a mere thought."

"Nice," I said, nodding my head. That little gift would have been useful hundreds of years ago during battle.

Three men came around the corner. Right away, I knew they were Vincent's minions. The life force was void in them, leaving only animated corpses that resembled bums on steroids.

The men and I prepared for an attack.

Six other minions closed in on our backs. Bloody perfect. Nine super-strength minions against five Spirians and one spirit trapped in a giftless human form.

"You underestimate us," said Khalen, having read my thoughts. "You also forgot the Angels."

He was right, of course. I wasn't sure how effective the Angels could be in the physical world, but I was sure to find out.

Another five minions came around the studio. Judging by the hum in the air, I knew we were in trouble. More minions followed. I didn't take time to count them.

Raphael manifested my sword from days gone past. Although the sword weighed only three pounds, this body was not equipped nor trained to wield it with much grace. My first swing nearly pitched me off balance. I was convinced that it would impede my ability to fight at all when a minion attacked my left side.

I swung around, both hands gripping the sword's leather-bound hilt. Instinct kicked in and I was back in the days of battle. I adapted quickly to this new, small body, and was able to fight with some dignity. I managed to cut down two thugs before a third nearly beheaded me.

Raphael blinded the man with dust, offering me enough time to slay him. The Angels proved useful with their ability to disadvantage our opponents by blinding, tripping or impeding them long enough for us to gain power.

The Spirians' gifts were equally impressive. Khalen had five minions on him at once, but quickly dispensed them as if they were nothing more than irritable insects.

The same could be said for the others. Ian and Aidan used a different strategy. They teamed well together and used more of their mind to distract the unsuspecting minions.

Arcadie barely broke a sweat as he downed one man after another. It almost seemed as if he and his brother were in competition with one another to see how many corpses they could accumulate at their feet.

Tetris had disappeared. Once the battle was over, however, he returned and cleaned the mess up with one swipe of his arm. The area that was littered with slain zombies was now miraculously clean and void of bodies.

"Where's Vincent?" Arcadie asked the old man.

"He scampered away when he saw me coming. I followed him into an alley, and then he just disappeared."

"He can't just disappear," Arcadie roared, still amped from the recent fight.

"Unless he was an illusion," Ian countered.

"I can bloody recognize an illusion," Tetris growled.

"Everyone needs to calm down and think," said Khalen, taking a few deep breaths himself.

"Baru is here," said Tetris. "I can feel him."

A hollow feeling filled my gut. I ran toward the karate studio door and pounded it. There was no answer. I saw nothing through the window and the studio was dark.

"Khalen," I called.

He easily unlocked the door and opened it with telekinesis. The studio was dark, still and eerily empty. It was if no one was ever here.

"He's gone," Tetris said. "Baru is gone."

"We've been duped," Ian said.

Case ran his fingers through is hair. "Where are the Angels?"

"We are here," Raphael called out, then manifested as himself before us. The other Angels also showed themselves; all young and impeccably strong. For beings that rarely battled physically, they looked formidable enough to challenge any army.

I had witnessed their power on many occasions and knew the strength of their protection. Now, standing before them, I could feel their power clear to my soul.

"The one you call Baru has taken Elle."

"What of the others?" I asked.

Raphael shook his head. "There were no others. They were an illusion."

"Baru is not an illusionist," said Case.

"It was Vincent who cast it. Baru and the minions were simply a distraction."

Archangel Chamael stepped forward. His black hair and dark eyes hardly depicted him as the Angel of protection from violence and war. "The darkness that surrounds him keeps us at bay. We are forbidden to enter. Gabriel follows them. His light can weaken their powers and perhaps lower Vincent's shield."

"Where has he taken her?" I asked, knowing he had many lairs in the area.

Chamael projected an image of Vincent's cabin in

Mazama. It was well hidden among the jagged cliffs and old-growth trees.

"Is it protected?" asked Khalen.

Raphael answered, "There are wards around the perimeter. The Angels and I can disarm them easy enough. There are over a thousand minions surrounding the house."

Aidan spoke up. "Neither Ian, I, nor Tetris recognized the illusion. How is that possible?"

Raphael adjusted his wings, then neatly folded them back. "Vincent is far more dangerous than we thought."

Arcadie shook his head. "We cannot fight him unless we know what we are up against."

Khalen looked at Aidan. "Contact your mate. See what she can tell us."

"She must be near the man to know his gifts."

"We can provide a link for her," said Raphael. "We Angels are omnipresent and are not restricted by space or time." He nodded at Archangel Michael. "Tell her that Michael will be by her side."

Aidan contacted his mate and informed her about the plan in less than five seconds—impressive. "She's tapped in," he said, relaying her thoughts.

Aidan placed his hands on either side of his head as if addressing a headache. His brows were pinched and his lips grew tight. Khalen noticed as well and looked concerned.

"Khalen, form a shield around her," Arcadie said. "Do it now!"

Khalen cast his shield.

Aidan screamed then dropped to his knees. Blood started trickling from his ears.

"No!" Ian cried, kneeling beside his brother.

"Tell Michael to break the connection," Khalen roared, rushing to Aidan's side.

"He does not respond," Raphael said with sadness in his voice. "I must go." He vanished.

"Contact Skye," Case told Khalen.

"She's already there. Sunjia is down, Michael had shielded her with his wings, but he is still and Skye cannot move him." He paused for a moment. "Raphael is with her."

Aidan writhed on the ground, holding his head. Archangel Raziel hovered over him.

In a moment, Aidan became still. The blood seeping out of his ears stopped flowing.

"Your mate is very skilled," said Raziel, his voice smooth as cream. "Most healers cannot work from this distance."

"She is connected to this man," Khalen explained. "He is her templar."

The Angel nodded in understanding. I watched in awe, feeling about as useless as a match in a storm. This level of magic was so out of my reach, I barely understood it. There was a time when I believed I was powerful. Today, I felt like an infant in a world I knew little about.

"Sunjia," Aidan called.

Khalen helped him stand. "She's all right. Skye is with her."

Raphael returned with Michael. "Your mate, Skye, is more Angel than Spirian," he said. "She taps into our energy so subtly I hardly knew she was there."

"She is rather seasoned," Case interjected. "She carries the blood of Shanuk."

The Angels nodded. "That she does. It is no wonder the old man speaks so fondly of her and the rest of you."

"What happened?" I asked Michael.

"There was so much darkness. I think Sunjia was detected by someone other than Vincent."

"Yes," Tetris intervened. "Baru protects him."

"The darkness is thick and dense around him. When he pushed her out, the blow was so fierce and fast, the pressure caused her head to bleed inside. I wrapped myself around her to keep her brain from exploding. I was careless and did not shield us from his next attack." He glanced up at Khalen. "If it were not for your shield, young man, we both would be dead."

Aidan growled after hearing what Baru had done to Sunjia. Khalen placed a hand on his shoulder, displaying a level of understanding and control.

"Sunjia is fine," Khalen assured him. "Talk to her." His expression changed. "My shield trembles. Baru is trying to breech it."

"Avel, activate your wards," Raphael said.

"From this distance?" I questioned.

"The power of our Father knows no bounds. Activate them as if you were there. Use your mind, Avel. Your intentions are what fuels the magic."

I felt foolish drawing a circle around me with my sword, but it was what I had learned and it comforted me with familiarity. Once the circle was drawn, my mind could focus. I felt protected and strong. I reached into my pocket and pulled out the single thread of Elle's blonde hair. The thought of her and the last moments we spent together crushed my heart. The pressure of it made it hard to breathe.

I squeezed my hand around the strand of hair. To want someone who no longer wanted me was almost too much to bear. I wanted to drop the hair and sever my connection to her, but my hand only clenched harder as if having a mind of its own.

I focused on the wards and connected them to the Angels. I felt the familiar hum of their activation and knew it was successful. My thoughts then shifted to Elle. I saw her in my mind, scared, shivering with cold and tied too tightly in a stone cellar.

"Father," I prayed, "please wrap her in your light and protect her from harm." I felt a tingle in the energy around me. "Be it so," I said, "as above, so below."

I opened my circle and stepped out. All eyes were on me like hungry mosquitoes. The Angels smiled.

"That was impressive," said Khalen.

I laughed. "Coming from you, who can ward off several thugs at once, cast a shield with a thought, and communicate with your mate over several miles, I'm honored. Thank you."

"You underestimate your own power, Avel," Raphael said. "You always have."

That snagged my curiosity. "What do you mean?"

The Angel had the audacity to laugh and fade away.

"Raphael?"

The other Angels faded with him.

Chapter 17

THE SPIRIANS DISCUSSED WHERE TO eat as if we had all the time in the world. My patience was at its end.

"There is a necromancer out there planning to rule the planet and you guys are thinking about your stomachs?"

Ian turned back to me and smiled. "We have to eat, lad. Ye know; keep up our strength and all that."

"We need time to strategize," Khalen explained. "Come up with a plan."

"How far is Mazama from here?" I asked. "We have been on the road for three hours already."

"About an hour and a half from here," said Case. "Calm your thoughts, boy, they don't serve you now."

"Elle is in trouble," I told them. "I had a vision of her."

"Yes," said Arcadie, "and you asked the Father to protect her. Have faith He will do so."

I did have faith. I just wanted to reach her and see for myself that she was safe.

They all laughed as if reading my thoughts. I had to remember to keep them to myself around all these

Spirians.

Khalen looked at me through his rearview mirror. "Is that not akin to asking the Father for patience, then demanding he grant it now?"

My eyes narrowed. "Perhaps," I admitted, knowing I had lost this battle.

We sat down in a restaurant that looked more like an expensive lodge. It was constructed entirely of long logs cinched together by complex clamps that needed to be tightened regularly.

A pleasant-looking hostess with dark hair and exotic eyes led us to a well-lit room that overlooked a colorful garden. "Will this do?" she asked Khalen.

"Aye," he said, "this is fine."

She smiled, obviously intrigued with his accent and attractive looks. "Can I get you gentlemen something to drink?"

"Give us a moment, love, will you?" said Ian, turning his charm on with turbo force.

Her face reddened. "Of course." She walked away, placing her hand over her chest.

I shook my head. The men hardly noticed the effect they had on that young girl. They spoke among themselves, giving her no notice at all.

When she returned, everyone ordered a beer. I ordered iced tea with lemon. Spirians may not be affected by alcohol, but I was in a human form and needed to keep my head clear.

The girl returned. Her blouse had been unbuttoned a bit lower than before. When she reached over the table to deliver the beer on the far end, she displayed an impressive pair of breasts that definitely gained the Spirians' attention. The conversation came to an abrupt halt.

Khalen and Aidan politely looked away. Case and Arcadie cleared their throats and reached for their beers, averting their eyes to something less alluring. Tetris and Ian made absolutely no effort to see anything but what she had to offer.

"Very lovely, m' dear," Ian commented, "but I must say yer efforts are sadly wasted. We are all spoken for."

She rose slowly, her face flush with embarrassment. Without another word, she walked away.

"Smooth as always, brother," said Aidan.

"Ye didn't want me havin' her flash her goods for nothin'?" His accent grew thick with emotion. He was riled and oddly uncomfortable with it.

I bumped his shoulder. "You're not spoken for," I said.

"Oh, aye, I am," he said. "I have a woman in Brazil."

That earned Arcadie's notice and a smile stretched across his face. "If you can earn her mother's blessing, dear boy, you deserve to have her."

"Erika is Arcadie's daughter," Ian explained. "I plan to join with her next summer."

"It sounds like her mother is not too happy about it."

"Oh, Kitta loves me. She just doesn't want to lose her daughter."

"Hmm," I said, not really sure what to think about that.

"Ye see, Kitta wants her baby girl to live in their clan. If we join, she will come live with me."

"Why can't you live with her clan?"

"That is a choice, but one I cannot make."

"Why?" I asked.

"I am bound to this clan."

Khalen chimed in, "You will always be bound to this

clan, Ian, whether you choose to live with her or not."

"It is customary for a female to live with her man," Ian said, almost defensively.

Aidan laughed, "And since when have ye ever been customary, brother?"

"Erika will live here with me," he announced, "and that is final."

Aidan and Khalen laughed.

Arcadie was more curious than amused. He watched Ian, but the young Irishman could not meet his gaze. Sensing the tension, he cleverly changed the focus to more pressing matters.

"We need a plan, gentlemen. I don't have to tell you the dangers of bringing down a Spirian Shadow when you don't know what his gifts are."

"Sunjia was able to tap into some of them before she was attacked," Aidan said. "The man is not an illusionist as we had suspected. He combines visions with shape-shifting—very rare. He can also materialize."

"So, who was in the studio?" I asked.

"Minions," said Aidan. "Made to look like people who you expect to see."

Scary, I thought. "Can someone who can materialize to another location take a mortal woman with him?"

"Baru can," said Tetris. "It is hard to do and very risky, but he has perfected the gift."

The waitress came to get our orders—her blouse buttoned back up. I had to smile to myself in noticing that when the rest of the men seemed oblivious. We ordered a refill of drinks and our meals. Once she left, we continued our conversation.

"Vincent must know he is a Spirian," I said. "Why does he continue to bring back the dead?"

"Not necessarily," said Arcadie. "His father was a voodoo priest. They believe in magic. Bringing back the dead is not devastating in their realm."

"His father has been dead for some time," said Case. "Who trains Vincent?"

"Baru," Arcadie suggested. "He is Javin's half-brother. It makes sense that Vincent would trust him."

"It takes time to develop such gifts," Case argued. "Vincent is young, yet he is as powerful as a centurion."

"There is another way," said Tetris.

The waitress returned with our drinks and meals. She eyed us suspiciously when we stopped our conversation. "Can I get you anything else?"

"No," Khalen answered. "Thank you."

She frowned at the sharpness in his tone, then walked away.

The shepherd's pie I had ordered did not resemble the ones in my faded memory. This was assembled in a fancy dish laden with mashed potatoes, cheese of various colors, and spices that smelled like basil and thyme. Hidden beneath was a thick beef stew-like substance in salty gravy.

Tetris sliced into his rare steak and took a bite. He chewed slowly, savoring the flavor. "Lord," he said, "there is nothing akin to American beef."

I slid a forkful of food into my mouth and was pleasantly surprised at the play of flavors. The texture was all wrong, but the flavor provided a tasteful distraction.

Everyone enjoyed their meal, seemingly disinterested in Tetris' last comment before our conversation came to a halt.

"Tetris," I finally prompted, "you said there was another way."

He nodded, stuffing another slice of beef into his mouth. Apparently Spirians took eating rather seriously.

"Well, what is it?"

My impatience earned a look of amusement from the elders at the table.

"My apologies, young Spirit. We continued the conversation telepathically."

Well, if I didn't feel left out before, I certainly felt it now. "Care to fill me in?" I didn't even try to keep the irritation from my voice.

Tetris wiped his mouth, then cleared his throat. "Spirians can transfer gifts to another blood relative. The process is called transference and can only be done once in a lifetime. Because the process weakens the body, it is typically done when the donor is dying and wants to pass on his gifts. It's a way of strengthening the bloodline."

"So, if this mystery Spirian passed his gifts onto Vincent, don't you think he would wonder where these gifts came from?"

"Voodoo priests often practice magic to strengthen their power," Case explained. "Vincent could easily attribute the powers to his own doing."

"Why would Baru keep Vincent ignorant about who he is?" I asked.

"Vincent is a pawn," said Tetris. "He believes he follows in his father's footsteps as a powerful priest. If he knew about his Spirian side, things would change."

"In what way?"

The old man finished his last bite. Satisfied, he neatly stacked his utensils on his plate before moving it out of his way. "Spirians inherently know about certain laws that should not be broken. These laws are obeyed by the Protected and Shadows alike. If broken, it could lead to the destruction of our race."

"Then why is Baru allowing Vincent to bring back the dead?"

"In there lies the mystery, young man," he said, sipping his beer.

"The woman is the link," said a voice. I recognized it as Archangel Gabriel. "She will be the one to bring Vincent's parents back."

"No," I said. "She would never do that."

"Not on her own accord," said the Angel. "Vincent will move the spell through her."

"Why does Vincent want to bring his parents back?" asked Aidan.

"Perhaps it's Baru who wants them back," said Tetris.

Aidan raised his hands, "Okay, why?"

"To cause a paradigm shift," said Gabriel.

"Explain," I said, suddenly losing my appetite.

"Life has a natural rhythm," Arcadie explained. "A series of natural disasters causes life to shift to survive. It prompts change. By bringing back Vincent's parents, he is causing a drastic, unnatural shift. The balance between good and evil will be so off kilter that the destruction will be monumental."

"And why would Baru disrupt the balance? What can he possibly gain?"

"Well," said Arcadie, "Baru has already transferred his gifts to Vincent, which tells me that Baru's time on Earth is short. If Elle delivers the spell, she will be the one who dies, leaving Vincent to rule along with his father. Because Warducca is not full Spirian, he will not be a threat. Vincent will overrule him. That allows Baru to live vicariously through his son."

Everyone was silent for a moment. I still had one

nagging concern. "What's the plan?"

Again, silence.

Case summed things up. "We have over a thousand minions to contend with, and two necromancers, one with impeccable strength and gifts, another with the same and perhaps a few mystery gifts. On our side, we have six Spirians, one spirit with impressive fighting skills, and the Archangels."

"Sounds like a barrel shoot," I said.

"For who," Tetris laughed.

"Us."

"Dear boy," he said. "Believe it or not, we are horribly outnumbered."

"Elle is not going to die," I said, slamming my fist on the table.

"Easy, Spirit," said Case. "We have not given up."

"We are running out of time," I reminded him. "She needs us and we are just sitting here, drinking beer and reminiscing as if we had all the time in the world. In Sparta, we faced armies that tripled this threat."

"If I remember, you died in one of them," said Case. "How many of those men were gifted?"

My eyes narrowed. "They were gifted in the art of battle," I argued.

"Battle is never an art," he said, "It is nothing short of a tragedy."

Khalen tapped his beer. "You said that Vincent would not attempt to bring back his father and mother until it was a full moon."

I nodded.

"That does not occur for another five days. We have time."

"The spell is more powerful on a full moon," I clarified,

"but it is not imperative that he wait."

"Baru knows of our presence," said Tetris. "He will not want Vincent to wait."

"I can handle the minions," said Khalen.

"There are too many. They will weaken you too much," Case retorted.

"I'll help him," I said.

"We need you to gather the book," Raphael chimed in. "Besides Elle, you are the only one who can touch it."

The waitress zoned in on our table, no doubt curious about the odd voice that had just spoken. An Angel's voice was like no other; it drew attention.

"Did you need anything else?" she said.

Khalen handed her two hundred dollars. "No, we need to go. Keep the change."

Her eyes widened as did mine. "Wow, thanks."

"Come," said Khalen. "We'll continue this conversation on the road."

I, for one, was grateful to be moving again, getting closer to Elle.

After we piled into the Escalade, I continued the conversation. "I can help Khalen with the minions, and then retrieve the book."

Case said, "Ian, Aidan, can you handle Vincent yourselves?"

Aidan shrugged. "I don't know what we'll be up against, but we can try. Keeping a necromancer in an illusion is like trying to capture a wave in a sheet of gauze."

"He's right," said Arcadie. "Tetris, can you keep an eye on them?"

"I'll be busy with that old fool, Baru, but I will try."

"Arcadie and I will help Khalen and Avel. Once the minions are out of the way, we will come in and help."

Case turned back to address the old wizard. "We have to take Vincent and Baru down. What is the safest way to do so?"

The wizard sat back and thought for a moment.

"Can't they die like everyone else?" I questioned.

"They can," replied Case, "but trying to kill them is like trying to stab a flying gnat with a toothpick."

"We can help," said Raphael. "Our presence will weaken their powers."

"I need you to shield Elle," I said. "She is your first concern." After the words poured from my mouth like the sludge from a coffee press, I wanted to take them back. The audacity of me telling the Angels their first priority was stupid at best, if not self-destructive.

"We understand your anxieties, Avel," Raphael patiently replied, "but our first concern, as you put it, is helping you and the Spirians complete this mission."

"Understood," I said. "Forgive my impudence."

Arcadie continued, "Why do I feel as if we are going into this battle blind, ignorant and unprepared?"

Tetris laughed, "Because we are, dear boy, good God."

The men were quiet for the last half hour of the ride. Each of us lost in our own thoughts. My only concern was of Elle, tied up and frightened in that dank room of stone and darkness. I tried reaching out to her like the Spirians could do with their mates.

A hollow void filled my core. Elle was not my mate, nor did she have any interest toward it. What we once had was clearly over. Her life was her own now, and I had to let her spirit fly to release her from my heart. God, the thought was like pushing a steel blade through my chest.

Today, this mission would end. The result of it determined the fate of this world. If we failed, the people would never know what happened or why. They would blame the wrath of God, no doubt, or perhaps the presence of Satan. They would not know how our small band of Spirians and Angels failed to protect them. We would all go unnoticed.

If Vincent survives and succeeds in restoring his parents' lives, the veil between realms would be torn. The mystical creatures of the underworld would roam freely. Humans would not stand a chance against the evil beings of other dimensions. The Spirians, alone, could not protect them. The gentle spirit of the human race would be replaced by fear and a raw passion for survival.

I smiled inwardly, remembering the many battles in Sparta where we were outnumbered and survived to fight another day. We humans have survived many such paradigms. With God's help, we would do so again, I was sure.

Khalen pulled off the road and onto a long dirt drive. "We stop here," he said, "and hike our way up."

The mile-long drive was steep and paved with loose black rock that crunched beneath our steps. We could feel the hum of the Angels as they neutralized the wards around the perimeter. Their presence brought a sense of peace in the midst of war. It always had. It was one of the reasons why I prayed for their help in every battle I fought. I silently thanked them for being there now.

Around us, trees towered toward the vivid blue sky. The bird song belied the perils that lay ahead. The land was laden with huge Douglas firs, spruce and cedars. The view from the land was vast and wild. There were no people in sight for miles. The mountain was young and jagged. Sparse undergrowth provided a good vantage of the property that surrounded a cold stone house. We moved silently toward it.

I saw movement through the windows and felt Vincent's presence. I wanted to reach out with my will and destroy him. Pawn or no in this game, what he planned was self-serving and destructive beyond mercy. No matter what outside influences convince us of doing, we are given the ultimate power and will to make the right choice.

"Get ready," Khalen seethed. "The minions are near."

Vincent had been busy. There were far more than a thousand thugs. The property buzzed with them like ants whose hill had been disturbed. We were surrounded.

I gripped my sword and said a silent prayer. A sudden gust of wind picked up, swirling all around our small band and away from us. We were in the eye of it all.

The minions shielded their eyes from the dirt that stirred and backed away.

"Now," Khalen roared then charged into the fury. We followed him.

Chapter 18

IN A MOMENT, I WAS surrounded. My body moved and attacked, mindless of the danger—just like old times. Flesh splayed from my sword as it found its mark again and again.

Khalen felled many of them without effort while Arcadie and Case downed others who were writhing in pain. Some of them were armed with blades and axes. I felt the sharp sting of one as it slashed across my back. I stumbled forward, but then quickly regained my balanced to thwart the next attack.

An axe swiped my ankles and I was down, my legs bleeding and unresponsive. Khalen, Case and Arcadie surrounded me, keeping the minions at bay.

I looked down at my injuries, clearly debilitated, and watched in amazement as they started to heal. I choked down the rising bile that burned my throat.

"Stand up," Khalen roared.

I grabbed my sword and immediately rejoined the battle. My body felt exhausted and spent, but the thugs kept coming, reeking of death and decay.

Khalen shoved me and shouted, "Get to the house. Find Elle."

I ran through the expanse of minions held back by nerve-numbing energy that the Spirians projected. The hum of it left me dizzy. I kept running, following the light of the Angels.

Ian and Aidan battled with Vincent, all of them moving as if in slow motion. It was odd. They were holographs of themselves, shifting and moving faster than my eyes could see.

Sparks of lightning shot through the house. I caught glimpses of the old wizard as he zoomed in and out of focus.

The Angels led me to Elle, tied up in the basement where Vincent's parents lay ceremoniously on stone tables littered with herbs and colorful flower petals.

"Avel," she called, her face streaked with tears and dust. I reached for her, then something struck me with the force of a freight train. Everything went black.

Moments later, I awoke, shackled to the stone walls.

Elle struggled against Vincent's hold, seething, "I won't!"

Vincent dragged her toward the tables supporting his parents.

"You will," he growled, "or your friends will die."

Ian and Aidan were surrounded by blue swirling light. They looked catatonic as if stuck in an illusion of nightmarish proportions.

Khalen, Arcadie and Case were shackled against the far wall, a hum of energy surrounding them. I sensed the pain they endured. Tetris was there, too, held by glowing bands. He struggled, but his efforts made the bands tighten, causing him great pain.

The dark basement hummed with so much energy my head felt ready to implode from the pressure. Now I knew what deep-sea divers endured at one-hundred feet below sea level. Every breath was an effort.

"Read," Vincent said, shoving Elle's face toward the book.

-Elle-

I CLOSED MY EYES, DRAWING UPON the memory of my prior research. "Help me, Hermes," I whispered. It was his book that had been adulterated. His words would bring back the truth, I was sure.

My body shook with the energy in the small, dank room. The power from Vincent, together with another force that stayed near him, pulled at my soul like a tornado. I concentrated on the cold stone beneath me, hanging on to my feeble link to the earth.

My friends had come to rescue me and now they suffered. Avel looked spent and void of expression when my eyes met his. I couldn't blame him for being distant. I left him without so much as a word or note and now it seemed that all was lost.

"Read," Vincent grabbed my hair and shook my head.

"The girl can't help you," Tetris roared, writhing in pain as a shard of lightning pierced his gut."

"Stay out of this, wizard!" boomed another voice. It came from a man, who suddenly manifested before us. He was not an Angel, of this I was sure.

Another, more powerful, hum filled the room, bringing with it an odd sense of peace. Suddenly, I was able to concentrate without fear. I was surrounded by Angels. I could feel them all around me.

"Hurry, Vincent, we haven't much time," the old man said.

"Read," Vincent commanded me, pointing at the wavering words in the book.

The letters blurred and I couldn't read them. Slowly, they became clear, manifesting into the infamous words of the Emerald Tablet, Hermes' life work that was soon acknowledged as the Sorcerer's Stone. The myth of the stone promised to bring power to those who believed and felt the strength of those words, but few ever could.

With a shaky voice, I started reading. "True, without falsehood, certain and most true, that which is above is as that which is below, and that which is below is as that which is above, for the performance of the miracles of the One Thing."

"No!" Vincent screamed.

"Vincent, stop her," the old man commanded. "Don't let her continue."

Vincent slammed the book down before me. "Read these words, or I kill your friends." He walked toward Avel. "Starting with this one."

Again, the next line of the tablet became clear. I started reading again, assured by the Angels that my friends would not be harmed. "And as all things are from One, by the mediation of One, so all things have their birth from this One Thing by adaptation."

Vincent's roar shook the stone walls. He aimed his hand toward Avel and fire flew from his fingers. The fire never found its mark. Light brighter than the sun radiated around Avel, deflecting the flame back to Vincent. He jumped back, grasping his hand now black and blistered.

The old man whisked the book away from me.

"Kill her," he told Vincent. "Kill her now!"

Words from the tablet flashed in my head. I spoke them as they appeared. "The Sun is its father, the Moon its mother, the Wind carries it in its belly, its nurse is the Earth. This is the Father of all perfection, or consummation of the whole world. Its power is integrating, if it be turned into earth."

Vincent reached for the book. He started to read the words.

"No!" the old man yelled. A band of light surrounded him, holding him in place.

"Keep reading," the soft, familiar voice of Raphael whispered to me.

I closed my eyes and recited the words revealed in my mind. "Thou shalt separate the earth from the fire, the subtle from the gross, suavely, and with great ingenuity. It ascends from Earth to Heaven and descends again to Earth, and receives the power of the superiors and of the inferiors."

The book flew out of Vincent's hands. The pages glowed orange.

The old man struggled within the light, clearly growing tired and weak.

Vincent screamed a few words in a language that made no sense. "Gasta, nuo, checume," he roared.

The powers he had summoned fell to the floor like dust in the rain.

"Read," the gentle voice told me.

"So thou hast the glory of the whole world; therefore, let all obscurity flee before thee. This is the strong force of all forces, overcoming every subtle and penetrating every solid thing. So the world was created. Hence were all wonderful adaptations, of which this is the manner."

Vincent tore at the pages, now burning in his hands. "No," he cried.

More words flashed in my mind. "Therefore am I called Hermes Trismegistus ..." And then I heard Avel's voice join with mine; "... having the three parts of the philosophy of the whole world. What I have to tell is completed, concerning the Operation of the Sun."

With that, the book burst into flames, and then vanished. Vincent fell to the ground.

Ignoring the horror of it all, I grabbed the keys from Vincent's belt and rushed over to release Avel from his shackles. I then moved to release the others. When Vincent had fallen, the light that held Ian and Aidan dissolved.

My bones ached and my hands shook. I wanted out of here, away from this place—now.

"You did it," Avel said, wrapping his strong arms around me. I melted into him, laying my head against his chest. He smelled of blood, sweat and death, but I didn't care. Somewhere in the midst of it all, he smelled familiar and comforting.

The energetic bands holding Tetris fell away.

"Now," he growled toward the old man who was aiding Vincent, "I rid this plane of you, necromancer." He cast a white-hot flow of energy toward the pale, weak man leaning over his young accomplice. In an instant, the old man vanished. Tetris fell to the ground.

Avel nodded to Khalen before approaching the dark young Vincent lying on the floor, his eyes now open and wide with fear.

Khalen gripped my arm. "Come," he said, leading me out of the cellar.

I heard Avel say, "I claim your life, Vincent Forei, son of Baru and Madrona. May the Father show mercy on your soul."

The swoosh of Avel's sword, and then the thump of what I assumed was Vincent's head, preceded an eerie silence.

"Oh God," I said, allowing Khalen to usher me up the stairs. "I'm going to be sick." I ran outside and purged the horror, fear and stress I had been warding off for several hours.

The grounds were littered with dead bodies. Again, I purged my stomach, now painfully dry.

"Ian! Aidan!" Khalen called.

My surroundings suddenly changed, as if I had stepped through a portal. I stood in the midst of a meadow filled with colorful, sweet-scented flowers. Not too far in the distance before me was a waterfall that resembled the tail of a white horse. It feathered over a steep gray wall. Rhododendrons bloomed along the edges of the cliff, mingled with various shades of green moss. The sight of it entranced me.

All I could hear was the crashing water. I didn't care where I was. I liked it here and wanted to stay. The details of how I got here didn't matter. I was at peace.

Chapter 19

-Avel-

BY THE TIME I GOT OUTSIDE, Tetris had the property cleaned of bodies and the ugly remnants of war. Ian had Elle in some illusion to spare her the trauma of death and gore. He stood beside her, claiming she would not remember anything. He then explained how he could wipe her memory clean of days past if it were required. I told him that would not be necessary.

The Angels manifested before us.

Khalen bowed. "Thank you."

"How were you able to enter the cellar?" I asked. "The darkness was thick as tar, I felt sure you couldn't enter."

"We all entered together," said Raphael. "With our combined light, we were able to smother the darkness. Doing so caused the Shadows' powers to weaken. It was Gabriel's plan. We weren't sure if it would work."

"And if it didn't?" asked Khalen.

"The darkness would have consumed us."

"I don't believe the Father is willing to give up his best Angels that easily."

"No," said Raphael. "It was His strength combined with our will that enabled that improbable feat to happen."

"I'm glad it did," I said, "or I would be toast a bit overdone."

Khalen confirmed. "We all would be."

Aidan drove the SUV up the driveway. Tetris spoke with Case and Arcadie. Each of them looked as if they had done battle with a rogue weed whacker. Slashes of blood stained their clothes. Tetris looked exhausted and battered.

I looked up at Raphael.

"Later," he said, placing his hand on my shoulder. I felt dwarfed in his presence. "You have many questions, Avel. Take care of Elle. We'll talk soon." He touched the hilt of my sword and it vanished. "You won't need that anymore."

"Thank you," I said as his image faded.

Ian held the door open for me. I climbed into the far back with Elle. She sat still, eyes closed, her breath slow and even. "Where is she?"

"Paradise," Ian chuckled. "I'll release her after we get out of here."

"Can you remove the memory of me killing Vincent?"

Ian nodded. "I can." He climbed in beside his brother.

The ride through Mazama was a quiet one. I was sure the Spirians were talking with their respective mates. I wrapped my arm around Elle and pulled her close to me.

She stirred a bit, opened her blue-green eyes and smiled up at me. "I had the most amazing dream," she purred.

I kissed the top of her head as she mumbled on about

flowers, waterfalls and various creatures.

We arrived back at the camp late that evening. The fires had burned down to embers, leaving a warm, welcoming glow. The night sky was clear and littered with stars that seemed to glow much brighter this evening than ever before. Balance had been restored and the world would rest in peace tonight. I breathed in the fresh, clean air, misted with dew.

"I'm tired," Elle said, clinging to my arm.

"Come, let's go to bed." I lifted her into my arms and carried her back to our cabin.

The fire had been stoked and built for us, leaving the cabin warm. A plate of fresh-baked cookies lay next to a bottle of 18-year-old Macallan Scotch. "God, I love the women of this clan," I said with animated sincerity.

Elle wandered over to the bed and searched for something she might change into for comfort. She looked lost and her hands started to shake.

I handed her a cookie and a glass of amber heat.

She took it, smiling. "What I really need is a hot shower and some clean clothes." She took a sip of the scotch and closed her eyes. "Oh, this is perfect."

"Come," I said, taking her hand. "Let's sit for a bit, then we can go to the showers. I'll give you one of my shirts to wear."

I brought over the tray of cookies and the bottle of scotch before sitting beside her.

"I've never tasted anything like this," she said, inspecting the glass of amber liquid as if it held some magic.

"It's a very expensive drink," I explained. "They age it for 18 years in seasoned oak barrels."

"I like it," she purred, snuggling up against me.

"At two-hundred bucks a pop, I wouldn't get too used to it."

Her eyes widened. "It doesn't cost that much!"

I laughed. "Knowing this clan, they probably buy it by the caseload."

Her fingers traced the ragged, bloody shreds of my clothing. "Are you hurt badly?"

I shook my head. "Skye is a healer. It was incredible. My back and legs were shredded. She was able to heal them in less than a minute. Even the Angels were impressed."

"I like her," Elle said sleepily. She sat up and looked at me as if I were a stranger.

"What happened?" she asked. "All I remember is being tied up in this dark and dingy cellar. I remember reciting the words of the Emerald Tablet and feeling as if I was in a lightning storm." Her eyes shifted as she pieced the fragmented memories together.

I wanted to stop her before she remembered too much. Ian said that he could only mask the memory, but not remove it entirely. "It's over now."

Her gaze was distant as she searched her memory. "I remembered asking for your father's help. I knew he held the answer. The words to the Emerald Tablet appeared in my head. The Angels were showing them to me. I remember being able to read them as clear as if they were written before me."

"Yes," I said. "The purity of his life's work was enough to destroy the evil that Vincent and his father enchanted."

"It was a different version of the Tablet than I remembered, though."

"Yes, there are many versions and translations." I smiled.

"Why are you smiling?"

"Because, I remember how my father made me memorize those words and recite them back with emotion in my tone. For many years, the words held little meaning to me."

"And now?"

I lifted her chin and gently kissed her cold nose. "Now, they hold magic and hope."

"It is said that those who live and feel those words hold the power of the Sorcerer's Stone."

My smiled broadened. "Ah, yes, the Sorcerer's Stone, a product of the illustrious Smaragdina Tablet."

Her pretty face skewed in confusion. "That was the original stone tablet, yes?"

I nodded. "The alchemical symbols hold much deeper meaning than the translations imply."

"Then why are the words so powerful?" she asked, taking a sip of her scotch.

"The words, themselves, are not powerful. It is the emotion and meaning behind them that make them so. Combined with the symbols and their hidden message, one could turn any substance to gold."

"Really? I thought that was just legend."

I looked at her and smiled. "Like the Angels, gifted beings, and the battle of good and evil?"

"So the legend is true?"

"The legend is true."

The sparkle in her eyes was like that of a child in the midst of a really good story. "Could your father make gold?"

"Oh, yes, and many more valuable things. He was a true alchemist."

"How did he do it?"

I pulled from my memory a snippet of the Tablet.

"And as all things have been and arose from One by the meditation of One: so all things have their birth from this One Thing by adaptation."

"Which means?"

"All things come from the Spirit, the creator of all things. My father called it Aeon Pneuma—Eternal Spirit."

"God?"

"Yes." I sipped my scotch, then set our glasses down on the table. I gathered a few toiletries, two towels, and a change of clothing. "Come, let's bathe."

She stood. "A hot shower sounds perfect."

I held my hand out to her and she hesitantly took it.

"Are you angry at me for running out on you?" she asked.

We wound our way through the silent camp toward the shower hut that lay nestled between a clump of trees.

"Disappointed, perhaps, but not angry." I squeezed her hand."

"I want you, you know."

I looked at her questioningly.

"There's just a fear in me—an emptiness that fights being filled."

"You will find someone, Elle."

She stopped, pulling my hand. "I want you."

At that moment, I read something in her eyes. Khalen had been right all along. Elle couldn't come to me on her own. The darkness in her prevented it. I had to pull her through it.

I gripped the back of her head and pressed my mouth to hers. It wasn't a gentle kiss. I wanted to let her know that tonight I would make her mine.

She pulled back a little, breathing more deeply now. Her body screamed no, but her eyes pleaded with me to take control. I gripped her hand and led her toward the showers.

When she started to head to the women's showers, I pulled her close to my side. "No," I said. "Tonight, we shower together."

She hesitated a bit but I wouldn't allow it. "Come," I encouraged. "It's all right."

We entered the warm area lined with cedar. Khalen had installed radiant floors that were lined with burnt-red ceramic tile. The showers were open and roomy with plenty of shelves for personal products, and rough ayate clothes for scrubbing the skin. I laid our things down on the bench, hung our clean clothes on pegs, along with our towels, and then gathered our soaps and shampoo from the bag.

I turned the water on to let it warm up. It smelled sweet and slightly tangy with minerals—remnants of the deep well from which it was pumped.

Elle looked ready to bolt. I gripped her arm. "Let me do this for you," I said. I began unbuttoning her blouse. I lowered it off her shoulders and allowed it to fall to the ground.

She was visibly shaking. I finished disrobing her, then quickly discarded my own clothes before leading her under the hot spray.

She closed her eyes as the water soaked her head and body. A low moan escaped her lips. God, I wanted to take her right there, but gritted back my urge. I had to go slow and stay in control.

I began washing her with the sandalwood-scented soap. Her skin was like silk beneath my hands. Her lips were trembling.

"You were not this nervous the first time I bathed

you," I said.

"I knew nothing would come of it. Tonight, I'm not so sure."

"I won't take you here, Elle. Relax."

She looked up and allowed the water to soak her face and head as I washed her body. When the touch became more intimate, she stiffened.

"I can reach that part," she said.

"Allow me to do this," I said in her ear. My grip around her hands tightened. A soft cry escaped her. I kept my task purposeful so I wouldn't alarm her. My own need was not so easy to tame.

I washed her hair and conditioned it with an herbal rinse scented with chamomile and vanilla. Her posture became more relaxed and she appeared much more comfortable with me. She looked up, expressing a hunger in her eyes that wasn't there before.

"My turn," she said, grabbing the bar of soap.

Her touch was gentle and far more teasing than I would have expected. I wondered if she knew what effect she was having on me.

"What were you like in your own body?" she said almost distantly as if asking herself the question.

I laughed. "Much different from this, I assure you."

Her hands roamed over my body like a sculptor smoothing the edges of her work. "In what way?"

"I was much taller, closer to Khalen's height. I had dark hair, blue eyes, and a muscular build."

She washed my hands, then moved to shampoo my hair. "What did I look like?"

I closed my eyes and rinsed my body. "You had jet-black hair that flowed down to your waist, and dark eyes to match. When you smiled, one did not need a lantern to brighten the darkness. You were slightly taller than you are now, and had a moderate, graceful figure."

She laughed and looked down almost nervously. "You must find me a bit of a disappointment, huh?"

I crooked my finger under her chin. "I did not fall in love with your body, Elle." She tried to look away. I didn't let her. "Stop running from me. I want you," I whispered, then kissed her.

~Elle~

When he kissed me, my world and all its nightmares ceased. My knees trembled and my heart raced as if anticipating a need I was unfamiliar with. Instinctively, I felt compelled to pull away, but his strong grip held me firm to him. The hint of panic that shot through me quickly dissolved. His hold and his kiss didn't soften until I yielded—completely. When that happened, I didn't want him to stop.

"Better," he said, releasing me and tossing me my towel.

Suddenly cold and flustered, I dried myself, trying to clear my head. I dressed in the shirt he had brought for me and looked for a pair of pants. There weren't any. I reached for my dirty pair, but he snagged them from my hand. The urgency in his eyes was both alarming and exciting. I wasn't sure if I should flee into the darkness, or into his arms. Instead, I just stood there, mouth open, and frozen still.

He smiled. "You won't need these," he said, stuffing them into the bag.

My head suddenly cleared. "You can't expect me to

walk back to our cabin in this!" I pulled the shirt out away from my body, emphasizing how it only fell to my mid-thigh.

"I most certainly do," he said, his smile turning wicked.

"I'm not comfortable with this," I said, slightly raising my chin to meet his greenish-gold eyes. That was a mistake. He could melt glaciers with that stare.

"Tough," he said, picking up the bag and gathering our toiletries.

At first I thought he planned to leave me. Then, like a vice, his hand gripped mine. I stumbled forward trying to keep pace with him.

"Are we in a hurry?" I asked.

"You are purposely dragging your feet, my dear."

I was. I just didn't notice until he brought it up. As we drew closer to the cabin, my heart beat double-time as if I were marching toward a death chamber. I tried pulling my hand from his.

"No, Elle. Not this time."

"I'm not ready for this," I said.

"That is your demon talking. I intend to drive it far away from you tonight."

I couldn't swallow. My throat felt as if he squeezed it with the same intensity as he did my hand. I couldn't breathe. "Please, Avel, don't do this."

He practically dragged me up the stairs. Panic filled me but I couldn't break free. "I don't want this!" I roared, my voice barely sounding like my own.

Once inside, he stoked the fire, still holding onto my hand. I fought hard to pull it away. He spun me around to face him.

"Look in my eyes and tell me you don't want me," he growled.

I looked into those languid eyes and choked on the words that struggled against my throat. "I—I—d—"

His lips crushed down upon mine, instantly melting the resolve I desperately clung to.

Somehow, we ended up on the bed. He made quick work of the shirt he had loaned me, and then discarded his own clothes.

His touch was gentle; his grip on me was not. In an odd sort of way, I was grateful for the restraint and his possessiveness. Without it, I would be out that door, I was sure. My soul wanted this, but my body didn't. As he continued to kiss me, I felt the thick walls around my heart start to crumble.

I returned his affections with equal enthusiasm, driven by an inner need that begged for its freedom. He took his time, expertly knowing how to feed that feeling until the need was replaced by a hunger that ruled all logic. My body started to tremble beneath his.

"I'm scared," I said.

His kiss was tender. "Don't be. Your heart will remember."

He was right, my heart did remember. We made love throughout the night until I fell asleep in his arms, my head resting against his chest.

I **AWOKE SEVERAL HOURS LATER** wanting more of what we shared earlier that night. My body craved him, wanted him. I was elated with that feeling. I awoke him by trailing soft kisses down his neck and chest.

A low, throaty groan of pleasure rumbled in his chest as he stirred. He opened his eyes, his pupils soft and inviting. "Hmm," he hummed. "I've created an insatiable female."

It didn't take long for him to take command of the situation, fueling my desire to another level. He liked to be in control. As far as I cared, he could have it. I willingly followed his lead, inwardly smiling at the odd admittance.

We were not disturbed that day and did not emerge until later that evening. Avel was grateful for the sliced cheese and fruit the women had left in the refrigerator yesterday evening. By sundown, however, we were both ready for something more substantial.

We wandered out toward the main fire where Khalen stood and talked with Arcadie, Case, Aidan and Ian. Skye, Eve and Sunjia sat on the far log, giggling and sharing stories with one another.

The conversations ceased as we approached. Khalen smiled broadly. "Ah, the couple emerges." He slapped Avel on the shoulder and followed up with a brief hug. He held his arms out to me and wrapped me in a bone-crushing embrace. "You look radiant, my dear."

A sudden flush of heat reddened my face. "Thank you."

"Come, have some wine," he said, pouring us each a glass.

Avel approached the ladies. "My sincere gratitude to you for the cookies, cheese, fruit, and fabulous scotch you left for us."

Skye nodded her head. "You are most welcome, Avel. We heard you had quite an adventure."

"More like a nightmare," Elle added.

"Come," Skye said, patting the spot beside her. "Tell us what happened."

Avel kissed my hand, then left to join the men in conversation.

I told the women slices of what I remembered, including how Avel, Khalen, Arcadie, and Case were shackled, and Tetris was bound in some kind of electrical bands that caused him pain when he moved. "I thought we were done for."

"So what made you think of reciting the Emerald Tablet?" asked Eve.

"I didn't. I prayed for Hermes' help. The Angels came and the words appeared before me."

"I bet Vincent was surprised," said Sunjia.

"He was furious. I thought he was going to kill Avel, but the Angels surrounded him with their light making Vincent's energy bounce right off him."

I took a sip of my wine, a light Burgundy. "I'm going to miss this place," I said, "and all of you."

"Are you going home?" asked Skye, a hint of sadness in her voice.

"Avel will return to the Father soon, and there will be no reason for me to stay."

Seth, Sunjia's oldest son, approached our group holding a book in his hand. "Ms. Alder, could you please sign this book for me?" he asked shyly.

He was a good-looking young man, almost mirroring Khalen in many ways, though not quite as tall. He held a copy of my latest novel, Emerald. I took it from him and the pen he offered. "I would be happy to, Seth."

He smiled.

I signed the book, and then handed it back to him along with the pen.

"Oh, you can keep the pen," he said. "I bought it for you."

The pen was heavy and encased in gold. "Wow, this is a nice gift, Seth, thank you."

"You're welcome, he said, exchanging glances with his mother before he turned and walked away.

Sunjia smiled, but it was a sad smile. "He spent his entire summer savings on that pen."

I frowned. "Why would he do that?"

She shook her head. "I'm afraid my son is smitten with you."

"No," I said. "He can't be more than eighteen."

"He's twenty-two."

"Well, don't fret over it, Sunjia, I'm taken." I placed the pen in my pocket. Avel would be leaving soon, but my heart would be taken for many years to come, I was sure.

The conversation fell into an uncomfortable silence as I sipped my wine. Subconsciously, I rubbed the raw areas of my wrists where the ropes in Vincent's cellar had chafed them.

Skye moved over and sat next to me. She placed her hands over my wrists and within minutes, the wounds were healed and the soreness was gone.

"Now that's a gift I wouldn't mind having," I said, trying to lighten the mood.

"You have a few of your own," said Sunjia."

"A few?"

"I see more now. It happens sometimes."

I waited for her to continue, but she calmly sipped her wine as if she had never opened that can of worms.

"Well?" I prompted, "What are they?"

"A strong intuition, a gift with plants, summoning the Angels, some kind of a protection force, and veiling," she said."

"I can summon the Angels?"

Sunjia nodded.

"What is veiling?"

"You can veil something and make it appear invisible. You also have a very strong shielding effect."

I pursed my lips. "And how, pray tell, do I manage to make things invisible?"

"Hold my hands," she said.

When I placed my hands in hers, Sunjia closed her eyes. Images flooded my mind like memory snippets. When she opened them again, I was left with an odd sense of knowing. My hands tingled as she let go of them.

"That was weird," I said.

"Try it," she said. "You know how now."

I focused on Avel's wine glass. Energy pooled in my belly, and then filtered out through my hands. With a slight wave, I threw the energy toward the glass. It faded, connecting to me with a subtle hum.

My eyes widened as the glass disappeared. When Avel reached for his glass, he swiped at air as if the glass was never there. We giggled as he looked around for it. His eyes narrowed.

"Okay, ladies, what did you do with it?"

I released the energy and pulled it back. "Right where you left it," I said, trying to keep the smile from my voice.

He glanced down and frowned. He retrieved his glass and walked over toward me. "Nice trick," he said, taking a seat beside me.

"Not a trick," I said.

His quizzical look was both charming and seductive.

"It's a new gift I've acquired, among others."

He leaned over and kissed me, then whispered in my ear, "I'm well aware of your new gifts, my love."

I shoved him away. "Have you no scruples?"

Skye and Sunjia laughed. Eve just smiled.

Sunjia told him about my newly acquired gifts, then

hesitated for a moment. "There is one more gift I didn't mention."

By the look on her face, I wasn't sure I wanted to know. The conversations around the fire ceased and all eyes were on me.

Avel took my hand, letting me take comfort in his nearness.

Skye started to smile, as did Eve.

"What?" I finally said.

"You have the gift of life," she said.

"The gift of life?"

Avel looked just as confused as I was. "She was touched by an Angel," he explained, probably thinking the same thing I was. She saw my immortality.

"You're pregnant," the woman finally blurted.

"Impossible," I said.

Avel half laughed and half cried.

"Wait," I said, trying to talk some sense into him. "It's not possible."

"You laid with him last night, did you not?" asked Sunjia.

My face flushed with heat. "Yes, but—"

"I can sense the life in you."

"Seriously?"

"Seriously," she laughed. "You carry Avel's young."

Chapter 20

THE OTHER MEN CAME TOWARD us. Khalen slapped Avel on the back. "Congratulations, my man."

I received another heart-stopping hug from him, then another from Case and Arcadie.

"This is all so unreal," I said. "The timing is all wrong. I shouldn't be fertile for another week." My face flushed. I couldn't believe I spoke that out loud.

"Some things," Arcadie explained, "are gifts from the Father. His timing tends to override our own."

Avel took my face in his hands and pierced me with his golden-green eyes. "It is a gift, isn't it?" He smiled. That look could melt butter, I thought.

I struggled to swallow, still not believing the truth of it all. "Oh God, yes," I said, almost breathless. "I'm going to have your baby."

"I pray it's a son," he said, closing his eyes.

"Me too," I said, no longer fighting the tears that pooled in my eyes.

-Avel-

SHE WAS CRYING. WERE THEY tears of joy or sorrow, I wondered? She seemed happy—confused, but happy. I held her as she shook and cried in my arms. The kisses I brushed against her head added small comfort, if any.

I thought about the time, soon to come, when I would have to return to the Ethereal Kingdom and what that would do to Elle. A pang cramped my belly as I remembered the day she took her own life and the life of our unborn son. I squeezed my eyes shut, silently praying for her strength to fulfill her promise to me.

"Come," a soft voice echoed in my head. "We must talk." It was the voice of Raphael.

I released Elle and brushed a kiss on her lips. "I'll be back in a moment."

She hesitantly let me go, her eyes swollen and red. The other women quickly gathered around her, offering their own kind of comfort. I was grateful to them.

Raphael led me toward the private lake where we could talk undisturbed. He appeared to me as himself; a form he often took when he was serious.

"Your time draws near, Avel."

I lowered my head. He was referring to my return. "When?"

"Five days from now, next Saturday."

I bowed to him. "Thank you for the time," I said, knowing he must have had something to do with extending my stay.

"The Father smiles upon you, my friend."

"Yes, in many ways," I said. "Elle is pregnant."

Raphael smiled. "Yes, we all know. She carries your

son, Avel."

A lump formed in my throat. "You mean Kael's son."

"No," the Angel said. "The child is of your spirit. He will look like you in many respects." He turned away to look at the shimmering lake and the two ducks who leisurely swam across it.

I stepped up next to him. "I am grateful."

"He will be important, someday. It is imperative that he survive. Will she have the strength to follow through with her promise to you?" he asked. "She has been made immortal, however, her will for death can overrule it."

"She will chose to live," I said without hesitation. My quick response surprised even myself.

Raphael turned to study me. "You seem quite sure."

"She has friends here. I want her to stay. I believe they can help her through it."

"But?" he added, sensing the hesitation in my voice.

"Khalen cannot allow it. She is human and once I return to the Kingdom, Elle will be alone."

"Elle is no longer human, Avel. She was touched by an Angel. She is more Spirian than human, now."

"I just need to convince Khalen of that."

"Can we help?"

"Perhaps." We stared at the water in silence for a moment until the Angel's previous words finally struck home. "My son is important?" I smiled.

The Angel smiled back. "In time, you will see."

Again, we stood in silence. My next question was one I already knew the answer to, but I had to ask it anyway. "Raphael?"

"Yes," he said, picking up a stone and skipping it across the lake. The ducks voiced their disgruntlement with a series of loud quacks and a flapping of wings as they scurried toward the far end of the lake.

"Is there any way I can stay?"

His expression was answer enough. "You know the answer to that one, Avel. Your time here is spent. What you and Elle have been given is a gift that few receive. Cherish it and take the memories with you."

I nodded and smiled inwardly, remembering last night and anticipating the nights ahead. "That I will, my friend."

When I returned to the fire, Elle had a bowl of elk stew on her lap. Another bowl rested on the log beside her. My wine glass had been filled and a plate of cheese biscuits sat on a stump table.

She beamed me a smile as I approached. "Is everything all right?"

"Everything is perfect," I said, grazing her lips with my own; deepening the kiss as one of many to remember.

"Wow," she said, lifting my bowl so that I could sit. "I never knew how dizzying an innocent kiss could be."

I smiled. "There is absolutely nothing innocent about that kiss, my love."

Her face reddened. "I waited for you."

"Really?"

"I wanted to share prayers with you; the way Skye and Khalen do."

I reached for her hands and bowed my head against hers. Before I could open my mouth, she began speaking.

"Father, thank you for all the gifts you have so graciously given us. Thank you for giving me new hope." She placed a hand over her belly. "A new life, and a new heart."

"Thank you for second chances," I added. She squeezed my hand, indicating she had said all that she had to say. I ended the prayer with, "Be it so. As above, so below."

She smiled. "That sounds familiar."

"It is how my father always ended his prayers. He claimed it was his way of trusting the outcome and sealing his intentions with utmost faith."

She handed me a biscuit, still warm from the oven. "Eve?" I asked, holding the fluffy bread in my hand.

"No other," said Elle. "The woman can bake."

I nodded, taking a bite. The sharp cheddar cheese added an interesting contrast to the sweet, dark wheat. The stew was spiced with an interesting mix of peppers and ginger. There was another flavor I couldn't identify.

Khalen read my thoughts. "Spicy sauce from Shanghai Restaurant in Port Townsend. Skye and I make a trip out there once a month just to buy more."

"It's good," I said, savoring the flavor of the sweet meat and buttery potatoes that surprisingly filtered through the contrasting sauce.

"Is there food in heaven?" Elle asked.

I nodded. "The Ethereal Kingdom is much like it is here, only more intense."

"Intense?"

The conversation ceased around the fire and everyone's attention focused on me. I was sure it was a topic of interest for most people, including Spirians.

"The colors are more vivid and alive," I said. "You have no physical body, but one can be manifested if desired."

"What do you do all day?" Gabrihen asked, sitting next to his mum.

"There is no shortage of tasks to be done. Some people tend the gardens, others care for the animals. We have cooks, carpenters, and other trades."

"Does everyone live together like we do?" young

Zhentu asked, crushing a biscuit in his tiny hand. His dark hair and blue-gray eyes resembled his mothers'.

"Yes and no," I said. Each spirit creates its own version of ethereal space. If we require the company of other souls, we merely have to think about them and call them to us, or we can go to them. There is no such thing as time or space. We are not bound to any given reality."

"Sounds cool," said Tanya, Eve's oldest daughter. She mimicked her parents' looks, having dark hair and obsidian eyes. She was only four years old, but stood taller than most kids her age and held herself with unusual elegance.

"It is," I agreed.

"Do you see people you know there?" asked Seth, a hint of fear in his words.

"You do."

"Even people you don't want to see?" he asked.

I glanced at his mother, hoping she would clarify his statement.

"He worries about seeing his father," she said. "He was a Shadow."

I nodded, fully understanding his line of questioning now. "Dark souls," I explained, "have their own realm. The darkness that surrounds them prevents them from entering our Kingdom."

His expression softened. "Like hell?" he asked.

"Some would call it that, but to those who are drawn to the dark, it is home."

"How can a place like that be home?" Gabrihen asked.

"I'm certain you have seen groups of people smoking together?"

"Yeah."

"To some, smoking is bad. They believe it destroys

your health, produces a foul odor on your breath and leaves a nasty residue on clothes and hair."

"Smoking is gross," another child said.

"To some," I explained. "To those who smoke, it is a social bond to others who do the same. It calms their body and clears their mind. It offers enjoyment."

"So it's not bad?" young Gabrihen asked.

"What is good for one soul may be bad for another and vice versa."

He wrinkled his nose. "So the Shadows' realm is good for Shadows but bad for those of us who are Protected?"

"Yes," I said. "It is part of the balance in all things."

"Have you met God?" Elle asked.

"Yes, as have you—all of you," I said as I looked around at the gathering.

She frowned. "Explain."

"God is not a person, Elle. He's the Source of all things, the energy that creates and offers life."

"So when we pray, we are not really addressing another being?"

"We address the Source, our Father."

"Who is not an entity," she said, trying to clarify but still sounding very confused.

"We give Him a name to better identify with Him," Arcadie explained. "Just as we do with the Earth, whom we call Mother. They are one and the same. They are both part of the Source."

"Well, aren't we all part of the Source?"

"Yes," Arcadie, Khalen, Case and I said in unison.

"The Source is all things, binds all things, gives life to all things, and is the creator of all things," I said.

Her confusion didn't lessen.

"Think of the Source as a body," said Case. "Other life

beings, such as ourselves, make up the cells, bone, tissue, blood and other fluids that keep the body alive. The body gives us food and enables us to function as a whole. When we pray, it is similar to a cell asking for a need. The body responds by eating food, drinking water, taking medicine, or anything else required to keep the cell happy and functional. In turn, the cell reciprocates by keeping the body alive and well."

She nodded, the confusion fading amidst a glimmer of understanding. "So when we give thanks, we inform the body, or the Source, that we are well and happy?"

"Yes," said Case. "And it has the same effect on the Father as it does on you when someone genuinely thanks you for something you have done. When they show you appreciation and gratitude, does it make you feel good and willing to do more for that person?"

She nodded. "Yes, it does."

"But when someone doesn't acknowledge your efforts, it has the opposite effect, does it not?"

"Well," she said. "It certainly makes it difficult to help them again."

"And that is where we differ from the Father. He is above such emotions. He gives us what we want, based on our emotions and intentions, hence the phrase, 'Be careful what you ask for.'"

"So," she said, trying to clarify. "You basically get what you give in return?"

"In most cases, yes."

"Life is not black and white," I said. "It's comprised from a myriad of colors, shapes and sizes; like a jigsaw puzzle whose pieces are constantly changing."

"Sounds confusing," she huffed.

"That's the irony," I said. "The simplicity of it all

creates the confusion."

"Simplicity?" she questioned. "Is that what you call it?"

"When you move your arm, you do so without much thought. If, however, you were to really analyze all that goes into moving that limb, and all the cells and tissues that must orchestrate their actions perfectly to create that graceful movement, the intricacies would blow your mind."

She raised her hand in a sign of mercy. "Okay, enough. I have plenty to mull over. Thank you very much."

The evening ended with much lighter conversation, laughter, and a spicy black tea that Eve had made with coconut milk and honey.

After helping with the dishes and putting away the leftover food, Elle and I bathed together, this time enjoying the process far more thoroughly. We returned to our cabin ready to settle in for the night.

I made love to her, taking my time and enjoying all she offered. I wanted to embed everything about her in my memory, to live it out again and again while waiting for her to come home to the Kingdom. I had no doubt that after this life, she would make it back to me.

"I never knew it could be like this," she said, rolling onto her side. "I watched people in love and thought it was a gift that was never meant for me."

I brushed a golden strand of hair from her damp forehead. "Now you know different."

Chapter 21

WE ENJOYED BREAKFAST WITH Khalen and Skye the next morning. Afterward, Skye and Elle left to brush the horse. I helped Khalen clean dishes.

"I have a favor to ask of you," I said.

"Another battle?" he said, smiling.

"No, nothing quite that fun."

He quirked a brow.

"Elle is happy here. She has friends and people to look out for her."

I could see the muscles in his jaw start to flex. "I know she is not Spirian," I continued, "however, she is no longer human, either."

"Our laws are clear," he said.

"The Spirian High Council has approved it," Raphael said as he manifested before us.

"It is risky," said Khalen. He glanced at me, showing a hint of discomfort. "In the future, if she becomes involved with a Spirian male, we don't know what will happen."

"She is more Spirian than human," Raphael challenged.

"Chances are good that she will become a true Spirian if she joins with a Spirian mate."

The thought of someone else claiming my Elle made my stomach churn. I took a deep breath and reminded myself that she should not have to endure this life without someone to love. I had opened that floodgate for her and it couldn't—shouldn't be closed again.

Khalen studied me, no doubt reading my thoughts. "We don't know that," he said, attempting to support my cause.

"There are many things we don't know," said the Angel. "Elle is pregnant. She will need support."

Again, Khalen flexed his jaw and closed his eyes.

"Khalen," I said. "I want her to find another mate." Thinking that and voicing it were two different things. I felt choked with sadness when the emotion rose to my throat. "You can help her and ensure that the one she chooses is a good match."

"The woman will mourn your loss," he assured me.

"Yes, she will need support. I'm asking you to share your clan. It is good for her."

"What makes you think she will want to stay?"

"I'm sure she won't voice it. You have seen her independent side. I need you to convince her to stay here."

Khalen turned and began drying the dishes. After a moment of silent consideration, he turned back to me and Raphael, concern dulling his eyes. "Ask me to be her templar, Avel. Then, I can ensure she is protected."

I knew that being a templar was a huge responsibility that one such as Khalen did not take lightly. As it was explained to me, a templar was designated during the union ceremony. If the man of the union died, the female automatically fell under the protection of her designated templar. He could either take her as his own mate, provided he was unmated himself, or he would find her another mate. Until then, he offered her protection and support.

"I am not Spirian," I said, "and cannot participate in a Spirian union."

"A templar can be assigned at any time. Tonight, after dinner, approach me with something that holds deep meaning to both you and Elle. At that time, ask me to be her templar. If I accept your offer, the contract is sealed."

He looked over to Raphael. "As a templar, I have the right to discipline her, should her gifts be used unlawfully. Will her angelic shield protect her from me as it did before?"

Raphael shrugged. "This is a first for me as well, my friend. According to the Spirian laws, a clan leader has authority of his region and cannot be disputed. Your acceptance to be her templar unites her with the clan. In a sense, she falls under your jurisdiction."

"Thank you."

Raphael quietly faded. I nodded my appreciation to him.

"I need to go into town today," I said. "and tie up a few loose ends."

"Do you need a car?"

"Actually, I was hoping you could drive me back to The Wellness Center so that I can pick up Elle's car and bring it back. She has expressed a need to continue her karate lessons."

"Yes," Khalen drawled. "Skye has told me all about your mate's skill with self-defense maneuvers."

"You sound disapproving."

Khalen shook his head. "My mate has an undying need to learn those skills."

"Sounds reasonable," I said, not really understanding his resistance to the idea.

"Skye is lethal as it is with her gifts. Add an additional measure of confidence, and she will want to be included in battles."

I smiled. "Why would a woman want to fight?"

He smirked. "You don't know my mate. Her independent nature has been the vessel of many an argument."

"Ah yes," I chuckled. "I know your pain. But in all honesty, would you have her any other way?"

"No," he said. "I would not."

We both laughed.

"I will take you into town," said Khalen. "I need to drop Arcadie and Tetris off at Bremerton Airport anyway."

He poured us each a glass of lemonade, and then clicked his glass to mine. "To stubborn, independent women."

- Elle -

SKYE PULLED THE HALTER FROM a nail in the grooming shed. "I'm sorry you missed your karate test."

I followed her out to the pasture where the mare stood waiting, ears pricked forward and her soft white nose flaring in a soothing nicker. Skye handed me a cookie to offer her. Following her instructions, I held my palm out flat to the mare, allowing her nimble lips to lift it from my hand.

"I need to wait another six months, but it's not such a

bad thing. My friend Jamie always tests with me, but she was not invited this time."

"You must miss her," Skye said, slipping the rope halter over the mare's head. I watched as she tied the simple halter without having to even look at what she was doing. She made it look so simple.

"I do miss her and the others in class. Karate has always been my social outlet."

She led the mare out of the pasture and into the grooming barn. "I asked Khalen if I could take lessons."

"And?"

She tied the horse loosely to each side of the grooming space, then handed me a soft rubber curry. "He said, no, of course."

"Why?"

"He believes it will be too dangerous for me."

"That's ridiculous."

"Spirian women do not fight," she added, starting to curry the off side of the mare.

I brushed Belle's neck in slow circular movements, loosening shed hair and dust from her coat. Her eyes softened. "I will speak with him tonight."

Skye peeked over Belle's neck at me. "Um, that might not be a good idea."

"Don't be silly. He needs to be updated to the twentieth century."

"Spirian ways are very different," she added. "He fears that if I learn to fight, the results could be quite fatal when coupled with my gifts."

"Which is great when your life is in danger."

"Yes, but a Spirian's gifts can be invoked at any time. It takes a great amount of control to keep them at bay when emotions get high."

"So you're saying that during practice, your gifts could turbocharge your efforts and do some serious damage?"

"Yes," she said. "Because I'm a healer, my gifts could easily be used to cause injury. Khalen is worried that my Shadow side could be seduced by the process of learning to fight."

I looked at her skeptically. "I don't think you have a Shadow side, Skye."

"Everyone has a Shadow side, Elle. Even you."

I thought back on the many times when I purposely hurt my family because I felt hurt myself. I wanted them to be just as miserable as I was. Their happiness made me angry. "I have gifts now. Do you think they will come out as I practice?"

She smiled. "Your gifts are intuition, herbal medicine, and veiling. The worst that will happen is that you will disappear as someone pretends to attack you."

We laughed.

"That's not such a bad thing," I said.

"We are forbidden to use our gifts on humans."

"Why?"

"If the wrong people find out about us, we would become subjects of study and could be thought of as a possible threat."

"Is that the only repercussion of showing our gifts?"

"No," she said, continuing to move along the mare's side. I matched her pace.

"What happens?"

"If Khalen or some other clan leader finds out, the person is punished and banned from their gifts for a certain amount of time."

"How do they find out?"

Skye smiled and shook her head. "They are tapped

into their clan. A leader knows your thoughts and Khalen knows your intentions. He will know what you do before you even do it."

I shuddered. We continued to curry Belle in silence. The thought of Khalen's wrath made my skin crawl. You could feel the power of the man just by standing next to him. I would not relish being on the receiving end of his temper.

"Don't worry," Skye said, trading our curries for firm-bristled brushes. "You are not a formal member of this clan. He will not discipline you."

My breathing eased a bit, feeling slightly less constricted. Using the short flicking strokes that Skye had shown me, I worked my way down Belle's soft neck. "I will miss you all when I return home."

"You will visit, yes?"

I smiled. "Yes, of course."

More silence filled the space. It was something we both seemed comfortable with. We switched to softer brushes, and then moved to comb Belle's mane and tail.

"Are you looking forward to returning home?" Skye asked."

"Yes and no."

Skye lifted the mare's front hoof and began picking it clean. "Explain."

"I look forward to my old routines, but I will miss the company and lifestyle here."

Skye's long braid brushed against the ground, though she didn't seem to notice. She worked on the horse as easily as someone with perfect vision, though she rarely looked at what she was doing. She used her hands to feel. There were times when I forgot that she was blind.

Maiyun ran into the barn, tongue hanging out of her

mouth and fur drenched. The smell that emanated from her held traces of something foul, like rotting fish.

"Oh, Maiyun!" Skye exclaimed. "Where have you been?"

Seth came running into the barn after her. "Sorry, Skye. I took Maiyun down to the beach. She found a dead seal and started to roll in it."

"Yes," she said. "That's exactly what she smells like."

"I was just about to bathe her, but when she saw me dragging out the hose, she bolted to you."

He smiled at me, almost shyly. "Hi Miss Alder," he said.

"Please, Seth, call me Elle."

"Elle," he said, drawing it out as if savoring the name.

Skye smiled. "Go with Seth," she told Maiyun.

Maiyun groaned as Seth reached for her collar. "Come on, girl. Let's get you cleaned up." He smiled up at me as he pulled the dog along with him. "Wanna help?"

I shook my head no. "Not this time."

"You're missing an adventure," he said, smiling.

I glanced down at Maiyun who reluctantly followed the young man out of the barn. "Have fun," I called out to him.

"Always," I heard him reply.

Skye smiled. "He likes you."

"So I've been told."

She cleaned the last hoof before untying the mare. I followed them out to the open pasture where Belle spent most of the day. She was comfortable with the playing children and enjoyed keeping them company as she ate the tender blades of grass that grew near the lake.

Skye released the halter, and then gave the mare a gentle pat. "Off you go."

We watched as she trotted out, her tail flying in brown and silver strands behind her.

"She's beautiful," I said, watching her run. "How long have you had her?"

"About six years."

"How old is she?"

Skye wrinkled her nose. "I'm guessing she's around thirteen years, give or take a few. She was an unfortunate victim of our last battle with the Shadows." She started leading me toward the lake. "Care to take a walk?"

"I told Avel I would be right back after we brushed Belle. He's probably expecting me."

"He and Khalen left to go into town."

I frowned. "He didn't mention it."

Skye shrugged. "He probably had some things to do."

"It must be convenient to be able to talk to everyone telepathically."

She led me down a path that bordered the lake and then took another path that led to the left. "If you stay with us, you will soon acquire the ability yourself."

"Really?"

"Really," she laughed.

The path was well worn and bordered by several medicinal plants, such as plantain, sheep sorrel and cleavers. In the distance, I heard children playing and Belle snorting as if trying to clear her nostrils.

A few moments later, a very wet dog came to join us. She shook before she reached us, then lightly pressed against Skye's thigh. She reached down and patted the dog on her withers.

"Hi Maiyun," she said, smiling. "You smell much better now."

"How does telepathy work?" I asked.

"When you live with Spirians, you become connected to them. This connection opens sort of a communication link that enables you to share thoughts."

"From how far away?"

"Everyone is different. I can communicate with Khalen over any distance because we are mated. I can communicate with Aidan more effectively than with Ian, because Aidan is my templar."

I shook my head, overwhelmed by the complications this lifestyle presented. "What is a templar?"

She placed her hand on my arm. "There is much to learn about our people. In time, you will understand. I felt the way you do only seven short years ago. Today, those years are like a blink in time."

"So you were not born a Spirian?"

She took another trail to the left that veered away from the lake. This trail was thick with Douglas firs and cedars. Their fallen seeds crunched beneath my feet. I wondered how she could walk barefoot so effortlessly without feeling pain. I never saw her wear shoes. I had asked her about that once, and she said she didn't like shoes. She was an odd bird, but I liked her.

"Yes, I was born a Spirian, I just didn't know it. I grew up with human parents."

"What happened to your real parents?"

"They were killed in a Spirian war. My grandfather, Shanuk, took me as a baby and placed me with parents who had just lost their newborn."

"Did they know you were special?"

She sadly shook her head. "No."

"How did you come to live here?"

"Shanuk found me after I got into an accident and was in the hospital with a broken leg. At that time, I didn't know who he was." She chuckled. "I thought he was an Angel."

"So he brought you here?"

"Not directly," she said. "I came to Belfair for vacation and ended up getting a job at The Wellness Center. Khalen worked there as the doctor before he became the regional leader."

"Let me guess. It was love at first sight?"

"Not even close," she laughed. "We nearly killed each other during our first year together."

"Why?"

"He tried to give me to Aidan because he thought that was what I wanted."

I mulled that one over for a bit, wondering how a man could do such a thing.

"Anyway," she continued, "I got mad, he got madder, and our energies merged into something akin to an electrical storm. If Case hadn't come, I'm not sure what would have happened."

"Sounds scary."

We rounded a bend and she led me down a path on the right. It took us back to the camp.

Eve, Jade and Ember were tending the gardens. They greeted us with familiar smiles. Eve offered us a glass of tea that had been brewing in the sun.

"Need any help?" asked Skye.

Ember tossed us each a pair of gloves. "With Eve's gift for acceleration, there is never a shortage of work here."

"Acceleration?" I asked.

Skye laughed. "Eve can speed things up."

"She's a Spirian form of Miracle Gro?" I said, trying to clarify.

"Yes," laughed Skye, "something like that. It affects

other things as well."

I remember how she was able to make bread so quickly without spending all day in the kitchen. "What about people?"

Eve frowned. "That would have adverse effects, I'm sure."

"I think that would be the dark side of her gift," Skye explained.

"What do you mean the dark side?" I followed Ember's lead and started harvesting vast amounts of beans.

"Everyone's gifts have a dark side and a light side," she said, handing me a basket for my beans. "How you choose to use your gifts determines if you are Protected or a Shadow."

I frowned, trying to determine my preference. I wanted to believe I was good, but deep down, my dark side was prevalent. It made me shudder. "What is the dark side to my gifts?"

All of them stopped and looked at me. I suddenly felt like a slug threatening the crop. "I'm just asking."

"Your dark side will reveal itself, if you so choose," said Skye. "It is best not to think about it."

The conversation grew silent for a moment. It was odd, but somehow I sensed that Jade and her sister Ember were humans, not Spirians. I wondered how it was that they were able to enter the camp when unmated humans were clearly forbidden.

During my first few days, the constant hum that emanated from these people was nauseating. I still had headaches from it, but they were becoming less prevalent. That hum didn't seem to affect these women at all.

"We have been here for many years," said Ember.

I stood and stared at her. "Were you reading my

thoughts?"

She smiled. "It was kind of hard not to when they were about me and my sister.

"But you're human. How is that possible?"

"I told you," said Skye. "When you are around us long enough, you develop that gift."

"But I thought that unmated humans were banned from the camp?"

Ember emptied her basket of beans into the cart. "I was mated to a Spirian once, before he was killed. My two sisters lived with me after that. Then, a new law was formed and we were forced to move away. Khalen allows us to visit but we cannot stay here or become involved with the men in any way."

"How was your mate killed?" I asked, emptying my basket into the cart, and then taking a sip of tea. It was brisk and sweet with a tang of lemon peel.

"A Shadow killed him while he was away on a business trip."

"God, that sounds awful. Did the police get involved?"

Skye emptied her basket. The cart, I noticed, was getting quite full. "The police do not get involved in Spirian matters," she said.

"How could they not when someone is murdered?"

"Spirians dissolve the evidence and we are careful not to be seen."

"What happens if you are seen and exposed?"

"You mean if you return to your life and tell others about a clan of gifted people that live on Harstine Island who can speak telepathically, heal wounds in seconds, and make things grow in rapid time?"

"Yes," I said. "I personally wouldn't do such a thing, but I'm sure there are others who would."

"Who would believe them?"

I thought about that for a moment. She had a point. If someone were to make such claims, they would no doubt be locked away and given ample amounts of drugs. "I guess no one."

"Exactly," said Skye. Occasionally, we are visited by authorities, but Khalen and Case quickly disperse them."

"How?"

"Clan leaders can control another's mind. If someone becomes too interested in our lifestyle, they simply remove that ambition and send them on their way."

"Interesting," I said. "I did wonder how you were able to live so far off the grid."

"They're not completely off the grid," said Jade. "They still pay bills and taxes, and have to work for a living."

I thought about the ample amounts of food and drink this clan seemed to have. Looking at the bounty of beans that were in the cart, the food abundance was a no-brainer. The constant supply of alcohol, however, was a mystery.

"Caleb works at the reservation. He is the buyer for alcohol and keeps us well supplied," Skye explained, having read my thoughts.

"Who pays for the utilities here?" I asked, hoping to glean a hint of how things worked.

"Khalen does," said Skye.

"Don't others have to chip in?"

"Everyone chips in. You pay for what you can, provide supplies for all to share, or work in a capacity that benefits the clan."

"I don't understand. Do the others give Khalen money to help pay for the cost of living?"

She grinned and shook her head. "We have one bank account that everyone contributes to. All expenses are taken from that account."

"How do you keep someone from spending too much money?"

All three women looked at me as if I had marbles pouring from my head.

"If Khalen were your clan leader, would you dare to cross him?" Ember asked.

I shook my head. "No."

"Exactly," said Jade.

"Lack of integrity is not forgiven," said Skye. "If a Spirian is cast from a clan, their life is compromised."

"Why?" I asked.

"Spirians must live in clans to survive. Without them, we become very sick and die. Also, if you are a female who is unmated, it is very dangerous to be alone. The Shadows are not picky about who they bring into their clans. Once they have their hooks in you, your soul is lost."

"So, it doesn't pay to be bad," I emphasized.

Skye emptied her basket into the now overflowing cart. "The thought of doing something wrong is like choosing to slit your own throat. There are some who would do it, but not many."

I felt strangely familiar with that feeling and it was unnerving to think of it now. "This cart is overflowing," I said. "What are we going to do with all these beans?"

"I sell them to the local produce stands," said Eve.

"The animals benefit from them as well," said Jade, tossing a few of the beans to the cows and goats peering over the fences.

We worked a few more hours in the garden after a quick lunch break, and then each of us went our separate ways. I wanted to take a shower and looked forward to having some down time with my computer. It had been a while since I had written a story, and I was eager to pick it up again.

Living with these unique people had inspired me to write something different—something more modern instead of historical.

Fresh from my shower, I sat cozily by the fire dressed comfortably in Avel's shirt and a pair of sweat pants that Skye had given me. Dinner would be ready in two hours, I was told, which gave me plenty of time to outline my story.

My email inbox needed attention. There were more than a few messages from my agent, James, who, for the most part, informed me that I had a new book tour starting next month. I would be visiting the northern states from Montana to New England. After that, he had me scheduled to tour Europe. I typically looked forward to traveling, but now I felt compelled to nest.

I rubbed my lower belly, thinking about the life inside. It was no larger than a pin prick, yet its presence was strong. I responded to my agent, and then replied to Jamie's constant nags about contacting her soon. I assured her that I would be in class this Saturday. We would have our usual coffee afterward.

I wondered if Avel would join me. It would be odd not having him in class. My stomach felt hollow and my heart heavy with the thought. What would life be like without him? I had only known him for a short time, but in that time we had lived a lifespan.

Although he occupied Kael's body, he was not Kael. He was a soul I had known and was familiar with. I had never believed in soul mates. Now, that ignorant perception had changed.

I closed my eyes and silently prayed, "God, help me

get through this. Help me remember his touch, his scent, his heart."

Chapter 22

-Avel-

I **QUIETLY STEPPED THROUGH THE** door of our cabin, welcomed by the glowing light of the fire. Elle sat huddled on the couch, sipping a glass of wine and reading something on her computer with the dim light of the screen reflecting against her bronzed skin. This life agreed with her. She looked healthy and glowed with a happiness that grew from within.

I smiled as she glanced up at me. Her expression changed to one of eager delight as she stood and greeted me with a rib-crushing hug. She had neatly braided her hair back—it smelled sweet like jasmine flowers. When she looked up at me, I pressed my lips to hers and savored the taste of them.

"I missed you," she said.

"I had some things to take care of in town."

Her expression showed worry. "Is everything all right?"

"Yes," I said, kissing her forehead, nose and mouth,

"Everything is perfect."

She didn't miss a thing. She saw me look across the room and over to the bed.

"Dinner will be ready soon," she sweetly admonished.

"I'm hungry now," I growled in reply. "And this meal, I don't intend to share."

She giggled as I lifted her into my arms and carried to the bed.

An hour later, we joined the others by the fire. Aidan, Ian, Case and Khalen sat with two other men we hadn't met yet. Khalen stood to introduce them.

"Avel, Elle, this is Caleb and his younger brother Drew."

Caleb, the taller man, looked slightly older than Khalen, had darker skin, and jet-black hair that matched his eyes. He jutted his hand toward me, and shook mine with intent and purpose. "We've heard much about you, Spirit. Khalen informs me you are an impressive warrior with a sword."

He then turned his attention to Elle. "My dear, you are much lovelier than words can portray."

Her face reddened. "Thank you," she said, shaking his hand.

"I'm Drew," the younger brother said, replacing his brother's hand with his own. He was not quite as tall as Caleb, but far more built. Both of them were Native American, and had the solid jawlines to prove it. He held Elle's hand for longer than I thought was necessary, so I offered him mine.

Drew reluctantly released Elle's hand and shook mine with such force, I felt sure he wanted to crush my bones.

Khalen held up two glasses of red wine. "Borolo?"

Elle's eyes brightened. "Yes, I love that wine."

I took the glasses from Khalen and handed one to her.

He gestured to the log on his left. "Sit."

Eve stood. "Can I get you two something to eat?"

"Yes, thank you," I said. "I haven't eaten since this morning."

Elle stood. "I'll help." She froze spotting her Miata nestled between Aidan's Jeep and Khalen's Escalade. "You brought my car?"

"I thought you could use it to get to town."

She came over and gave me a hug that nearly knocked my wine from my hand. "Thank you."

"You're welcome, love." I watched as she and Eve walked toward her yurt.

Drew's brows arched. "She's easy to please."

Skye walked toward us carrying a very sleepy-looking Zhentu. Gabrihen, Shaiya and Kaili walked beside her, all smiling as if they shared some wonderful secret.

Khalen reached out for his youngest son. "Time for bed?"

"Mummy said we could stay up with Seth for another hour and listen to stories," Kaili explained.

Shaiya held up a bag of marshmallows and chocolate. "We're gonna make some-mores," she said.

"S'mores, huh?" Khalen laughed.

Gabrihen showed the graham crackers he held in his hand. "I have the cookies," he said.

"Sounds like you have all that you need." He smiled as the three of them scampered away toward Seth and the other children.

Zhentu sucked his thumb and buried his face against Khalen's chest. Khalen very gently removed the thumb from the boy's mouth, and then held his hand affectionately. His brows furrowed when he kissed Zhentu's forehead.

"He feels warm."

"Teething," Skye explained. "I was hoping you could help him sleep?"

"Ah," said Khalen. "Of course." He nodded toward us and the others. "Excuse me."

Skye smiled watching them leave.

"You have a beautiful family, Skye," I said.

"Yes," she said. "I think so, too."

Eve and Elle came back with two plates filled with chicken, kasha and steamed broccoli.

A few moments later, Khalen returned.

"That was quick," I commented.

Skye laughed. "Khalen has a gift to cause someone to sleep deeply." She eyed him with a knowing glare. "Whether they want to or not."

I decided to let that can of worms stay closed. "This food is great, Eve. Thank you."

She smiled and nodded. "You're quite welcome."

Case wrapped his arm around her shoulders and drew her into him. The love that bonded their souls was evident.

A familiar ache weighted my chest. Elle and I would never know that strong of a bond. There simply wasn't enough time for us. Even the few short years we had many lifetimes ago was nowhere near long enough. It was an odd hand of fate we had been dealt, yet still I felt blessed. There were so many who never felt love that spanned the space of time.

I finished my meal before Elle had consumed half of hers. She pushed her plate toward me, offering her uneaten portion.

"No," I said. "I'm fine."

She continued to eat, speaking quietly with Eve and

Skye. Sunjia and another woman were spending time with the children, laughing and enjoying Seth's stories.

I focused on Khalen, silently asking him if now was a good time to ask him to be Elle's templar.

He looked at me and nodded.

I stood and retrieved a small envelope from my pocket. Upon it I had drawn alchemical symbols to seal the contents and the promise it held. I walked toward Khalen and respectfully bowed my head. Presenting him with the envelope, I said, "Khalen, leader of the Grahdun clan, I formally ask you to be my mate Elle's, templar."

The shocked look on the surrounding faces stilled the conversations.

"Avel?" Elle queried with concern in her voice.

I met her eyes, silently pleading her to remain quiet.

Khalen stood and accepted the package. "I, Khalen Dunning of the Grahdun clan, honorably accept your request, Avel, son of Hermes," he said. His attention turned to Elle. He gripped her wrists. "Elle Alder, mate of Avel, you are now formally under my protection and the protection of this clan."

A faint blue light encircled them. Elle inhaled sharply. When the light faded, Khalen released his hold. He had made a connection with her, which enabled him to protect her over any distance.

The announcement gained the attention of the whole clan. Soon, we were surrounded by people offering congratulatory hugs.

Skye gripped Elle's quivering hand. "That makes us sisters," she said excitedly.

Elle grabbed my arm. "What does this mean?"

"It means you can live here for as long as you like. Khalen will protect you and find you a suitable mate."

"I don't want another mate," she seethed. "I belong to you."

I held her upper arms and forced her to meet my eyes. "Elle, we both know my time here is done. I must return to the Kingdom."

She closed her eyes. "It doesn't matter. I will always belong to you and only you."

I held her tightly, kissing her head. "A lifetime is too long to be alone," I said. "When the right man presents himself, I want you to let me go."

"I won't," she said. "Ever!" She started to shake.

The crowd slowly returned to their respective fires, leaving only our small group to talk.

"What did you give him?" Elle asked me.

"The promise you had made me back at your parents' cabin."

She looked confused for a moment, and then her face softened. "You saved that?"

"Absolutely," I said. "It means something to me, and hopefully to you as well."

She placed her hand over her lower belly. "It does."

"Have you thought of a name for him?" I asked.

Her face brightened. "Him? What makes you think it's a boy?"

"An Angel told me," I smiled.

She glanced down and shuffled her feet as if troubled by the questions in her mind. "Is he—yours?" The last word was emphasized.

"Yes. The child is of my spirit, not Kael's."

She covered her mouth and choked out a sob. Tears began to pool in her eyes. Her arms circled my waist and tightened around me.

I held her for a while, allowing her emotions to flow.

We had only two short days left. She didn't know that, and I wasn't willing to tell her.

She released me and looked up into my eyes. Hers were swollen and bright with tears. "Did we have a name chosen for our unborn son—before?"

I smiled. "Yes. We were going to name him Connor."

"Then Connor will be his name," she said, wiping away the tears. After taking a few deep breaths, she was composed enough to return to the group.

Skye brushed Elle's arm. "Hey, you okay?"

Elle nodded. "Yeah, I think so."

She looked over at Khalen and waited for him to acknowledge her before speaking. "Do I have to live here?" she asked him.

"No," he said. "You do not, but it is dangerous for you to be alone. The Shadows will not take long to notice you're not entirely human."

"Do you not want to live here?" Skye asked, trying to keep the hurt from her voice.

"I have a home," said Elle, "and friends. My life is in Port Orchard."

"Your life changed the day Archangel Jeremeil touched your soul," Khalen explained. "Take some time to settle yourself, but know that living here with us is your best option for you and your son."

She looked at the ground and shifted her eyes as if pondering her options.

"Please, Elle," I said. "Stay here where I know you will be safe and looked after."

"I don't want to be looked after," she said.

I closed my eyes and took a deep breath. "It is your choice, love. I cannot force you. I can only ask for your compliance."

"God, don't say it like that," she said. After a few silent moments, she finally said, "I'll think about it."

Chapter 23

THE NEXT TWO DAYS, I didn't leave her side. We took long walks, spent a day in Seattle, and strolled along the beach. We kept our conversations light and did our best to avoid the inevitable.

Khalen offered us his beach house for our last evening together. Elle was sipping a glass of Petit Syrah while I fried shrimp and rice in a pan.

"Are you going to karate class with me tomorrow?" she asked.

I shook my head. "No, love, I have some things to take care of in town."

The brightness in her eyes faded a bit. "That's too bad. I told Jamie we would join her for coffee afterward. She is chomping at the bit to hear about all our adventures. You know how she is."

I rolled my eyes, remembering the boisterous female with a mouth that lacked the ability for silence. "Yes, I do."

"When I told her I was having a baby, she nearly

exploded on the chat window. I really thought she would come through my computer."

I laughed. "I wouldn't put it past her."

Elle frowned. "What's wrong?"

I looked back over my shoulder. "Nothing, love, why?"

"You seem off all of a sudden. Do you want me to skip karate tomorrow?"

"No," I said. "It's time we return to our old routines." I stirred the food in the pan, fighting back the sting in my eyes.

When I turned around to fill our glasses, Elle's face had turned pale. "I don't want our old routines," she said.

I couldn't meet her eyes. Instead, I forced a smile. "Then we'll make new ones," I jested.

Her face brightened. "I like that idea."

"Are you ready to eat?"

She slid off her stool and carried our wine out to the patio. "God, I could get used to this view," she said, taking a deep breath and staring out at the crashing waves.

"Khalen has several houses on the peninsula. I'm sure he would be willing to open them to you any time you need some peace."

She scooted her chair beside mine and sat. "Do you mind if I sit next to you?" she asked.

I pulled her chair closer to mine and smiled. We held hands and prayed. "Father," I said, "thank you for the abundant blessings you have bestowed upon us. Let us appreciate them wisely. Be it so, as above, so below."

"You told me what that closing phrase means to your father, but what does it mean to you?" she asked.

I served her a portion of food, and then filled my plate. "It means that whatever we project to the heavens is reflected here on Earth."

Her frown didn't soften. "Hmm, I was kind of hoping that Heaven would be much more pleasant than here."

I smiled and took a sip of wine. "Heaven is what you make of it. You don't have to die to experience it."

"Meaning?"

"Peace, beauty, love and fulfillment all come from within. What we project, we receive threefold. So when I say, 'As above, so below,' I'm projecting what I want to the Heavens so that it can be reflected and magnified here on Earth."

She nodded. A sparkle of understanding shone in her eyes.

We ate a bit in silence, watching the seagulls vie for food that was scattered on the beach. A soft breeze cooled the air but the skies were clear—a rarity on the coast.

"Avel, when you return to the Ethereal Kingdom, will you be able to see me?"

"Not physically," I lied. "But I can feel you. I'll know if you are happy, sad, or anything in between. Our hearts are connected as well as our souls." I knew that if she believed I could see her, she would never allow herself to love another. I didn't want that for her.

"Will I be able to talk to you?"

"Always," I said.

"Will you hear me?"

I shook my head. "I can only feel the emotions behind your words," I lied. If she knew I could hear her, she would find it hard to move on once I was gone.

"Sunjia said I can call upon the Angels."

I nodded. "Yes, you can."

"Could I do so to send you messages?"

"The Angels serve the Father, Elle. You have the ability to call them, yes, but not the right to use them for your own personal gain."

Again, her expression fell to despair. "How long do we have, Avel?"

I was hoping she would avoid that question. "Not long," I said.

"How long?"

"Tonight is our last."

She pushed her unfinished meal away. "No. I—" She slid her chair out and ran inside.

I knew there was little I could say. I didn't want it to end like this. I wanted one more cherished evening with her. I stood and began clearing the dishes.

Elle had ran to the bedroom, crying. I set the dishes in the sink to soak, and then went to comfort her.

She lay curled on the bed, shaking with sobs. I lay beside her and held her in my arms. "Shh," I cooed. "Don't let it end like this, love. I want to remember you happy."

She turned to face me. "This is so hard," she sobbed.

I kissed away the tears from her face. "I know, love. It is for me as well."

"Make love to me," she said. "I don't want to sleep tonight."

I propped myself up onto my elbow and quirked a grin. "I have stamina, love, but all night?"

"Yes, she said. I want to be distracted from all this. I want all of you."

"Hmm," I purred, rolling on top of her. "I'll certainly do my best."

As promised, we didn't sleep much all night. My body was spent and sore. Elle looked exhausted, elated, and beyond any capacity for worry or fear.

I brushed the damp tendrils of hair from her forehead and smiled. "Again?"

She giggled. "Yes, but I don't think either of us is capable."

"Let's try."

By ten o'clock that morning, we were packed and ready to leave. We drove away in silence, both knowing we would never return here together again.

Elle stared out the window, doing her best to stay positive. She had promised me no more tears. It was a feeble promise, but one she was trying hard to keep.

I reached over and took her hand. "We're going to be all right."

She smiled at me. "Yes," she confirmed. "We are."

"I'll drop you off at the studio."

Her hand tightened around mine. "Don't leave without saying goodbye."

"I'll be outside by the end of class."

She nodded. "I don't want to go to class. I want to be with you."

"It's best if you're not."

I pulled up to the karate studio and kissed her goodbye. "I'll be here when you come out," I assured her.

She nodded, tightened her lips, and then grabbed her bag from the behind the seat. "I love you," she turned to say, just before entering the studio.

"I love you, too," I replied.

I saw Jamie give her a hug that nearly knocked her off balance. My reflection faded from the glass door as I backed the Miata up and drove away.

The errands I had to run were quick, but I didn't tarry with the tasks. When I returned to the condo, I made sure things were returned the way Kael had left them. It was imperative that I removed all traces of me from his life.

My last task was to pick the bike up from the repair shop, then return to the studio.

I arrived just minutes before class ended. Elle did not dally. She was behind me as I lifted the bike from the car. I heard her bags drop to the ground.

Jamie ran out. "Kael," she screamed then assailed me with a fierce hug. "You have been holding out on me," she said, waving a finger. "I knew you two had a thing going on."

"Jamie," Elle said, rescuing me from the woman's onslaught of words. "Why don't you head to the coffee shop. Kael and I will be there soon." She smiled at the boisterous woman. "We can talk then."

Jamie clapped her hands together and jumped like an excited child. "Okay. I can't wait to hear all about you two."

We watched her drive away.

Elle traced her fingers over the renewed bike. "It looks good, like nothing ever happened."

"Yeah, they did a good job."

She wrapped her arms around me. I lifted her chin and slowly, tenderly, pressed my lips to hers, savoring her taste one last time. "I have to go," I whispered. "Our love will live on, forever."

She nodded, "Forever," she said and stepped away. I could feel her pain, a mirror of it reflected in my heart, feeling like a thousand shards of glass cutting it away.

I turned the bike around, gave her one last look, then mounted up and rode away.

"Goodbye," I heard her say. The finality of it caused my eyes to burn. I no longer held the tears. I allowed them to flow freely down my face. It felt good to cry.

Chapter 24

-Elle-

PART OF ME WANTED TO follow him, another part wanted to fade away. Mindlessly, I turned the ignition key and drove toward the coffee shop where Jamie was waiting. I said a silent prayer that Avel would be there as well. "Father, please let him stay," I said. It was a feeble request, and I knew it.

As I turned left at the light, I heard the sound I had pushed back from my memory—the sound of metal crushing metal, tires screeching, a woman's scream, the bustling of curious bystanders.

My heart pounded as I jammed the car into park and ran toward the chaos. Avel lay on the street, his bike mangled in a heap of twisted metal, spokes and shredded tires.

I fell beside him and lifted his head into my arms. "Avel," I cried. His head was bleeding, his body mangled. He opened his eyes for a brief moment, and smiled.

Archangel Raphael stood beside him. He wrapped his wings around Avel's body, and then faded.

"I called 911," a person said. "Do you know him?"

No response. I just wanted to hold him and never let go.

"Miss? Did you know him?"

The chaos around me faded. I felt numb, stunned, and void of life. My love was gone. Darkness consumed me like a welcoming veil.

I AWOKE IN THE HOSPITAL WITH an IV stuck in my arm. A warm, familiar hand stroked my forehead, leaving behind a comforting tingle. I recognized that energy. "Skye?"

"We're here," she said.

"How are you feeling?" Khalen asked.

I squinted against the bright lights of the room. "Confused." I started to sit up. "Where am I?"

Khalen pressed a button on the bed to elevate my back. "Harrison Hospital."

"Avel is gone," I said, not even trying to hide the pain in my voice.

"Only from this world," said Khalen. "His spirit lives on and remembers you."

"What happened? Why am I here?"

"You went into shock," he said. "They're keeping you for observation."

"I want to go home."

Skye squeezed my arm. "You'll be released today. Khalen has assumed your care. We are just waiting for the paperwork to be completed."

A woman peered into the room—the sullen look of

Jamie. The expression she bore did not fit her exuberant personality. "Elle?"

"Hi Jamie."

She padded into the room and nearly pushed Khalen aside to give me a hug. "Oh, honey, when I heard what happened, I was so—" she broke down and started to tremble.

"Hey," I said. "It's okay."

"I'm so sorry," she sobbed. "God, you don't deserve this."

I allowed her to carry on, knowing there was nothing I could do or say to stop her. Jamie's drama had to run its full course.

After a few moments, she rose and looked between Skye and Khalen. "Brother and sister?"

"Well, yes and no," Elle said. "Skye is my sister, and Khalen is her ma—husband." I quickly corrected myself; Jamie would never understand the concept of mates.

She hesitantly held her hand out to Khalen first. "I'm Jamie."

Khalen smiled, pouring out his usual charm that could melt the coldest glacier. "Jamie," he said, "delighted to meet you."

"Oh, I love the accent. British?"

He nodded.

She then turned to Skye and presented her hand. "Hi, Skye. It's nice to meet you." The look on Jamie's face depicted confusion.

Skye smiled and lightly shook her hand. "Nice to meet you too. Elle speaks of you often."

Jamie smiled. I could tell that she wanted to mention that I never spoke of my family, but she held her tongue.

The silence that followed caused my chatty friend to

shuffle. "Well, um, I guess I should be going." She smiled at me. "You look good, Elle."

"I'll be going home today. I'll give you a call later, okay?"

Her face brightened. "Okay." She gave Skye and Khalen one last look before turning to leave.

Moments later, an older gentleman with salt-and-pepper hair walked into the room. "Elle Alder?"

"That's me," I said.

He smiled and introduced himself, "I'm Doctor Cabbot." He looked at Khalen. "You must be Doctor Khalen Dunning."

Khalen shook the man's hand. "I am."

"I've heard much about you," said the doctor. "Your reputation is quite impressive. You own The Wellness Center in Belfair, correct?"

"Yes."

Doctor Cabbot flipped through the pages on my chart. "Well, Miss Alder, you've had quite a shock. How are you feeling?"

"Fine," I said. "I'm ready to go home."

He smiled. "Hospital food doesn't appeal to you?" he jested.

"Hospitals don't appeal to me."

He laughed. "Understandably." He signed a page on my chart then clicked his pen and slid it into his pocket. "I have released you to Doctor Dunning's care. A nurse will come in a moment to discharge you."

"Thank you," I said.

He smiled. "Take care."

When we returned to the camp, my car was parked in front of the cabin that Avel and I had shared. My heart sank.

Skye laid her hand on my arm. "You won't be staying there tonight. We have a spare room in our home. Khalen wants you close."

"Thank you," I said, giving the old cabin another look. To be honest, I wasn't sure if I could ever enter that place again without Avel. There are just too many memories.

Skye showed me to my room. Their yurt was much larger than any of the others I had seen. It was like multiple yurts had been joined by long corridors. We left the main living space and headed down a wide hallway that opened to another large space. There were no pictures on the walls and it made me curious.

The room was spacious with a long queen-sized bed on a cherry-wood frame. Two matching end tables sat on either side. The simple design added to the airy feel of the room. A large window to the left looked out at the forest and provided ample privacy. A dresser stood at the far end of the room.

Skye opened a closet constructed of accordion doors that also served as an attractive wall. To save space, the closet was part of the entire wall.

"Wow!" I exclaimed. "I've never seen anything like that. If you wouldn't have opened the door, I would have never guessed that space was behind it all."

Skye beamed with pride. "That is my mate's doing. Most of the walls in this yurt serve as a place for clothing or other items." She walked to another wall and opened the panel. Towels, linen and extra pillows lay neatly organized on shelves.

"Impressive," I said. "That explains why there are no

pictures on the walls."

"Khalen doesn't care for a lot of pictures, and I cannot see them."

"Oh yeah, I keep forgetting you're blind." It was an odd thing to say, but I felt so comfortable around the woman, it was like talking to a sister I had grown close to. My biological sister and I could never seem to get along. In my family, I always felt like the odd one out.

She giggled. "I'm happy that you forget I'm blind."

Maiyun came trotting through, curled tail wagging, and her tongue hanging out of her mouth. She pressed against my leg.

I rubbed behind her ears and felt her warmth and comfort. "Hi, Maiyun."

"I have unpacked your things and have placed them in the drawers. There is one more load in the dryer. I will bring them when they are done."

"You've been busy."

"We were—prepared. It is hard losing someone you love." Her hand pressed lightly on my belly. "But Avel did not leave you alone."

I smiled, suddenly remembering the tiny life inside of me. Avel's son. A warmth spread through me, offering new enthusiasm and strength. "No, he did not."

I reached over and held the woman close to me. I needed to feel her. The emotions that welled in my heart burst the dam of my will and trembled throughout my body. I sobbed until time was no longer a factor.

"It's good to cry it out," she said, her voice low and comforting.

Maiyun licked my hand and pressed her body against me, offering her own kind of comfort.

"I almost thought, with all the miracles I had witnessed

these past two weeks, that somehow Avel would return to me—that our story would continue."

"Your story does continue, Elle. It is not over. This physical existence is temporary. We all understand that at some level. Avel's body has been gone for many years. What you have grown to love is his soul, something that cannot be destroyed. Whether his body is here or not, you two are connected and always will be."

I released my hold on her, feeling the absence of her warmth. "Right now, I don't feel so connected with him."

"Give it time."

She sat on the bed, patting the space beside her. I took the invitation and joined her.

"When Shanuk died," she continued. "I felt a part of me die with him. I thought I would never see him again and that my memory of him would fade over time."

"From what I hear of him, he would be a difficult man to forget."

She smiled, and then laughed. "He was well liked and very well respected. I feel him with me, always. I cannot touch him, but he is always here." She placed her hand over her heart.

"Yes," I said. "That is where Avel said I would feel him."

"You will," she assured me, "when the grieving stops."

She stood and patted my hand. "I'll make you some tea and let you get settled. Come to the main room when you're ready. Eve and Case will be coming over."

I nodded and took a deep breath. "Okay. Thank you, Skye—for everything."

She smiled back at me before turning to leave the room. Maiyun rubbed her head against me, and then followed her mistress down the hall.

I looked at my computer on the dresser. It had been plugged in to restore the charge. Skye had thought of everything. In the short time I had known her, she had observed my habits, my likes and dislikes, and had truly gotten to know me. Not even my own family or friends had exerted such an effort.

I frowned, suddenly realizing that I never allowed them to know me. When someone got too close, I pushed them away. Somehow, Skye had filtered through the cracks in my armor. I tried imaging myself pushing her away. The thought produced a smile. Pushing Skye away was improbable at best. She was subtle, but she had a strength about her that I couldn't thwart—nor did I want to.

I unplugged my computer and carried it over to the comfy chair in the corner of the room looking out toward the open window. The late day had grown cloudy and cold, promising an even colder evening. I kicked off my shoes, and reveled in the warmth that radiated from the hardwood floors.

I opened my computer and glanced at the myriad of messages in my inbox. Life continued on as if nothing had changed, I thought. So many people, including my editor Evelyn, were oblivious to my pain, my loss. The forwarded jokes that typically made me laugh held no interest for me today.

There were a few messages from Jamie, two from days past, and one that arrived today. I opened that one. It was short and terse, very unlike my friend who wrote it.

Skye. Your sister? Seriously?

Call me,

Jamie

That was it, the entire message. It had to go down in history as Jamie's shortest email ever. Unfortunately, I was not in the mood to speak with anyone. The call she had requested would just have to wait.

I opened my newest novel and read the last few paragraphs. I had been on a roll during my last writing session. The emotions I had been feeling at the time returned now in full force. Never in my life had I known such happiness. Avel and I made love that morning, multiple times. I was sitting in the front room with a hot cup of coffee, staring out at the ocean. The sun was just starting its ascent, casting a luminous glow to the reflecting western sky. Avel watched me write, sipping his coffee with a silly grin on his face.

My stomach wrenched at the memory of something that never would happen again. I tried to shake it off and concentrate on my work.

Khalen knocked on the door and opened it wider, revealing his massive frame. He was a foreboding man and one I never wanted to cross.

"Come," he said, "be with the family."

"I really don't wa—"

He walked into the room, boldly closed my computer, and placed it back on the dresser. "You need to be with people," he said, his voice more commanding than was comfortable. "Come."

I stood and followed him out of the room. "Are you always this commanding?"

"Yes," he replied, leaving no room for argument.

Skye gestured for me to sit across from her on the leather chair. She had placed my cup of tea on the table, next to a plate of brownies that Eve had, no doubt, brought over.

"I'm glad to see you joining us," said Case, a brilliant smile on his handsome face.

I glanced over at Khalen, taking a seat next to Skye. "Your son can be very convincing."

Skye laughed. "You have no idea."

Chapter 25

We attended the funeral and endured the speculative looks from Kael's parents. During the memorial reception, his mother, a thin, fashionable woman with dark hair and eyes to match, approached me.

She held up an envelope. "My son had the good graces to inform me that he was now married. I'm assuming you are the woman?"

I forced a smile and extended my hand. "I'm Elle. You must be Tamina, Av—Kael's mom?"

"Tami," she corrected, curiously eyeing me like a cat about to pounce on a tasty morsel. "Odd how he never mentioned you before."

I shrugged. "We had a very unique relationship."

Kael's father joined us. His gray suit matched his eyes and accented his nearly white hair. He was a short man, much like Kael, but handsome in his own right. Kael had clearly acquired his father's looks and his mother's eyes.

The man held out his hand. "I'm William, Kael's father."

"Elle," I said, taking his hand. I then gestured to Skye and Khalen. "This is my sister, Skye, and her husband, Khalen."

They all exchanged polite shakes, and then the old man's eyes focused on me. "I hear you married my son?"

I swallowed past the annoying lump in my throat, not really knowing what story Avel had given them. "Yes."

"Recently?" he asked.

"Yes," I replied, not wanting to talk myself into a corner.

"When?"

Perfect. A woman should know her own wedding date like she did her birthday. My mouth hung open like a Venus Flytrap.

"August 13th," Khalen chimed in. "I performed the ceremony."

"We were not invited?" Tami said.

"It was rather impromptu," I said.

"It is unlike my son to be offhanded," said William.

True, I thought. There was nothing spontaneous about Kael. He planned everything to the smallest detail.

"It was my idea," I said, smiling, feeling rather pleased with the response.

"Why?" asked Tami. "Are you pregnant?"

"My sister is not pregnant," Skye retorted. "She and Kael were in love. My husband offered to perform the ceremony, and they both accepted. There is nothing more to it than that."

Both Tami and William stood back a bit, obviously stunned by the quiet woman's response.

"I see," said Tami. She took William's hand and led him away.

"What was all that about?" I asked Khalen.

"I'll explain later."

"He did what?" I asked, listening to Khalen reveal Avel's doings.

"Kael's family is quite wealthy," he explained. "I gave him the name of our lawyer in town. We filed a legal marriage certificate so nothing could be disputed."

"Why did he do this?"

"He wanted you and your son to be cared for," said Khalen. "To never be without."

I held the papers in my hand detailing all that I now owned: his condos, cars, and monthly allowance. I knew Kael had been well off, but dang. "What am I going to do with all this?"

"He wanted you to pursue your passion. Buy the biggest greenhouse you can find. Make medicines, write books, live the life you always dreamed of."

I forced myself to breathe. My body trembled. "God, I don't know what to do with all this," I mumbled.

Skye laid her hand over mine. She always seemed to have a calming effect. "Relax, Elle. Khalen is a master at investments. He can help you."

I sat down on the couch and accepted the hot cup of tea Skye handed me. "So much has changed in the span of a week."

After a bout of morning sickness, I returned to class for more of Master Mac's abuse. He was being particularly hard on me today. I wasn't sure if it was because I had thwarted his last attempt to date me or because I had to visit the bathroom too frequently.

No one but Jamie knew I was pregnant, and Khalen

was adamant about me taking a break until the baby was born. I craved the distraction, and the exertion that karate had offered. I needed some normalcy in my life.

My body pounded the ground as Master Mac demonstrated a lethal blow. After that, everything was a blur. The next thing I knew, I was standing above Master Mac, holding him to the floor with a one-finger hold on a pressure point to his neck. The studio was oddly silent and the weight of five focusing stares pressed against me like heavy fog.

I released my hold and rushed toward the bathroom once again.

Class ended early, and Master Mac disappeared into the back room.

"Coffee?" Jamie asked.

I nodded.

As much as I loved coffee, I ordered a cup of peppermint tea instead, hoping it would settle my stomach.

Jamie returned to our table with two cranberry scones and a steaming vanilla latte. She pushed a scone toward me.

"So," she said, "care to tell me what the hell happened in class today?"

I sipped my tea and feigned innocence. My cell phone rang. The charming tone of Beethoven's Fifth indicated it was Khalen calling—no doubt to berate me for my overexertion today.

"I have to get this," I groaned, then pressed the Answer button. "Hello, Khalen."

"Stay where you are," he said, his tone indisputable.

"Um—okay." The phone clicked off. "He just hung up on me," I said. "The man is abrupt and impatient at times, but that was just rude."

Jamie snorted. "He's intense. I don't know how your sister lives with him."

"So," Jamie said, wrapping her hands around her coffee cup to stay warm. The temperature in the shop seemed to have dropped several degrees. "Tell me how you did that with Master Mac."

Three young men entered the shop. They reminded me of rebel teens looking for their next distraction from a life they couldn't escape. They dressed in black leather studded with gaudy metal bling, and their hair looked as if it had been caught in a windstorm, then sprayed to stay that way. The oldest and tallest of them looked right at me, his dark eyes seemed to glow like hematite.

I looked away and shivered, feeling the weight of his stare.

Jamie looked over her shoulder. "Hmm. It looks like you have an admirer."

"Don't look at him," I hissed.

The man sauntered toward us and extended his hand. "I'm Blair," he said, displaying a confident smile that could pass as charming in another circumstance.

My instincts warned me not to touch him.

Jamie, on the other hand, reached out and met his greeting with the enthusiasm of a sex-peaked teen. "I'm Jamie."

The man frowned and released his hold on her. His eyes returned to mine. "And you are?"

"Not available," Khalen said, storming his way toward him.

The man stepped back. "Khalen," he nodded, keeping his eyes down. Ian and Aidan stood behind the other two men, smiling with anticipation.

"The peninsula is off limits to you, Blair. What brings

you here?"

Blair's eyes shifted toward me. "A feeling," he said, smiling.

It was a look that made my insides twist with fear. I felt the hum radiating from Khalen. I was familiar with it and found it oddly comforting now.

Jamie felt it too, but I could tell it made her head ache, the way it used to affect me.

"By all rights, I could take you down," Khalen growled.

Blair looked around at the people taking notice. "Here? That should be interesting."

Everything went quiet and for a moment, I felt peace and stillness. It ended just as quickly as it came. Khalen, Ian and Aidan sat at our table, each with a cup of coffee. Everyone around us paid no attention. Even Jamie seemed unaffected by what had transpired. She and Ian were talking about a movie they had both seen recently.

Good Lord, I thought. I'm losing my mind. Where had Blair and his gang gone? Were they even really here?

Khalen leaned toward me. "You pushed it too hard today."

"I'm fine," I assured him.

His jaw tightened. I could tell there was so much more he wanted to say, but our environment checked his tongue. I had not been staying with the clan and, therefore, had not developed the ability to telecommunicate. Now I wasn't sure I wanted to.

Jamie stood. "Well, darlings, I have a bid I must rush to." She looked at me. "We'll chat later, okay?"

"Okay," I said, watching her leave.

Ian gathered our cups and trash and tossed them away.

"Let's go," said Khalen, grabbing my arm rather painfully.

I tried pulling away. "Khalen, you're hurting me."

"You're lucky I don't bind you to your cabin for the next nine months," he seethed.

I twisted away from him, and then froze as a jolt of energy flowed through me. It didn't hurt, but it certainly rendered me useless. He plucked the keys from my hands and tossed them to Ian. "Bring it to the camp."

"No," I said. "I want to go home."

"Aidan, take care of the others. Return to the camp with her things."

The older brother looked at me with a measure of sympathy and nodded.

With the strength of an iron vice, Khalen gripped my arm and nearly tossed me into the passenger seat of his SUV. I watched as he buckled me in, still unable to move.

"You will not be coming back here alone," he said, pulling away from the coffee shop. "You are to remain in camp, unless accompanied by myself, Ian or Aidan." His eyes pierced mine. "Understood?"

"I have a class tomorrow," I retorted. "I need to attend it to qualify for the test. I already missed the—"

"No," he roared. "You have already seen how quickly things can get out of hand. Your gifts are unpredictable and it is too risky."

"Khalen, this is my life. You—"

"Not anymore," he interrupted again. "Your life changed the moment that Angel touched you."

"You don't own me," I argued.

His eyes glowed so brightly they mirrored the sun. "I am your templar. You are my responsibility."

"Avel is dead. Your obligation to him died along with him."

His lips tightened. "It doesn't work that way, Elle."

"Then how does it work?"

"I vowed to protect you and your son until a suitable mate can be found."

"I won't mate another," I said defiantly.

He verbally growled. Literally, like a great big bear, he growled. I felt the rumble of it clear to my bones.

"Avel told me you were stubborn, but he failed to mention you were unbendable."

"I would expect a man of your stature to fully look into a commitment before agreeing to uphold it."

His brow arched. "Oh, I intend to uphold it, my dear. Believe me."

"Against my will?"

"Yes, if necessary."

The finality of his words stuck in my throat, threatening to choke me.

Chapter 26

WE ROLLED INTO CAMP AND I was dutifully escorted back to my cabin. My things had been unpacked and there was a tray of food on the counter.

"Stay here," Khalen demanded, closing the door behind him.

I mocked a salute. "Sir, yes Sir." Looking up to the heavens, I said, "Avel, at the end of this lifetime, we will discuss this—arrangement." I tossed my bag onto the couch and rummaged through my things, hoping to find my computer.

A knock sounded on the door. "Elle, it's me, Skye."

"Come in," I called over my shoulder, still searching for my computer.

"Hi," she said, timidly.

I growled in response. "Your mate is an—"

"Ass?"

"Yes," I said. "A big furry one with a head the size of Texas."

She laughed. "He is angry," she sighed. "You're lucky

he's only bound you to this cabin."

I glared. "He wouldn't dare?"

"Oh yes, I assure you, he's bound you here until he calms down."

"I have to pee," I said. "He can't hold me here."

She covered her mouth and laughed.

"What?"

"He told me to tell you to use a cup."

My eyes widened. I walked toward the door.

"No, Elle. Don't—"

A wave of energy hit me so fiercely I fell back onto the floor as if a semi had plowed into my chest. My hand that had clutched the door handle stung with the ferocity of a hundred bee stings.

"God Almighty, what was that?" I huffed.

"Khalen's ward," she said. "Actually, you got off easy. I don't think your next attempt will be that forgiving."

"Forgiving? Is that what you call this?" I held up my still-stinging hand. With little dignity or grace, I hauled my body up from the floor and dusted it off. I offered her a sideways glance. "You don't seem to have any issues with the door."

"The ward is not meant for me," she said, almost too smugly.

"What if you open the door and I run through?"

"He said that's a fabulous idea and is encouraging you to try it. Personally, I do not recommend that plan."

I paced a few times, trying to keep breathing and forcing my emotions to calm. "Can he do this?"

She nodded. "He is your templar and the leader of this clan. He can do anything within his power to keep you safe and protected."

"Safe and protected," I muttered. "He has a warped

sense of both." I paced a few more times. "Honestly, Skye, if he were not your mate, I would turn him in to the authorities."

Skye laughed. "And what, pray tell, do you think they would do?"

"Arrest him!"

"Hmm," Skye remarked. "That would be interesting."

"You don't seem too worried about it."

She shrugged. "Do you remember what happened in the coffee shop today?"

"Yeah, three thugs entered and the oldest one zoned in on me like I was his next meal."

"How about what happened next?"

I sighed, feeling that all this was irrelevant to my current situation. "Khalen said he could take him down and Blair said, 'That should be interesting,' or something like that."

"What do you remember after that?"

My face paled. "The three men were gone and no one seemed to notice anything."

"Exactly," said Skye. "On top of that, more than half of the police force are Spirians, Elle. They fall under Khalen's domain. "Whose command do you think they will follow?"

"Who were Blair and his friends?"

"Shadows. They sensed your power and zoned in on you."

"My power?"

"During karate class, your instructor invoked a protective response. Your gifts kicked in, sending out a wave of energy that could be felt by any Spirian within fifty miles."

I walked to the kitchen and poured myself a cup of

water. "And the Shadows felt it?" I eyed the fruit and cookies on the counter.

"We all felt it," she added. "Are you hungry? Eve and I placed some sandwiches in the fridge."

My stomach growled, reminding me that the little food I had consumed this morning had been quickly purged during class. I had only looked at the scones at the coffee shop, never having the time to enjoy them. The tray in the fridge was colorfully prepared with various sandwiches, veggies and fruit. I began eating without ceremony. "Want some?" I said between bites.

She smiled and shook her head. "No, those are for you. Khalen asked me to join him for lunch in an hour."

"And does Khalen always get what he wants?"

She pondered that question for a moment, then stifled a laugh. "Despite my many efforts to deny him at times, yes, he always gets what he wants."

"That must be frustrating."

"At first, it was infuriating. It's not easy being mated to a regional leader. Khalen's gifts are powerful, and his will is even stronger. I shudder to think how indomitable our children will be when they mature."

I cringed thinking about stubborn teens with an attitude and gifts to boot. "Would they ever challenge your mate?"

She pulled a stool out and took a seat. "I have no doubt they will try."

I refilled my water glass and took a long swig. "I hope I'm not around to witness it."

Skye frowned. "I hope you are," she replied quietly.

I walked around the counter and laid my hand on her arm. "Skye, I can't stay here. My life is elsewhere."

"You saw what the Shadows are capable of. Living on

your own is too dangerous."

Remembering the power of that Shadow called Blair was unnerving. If Khalen hadn't arrived, I'm not sure what would have happened.

"You would have been consumed by them," she said, having read my thoughts.

"Consumed? As in, eaten?"

"No. They don't eat you, they manipulate you into following them, then slowly eat away at your soul until nothing is left."

"Sounds like you speak from experience."

"I know a woman they took." Her face showed pain. "I came close to following her fate. Khalen saved me."

She stood and offered a hug. "I need to go. Khalen and Case will be by later to talk to you."

"About?"

"Your options."

I finished the rest of my sandwich then put the rest back in the fridge. I still had to pee and eyed the glass I had been drinking from. "That's just wrong," I said.

AFTER RUMMAGING THROUGH EVERY drawer and cubby space, I finally found my computer. It was under the bed of all places. The cabin had been rearranged and cleared of all traces of Avel. I still felt him, though, clearly as if he were standing beside me.

The queen-sized mattress was replaced by a full-sized day bed against the opposite wall. The curtains were lighter and covered with white lace. Even the furniture was different. Old tables were exchanged with newer, modern ones, and an oak armoire took the place of the original dresser.

Colorful throw rugs covered the hardwood floors. The clan had taken great effort to change the place so that it wouldn't remind me of Avel. I had to admit knowing that we never shared that bed together added some semblance of comfort.

I remembered how hard it had been returning to my parents' cabin and entering the small room that Avel had occupied a few short weeks ago. My heart sank at the memory of him sitting in that bed, shirtless, and grim-faced after our verbal bout with each other.

The promise I had made him was stated in earnest. I would fulfill that promise at any cost and I think he knew it. That was why he made me say it out loud.

I stoked the fire, added another log, and then curled up on the couch to catch up on my work. Jamie was online but I didn't feel like chatting with her. I kept myself signed out.

James, my agent, politely reminded me of my deadline that had passed two days ago. I sent him a message, ensuring him that I would have something to him soon. He would not appreciate that response, I was sure, but it was all I had to offer right now.

Closing all other windows, to remove distractions, I opened my current novel and began typing. Life disappeared as I entered the realm of my creation. I became the characters and they became aspects of me. Imagination drove us from one scene to the next. My fingers barely kept up.

A knock sounded on my door. I glanced over at it and continued to type. I figured if I ignored the intruder, he would take the hint that I was busy and would go away.

The door flew open. I jumped, nearly dropping my laptop to the floor. "I don't remember asking you to enter," I said, righting my computer on my lap.

Khalen waved his hand, and my computer closed and flew on its own volition toward the bed. Thank God it landed softly.

"Hey," I objected. "I hadn't saved my work yet."

"Too bad," he replied, waiting for Case to enter before slamming the door closed.

I swallowed, gauging the anger his expression displayed.

Case walked to the liquor cabinet and poured three glasses of wine.

"None for me, I'm pregnant."

"That's right, you are," Khalen seethed, taking the glass Case offered. "Perhaps you should consider that the next time you ignore my warnings."

"I'm pregnant, Khalen, not dead. Attending karate class should not have been a problem."

"You lost control today, Elle. What would you have done if you had killed your instructor instead of rendering him helpless?"

"Or worse," Case added, "what if you landed wrong and lost Avel's son?"

Avel's son. God, the sound of it was as effective as waving a blinding reminder of his absence right in my face. I swallowed and fought back the tears stinging my eyes.

"No more karate. No more leaving this camp unless you are escorted. Am I clear?" Khalen asked.

"Do I have a choice?"

"No, you do not."

"What happened today," Case explained, "not only placed you at risk, but this entire clan."

"I don't understand."

"You lost control. Doing so leaves a wake of complications. Aidan had to remove the memory of the event from your teacher and his students. That memory wipe removes other memories as well, including their memory of you."

"Jamie still remembers me," I said.

"Not anymore," Khalen added. "If she spoke to anyone about what she witnessed, our clan would be in danger."

I sank down into the couch.

"Khalen killed three Shadows today. Their clan will want to retaliate."

"You killed them?" I asked.

"If I hadn't, they would have returned with news of your existence. Shadows are hungry for unmated females with gifts. If they find you, they will kill your child and take you for their own."

I found it hard to believe that an entire race of people could do such horrible things right under the nose of others and not be noticed. Yet I was being chastised for using gifts I could not control.

"Spirians share this planet with humans," Khalen explained, "but we live under their radar. We govern our own. We are forbidden to use our gifts in their presence."

"I did not mean to use my gifts," I retorted.

His eyes glowed bright yellow and I felt stings piercing my body. I wanted to speak but couldn't get my mouth to work. The pain increased.

Case frowned. "Khalen," he said, raising his hand.

The pain faded. I took a deep breath and tried not to show any signs of alarm or fear. I would not give him that satisfaction.

"You will learn to speak respectfully," Case said, his tone even and calm. "What Khalen is trying to say is that you have no control of your gifts. Putting yourself into situations that cause a protective response is not permitted. You will do what he asks you to do."

I opened my mouth to speak, but his piercing warning stifled my words.

"I will remove the wards," Khalen said. "Give me your word that you will not leave this camp unescorted."

These men were unmovable as mountains and about as predictable as tigers looking for their next meal. I suddenly felt like a helpless rabbit in their path.

"Do I have your word?"

"You leave me no choice," I said. "You have my word."

"Excellent. I will tell Skye that you will be joining us by the fire this evening." It was more of a command than a statement.

The two men finished their wine, and then took their leave.

I wanted to slam the door behind them, but thought better of that idea. I relished my freedom too much to risk it again.

After a long, soothing shower, I joined Skye, Sunjia and Eve by the fire. Sunjia and Eve wanted to learn more about the day's events. I told them my side, and Skye filled them in on the rest.

Khalen finished his conversation with Drew and Caleb then walked over and handed me a glass of wine.

"I shouldn't."

"You are not human anymore, Elle. Wine and spirits will not have the same effect on you."

"It won't harm my child?"

"No," he assured me. "Just don't overdo it."

"Thank you," I said, accepting the glass.

He then walked over to Skye, pulled her next to him,

clinking his glass to hers before claiming her mouth in a long, demanding kiss.

Eve and Sunjia chatted away as if this was an average occurrence. I had never been around affectionate people and felt a tad uncomfortable.

Seth walked toward me, a shy smile on his young but handsome face. "Would you like to join our fire?" he asked.

"I have something to discuss with her first," said Drew.

Seth looked at him, shuffled his feet a bit and lowered his eyes. "Of course." He glanced over at me before turning to leave.

Sunjia looked after her son, disheartened. I could tell she wanted to go after him, but decided to give him some space instead.

I felt like a new toy in a playground of aggressive children.

"Come with me," Drew said, sliding his hand through my arm.

I walked with him to the lake.

"Khalen has asked me to take you as a mate," he boldly stated.

"He did what?"

"I believe it is a good match."

"I don't care what you believe. I'm not mating anyone, ever."

The man had the audacity to laugh. "Yes, he said you would say that."

"Ever!" I repeated with more conviction in my voice than was probably necessary.

"Needless to say, I will pursue," he said. His hands sneaked their way around my arms. "I find you—intriguing."

I tried to pull away, but his hands held firm. Then

I remembered he was a mason worker—all muscle and brawn. Perfect.

"I'm flattered you think so, Drew, but I'm not ready for this, nor do I think I ever will be."

"Well, if there is one thing us Spirians have, it's time. I will wait it out." He released his hold.

"Just don't hold your breath." I started to walk back to the fire, but he stopped me.

"Seth is interested in you."

"Yes," I said, "I've been told."

"He is not a good match."

"No one is," I assured him.

"Don't be so sure." His eyes glowed like deep amethyst, preventing me from looking away. It was suddenly hard to breathe.

A smile stretched across his face. "I believe Khalen is right."

I didn't want to know what that meant and kept my mouth shut. "Can we go back now? I'm getting cold."

He wrapped his large arm around me. "Of course."

When we passed Seth, Drew gave him a warning glance then tightened his hold around me. Something snapped and suddenly I found myself surrounded by people. Drew lay sprawled on the ground.

Khalen and Case pulled me away while Skye tended to Drew.

"What happened?" I asked.

"Pregnant or no," Khalen stated, "you start training tomorrow."

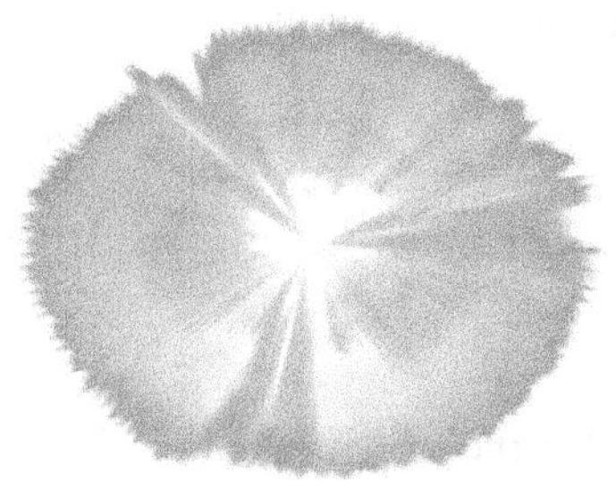

Chapter 27

I DIDN'T KNOW THE TRUE impact of that statement until the following week. Case and Khalen were relentless in their training. My body never knew such pain.

Between the mélange of Qi Gong, energy wielding, and shielding exercises, I managed to sneak in a few meals and a bit of rest. There was still no trace of telepathy and I was beginning to wonder if it would ever happen.

A knock sounded on my door. I was still enjoying my first cup of coffee after doing an hour of Qi Gong. I wasn't expecting Khalen for another thirty minutes. "Come in."

Skye entered with a tray of hot cookies. "How are you holding up?"

I breathed in the comforting aroma of oatmeal, cinnamon and cranberries. "About as well as an old bridge in its last year."

She carried the tray to the kitchen to serve us each two cookies.

"Help yourself to coffee, if you want."

She poured herself a cup before coming over to join

me. “Training is difficult,” she said. “I cannot imagine doing it while pregnant.”

“I’m not sure who is more unbending, Case or Khalen.”

“Impatient as they are,” she said, “they are still the best when it comes to helping you develop and control your gifts.”

“I just hope I survive the ordeal.”

We sipped our coffee and enjoyed the cookies in silence for a while. Skye was one of the rare people with whom I could enjoy quiet time. She seemed very comfortable with it, and that comfort transferred over to me somehow.

“There were three men in the yard this morning, practicing fighting techniques,” I mentioned. “I’ve never seen that style of fighting.”

Skye nodded. “Yes, that was Drew, Caleb and a young man from a neighboring camp. Drew is the appointed trainer for all types of fighting. He is the one who taught Khalen, Ian and Aidan.”

“I thought he was a mason worker?”

“Oh, he is, and a general contractor. He wears many hats around here.”

“Why is he not mated?”

“He’s a man of high stature,” Skye explained. “His mate must be very strong and spirited to be a good match. That’s why Khalen believes you and Drew are good for one another.”

“I’m not available,” I countered.

“Finding another mate does not mean you need to release Avel from your heart, Elle. Spirian women are vulnerable when they are unmated.”

“I’m not a true Spirian, Skye. I can’t even read minds yet—nothing. It’s very frustrating.”

"You may not have been born a Spirian, Elle, but you have an energy around you that attracts our kind."

"I just want to raise my son and be happy until the day I return to Avel."

"And being happy requires you to live alone, without another being to love?"

"I'll have my son."

"Khalen will not allow you to mourn Avel forever."

"I don't intend to," I said. My coffee had grown cold, much like the conversation. I walked to the kitchen to pour us a warmer.

"Besides," I added, "what can he possibly do?"

"You ask that now?" she said, incredulous. "After a week of training? Do you not understand his position?"

"I understand it quite well," I said, not really hiding my stiffness as I sat.

"He can force your union with Drew."

I choked on my coffee. "He wouldn't dare."

"He most certainly would."

Epilogue

-Avel-

THE SOUND OF HER VOICE pierced my heart like a jagged dagger.

"Avel, please. I need you now." She sobbed and I felt the pain in her heart.

Every fiber of my soul wanted to manifest before her and offer solace. It was a selfish need and one that would make her life miserable. Showing myself would only prolong the pain she felt. She would learn to rely on my feeble manifestation, one that could not provide physical comfort. I didn't want that for her.

"She calls to you," said Raphael.

"Yes."

"It is right for you to stay away," he offered.

"It pains me to do so."

He frowned. "Would it be better to shield you from her voice?"

"No. I never want to be severed from her. Painful as it

is to stay away, hearing my name on her tongue is a strong antidote."

He nodded and laid his ethereal hand on my shoulder. "Understood."

-Elle-

EVEN IF AVEL DID HEAR my words, he wouldn't come to me. I knew that. I continued to sob until my tears were spent.

"I know you can hear me," I said, sniffling and looking up at the stars. I rubbed my swollen belly. "Connor grows quickly now; he will enter this world in two more months."

I looked down and allowed more tears to flow. "I miss you. I pray you can see our son when he's born. I know you don't want to interfere, but that is one thing I ask. Please be there, even if I cannot see you. I want to feel you are there."

My hand covered my chest. "You were right," I smiled. "I feel you here, in my heart, always." The stars were particularly bright this evening in the absence of moonlight. One shone brighter than the others.

"I love you," I sighed. "I will always love you."

-Avel-

MY HEART FILLED LIKE THE belly of a lion after a solid hunt at the sound of those words. They were said with strength; I could hear it in her voice.

"I love you too, my angel. My heart has always belonged to you."

She would never hear those words, but I knew she felt the intent behind them.

Elle would survive this life and fulfill her destiny. Of that, I was certain.

-The End-

A Note From the Author

I hope you have enjoyed reading *Aeon Pneuma*. This story was about a young woman I knew who was always unhappy. She eventually took her life and the life of her unborn child. I meditated for several years over the incident, trying to understand why there are those among us who cannot find happiness. I wrote down what I learned and developed this story around those writings.

For those of you who believe they live in their own kind of hell, please find hope in these pages and know that God never gives up. Choose to live your life as promised. Every one of us has gifts. Discover yours and make them stronger. Life is a treasure that shouldn't be wasted.

Many of us have a story to tell but are afraid tell it for one reason or another. My goal is to encourage and inspire you all to tell your story, be it as a memoir or as a fictional tale such as this one.

About the Author

Rowena started writing at a young age, feeling an inherent need to tell stories that inspire and reflect aspects of life that are rarely considered.

Being a descendant of James Hudson Taylor, author and founder of the China Inland Mission, Rowena comes from a long line of story tellers, including her mother and father. The tradition of writing continues through her daughter, Erika.

Rowena's goal is to inspire others to tell their stories and share the wonderful gift and adventure of life. She often speaks before groups, sharing her experiences of writing and telling stories. It is a passion of hers that she shares with her mate, Gregg.

Together, they are writing a book entitled, *Finding Peace Among Chaos*, due to be released in Spring 2013.

Though she is over seventy-five percent blind, she doesn't allow that to derail her ambitions. Her husband is deaf, so they make the perfect pair. They live on the Olympic Peninsula in Washington with her guide dog Skye-Bear.

Other Books by Rowena

Protected
Union
Legend
Illusions
Fealty

www.Rowena-Portch.com

Book a Speaking Engagement with Rowena and Gregg

Rowena and Gregg love to inspire people to tell their story and to follow their passion no matter how unobtainable it may seem.

Both of them have been on their own since age fourteen and have some incredible stories to share. Though both of them are disabled—she's blind and he's deaf—neither of them allow their impairments to deter them from their dreams.

If you want Rowena and Gregg to speak at your next event, please email them at:

Rowena@Rowena-Portch.com

www.ingramcontent.com/pod-product-compliance
Lightning Source LLC
Chambersburg PA
CBHW060403260626
47160CB00006B/2417
9780988627536